If he was arranging for contraband to come ashore, it would be best the stranger did not see it.

Morwenna moved towards him, pretending to trip and falling into his arms. He caught her and held her. She looked up and the heat in his eyes startled her. A fierce shaft of heat shot through her and she gasped. The next moment he had her pressed hard against his body and his arms were about her. She ought to push him away, but if she did not distract him he might notice the flashing lights.

Now he was bending his head, and his mouth was on hers, taking possession of her lips, sending little thrills of heat racing through her body. She moaned with pleasure, unable to pull away or tell him to stop. It was as if a sudden fire had begun inside her and she was burning up with the need to allow his kisses and so much more. She wanted him to hold her for ever, to take her here on these cliffs and kiss her senseless… She wanted to love him, to stand by his side and keep the world at bay.

No—how stupid of her. She was allowing her loneliness a̶ ̶ ̶ ̶ ̶tration to take over her mind. To 1̶ ̶ ̶ ̶ ̶ ̶ ̶ ̶ ̶ ̶ ̶ ̶lead to only one th̶ ̶ ̶ ̶ ̶ ̶ ̶ ̶ ̶ ̶ ̶ ̶ ̶ ̶as she did, e̶ ̶ ̶ ̶ ̶ ̶ ̶ ̶ ̶ ̶ ̶ ̶ ̶ ̶ ̶ ̶ ̶1l. She r̶ ̶ ̶ ̶ ̶ ̶ ̶ ̶ ̶ ̶ ̶ ̶ ̶ ̶ ̶ ̶ ̶ ̶e.

Anne Herries lives in Cambridgeshire, where she is fond of watching wildlife, and spoils the birds and squirrels that are frequent visitors to her garden. Anne loves to write about the beauty of nature, and sometimes puts a little into her books, although they are mostly about love and romance. She writes for her own enjoyment, and to give pleasure to her readers. She is a winner of the Romantic Novelists' Association Romance Prize. She invites readers to contact her on her website: www.lindasole.co.uk

Previous novels by the same author:

A STRANGER'S TOUCH

Anne Herries

First published in Great Britain 2012
by Mills & Boon, an imprint of Harlequin (UK) Limited.
Harlequin (UK) Limited, Eton House, 18-24 Paradise Road,
Richmond, Surrey TW9 1SR

© Anne Herries 2012

ISBN: 978 0 263 89286 4

A STRANGER'S
TOUCH

Prologue

'You understand, Melford? This mission is important for there are dangerous men at work. If they discover your true identity and why you are in Cornwall, your life could be forfeit.'

'Yes, I understand that, sir. I shall keep a close mouth. I know that his Majesty's life could be at risk and I have given my promise that I will serve both him and the Government of England with a true heart.'

Lord Rupert Melford frowned. His family had a long history of serving the crown. When Henry Tudor took the throne from the last ruling Plantagenet, Sir Robert Melford had stood with him. The family had prospered since those times and was extended over England, with branches of the family living in France and the

New World. Rupert had never met his cousins from the Americas, though he'd heard they did well. However, he knew his French cousins, and had been on the verge of departing for France to visit Stefan de Montfort, the present lord, when he was summoned to Lord Henry Cecil's house.

'I knew your grandfather Anton and your father Richard,' Lord Henry continued. 'Losing his first wife was hard on him, but fortunately he met and married your mother. Your birth and that of your sister was a blessing to him.'

'Thank you, sir. My father was a good man.'

'And you are very like him. When this unfortunate business was first brought to my attention, I knew you were just the man for this work. I know you are brave and intelligent, but we also need discretion. There are rumours, but nothing definite. If these rogues had any idea that we knew of their existence, they might go into hiding and we should lose them.'

'A family of two brothers and one sister,' Rupert said. 'All of them smugglers and ruthless, you say?'

'If smuggling were all it was it would be a matter for the Revenue Officers. A few barrels of French brandy or some silk that does not pay tax is one thing, but these Morgans are at the heart of a nest of spies and vicious enemies of the Crown. They are the means by which the spies enter and leave the country in secret— and it is these ruthless men who plot to bring down the King.'

'King James is not popular with everyone, particularly some Catholic families,' Rupert said. 'However, he was the only heir to our Gloriana and is therefore England's rightful king. These men deserve to hang if they harbour traitors. Why do you not simply send soldiers to arrest them?'

'If I ordered their arrest, they would disappear into the sea mist or one of the caves that abound on that coast. It is a wild rugged part of the country, Melford. As I said, if it were merely smuggling I'd say be damned to them and leave it at that, but the smugglers are too clever for the Revenue and too many of our men have lost their lives to this already. It will not be easy for you to discover what is going on and get away with your life.'

'Is the whole family involved—even the girl?'

'I believe the ringleader is the eldest brother— Michael Morgan—but do not trust any of them or anyone else in the area you meet for that matter. They stick together in that part of the country, which is why we can never get close enough to catch them in the act.'

'I shall do my best for you, sir. As you know, I have a small talent for sketching and I shall let it be known that I have come to draw and paint the charm of the Cornish coast.'

'Charm?' Lord Henry shook his head impatiently. 'In my opinion 'tis a god-forsaken place, but I dare say the excuse will make a good cover for you. I wish you well, Melford. If you discover anything important, get word to me as soon as you can.'

'I shall make arrangements for my men to travel independently and if there is anything to report one of them will bring word to you at once.'

'Then all I can say is God keep and save you. His Majesty is in your debt, sir.'

'I ask for no reward,' Rupert replied and grinned, his blue eyes dancing with humour. 'In truth the mission is reward in itself, for I was bored and restless.'

'I heard that you lost the lady you were to wed. I am sorry for it, Rupert.'

'The marriage was arranged when we were born,' Rupert replied and a cloud passed across his face. 'I loved my sweet Jane, but the fever claimed her before we could marry. I am sorry for it—and no doubt it is a part of the reason I felt I needed something more in my life. Had I not received your letter, I would have been on my way to France tomorrow to visit my cousins.'

His true reason lay deeper, but was not one he wished to discuss for it was a festering hurt that lay buried deep inside him; one he had tried many times to dismiss, but which returned to haunt him when he least expected it.

'Then I was fortunate to find you in England. I shall bid you good day, sir—and good luck.'

Rupert nodded. He was thoughtful as he left Westminster Hall and began to make his way through the streets of London. His ship was provisioned and waiting for him. He would travel to his destination by way of the sea rather than on horseback. His trusted men could take the land route and establish themselves in the area quietly. If dealing with smugglers, it might be useful to have his own ship close at hand just in case.

For a moment he thought of Jane Follet, the young woman he had been betrothed to since they were both little more than children. As fond as he'd been of Jane, it had not been a raging passion. He had wanted to wed her, to give her the care he sensed she needed, because the children they would have might fill the emptiness inside him. Fate had decreed it was not to be and he had accepted it. He had promised he would marry a girl of good family for the sake of the family and in time he would keep his word, but as yet he had not been able to bring himself to offer for any of the young women brought to his attention.

An oath left his lips, for the matter was one that troubled him, though he tried to ignore it. He'd given his word and must keep it, because of that dark happening in his past. Not yet! He was not ready to take a wife. It was too soon after poor Jane's death.

Rupert had his mistress, a feisty dark-haired wench he visited when the need took him. Since he would be away for some weeks, perhaps longer, he might call on Mollie and make certain she had enough money to tide her over until she could find a new protector—just in case he did not return.

Mollie was the only one who would miss him. The only one who would care—and perhaps she only cared because he kept her in luxury?

Was it possible to find love? To find someone who would make his heart sing and his body throb with needy passion? Mollie satisfied his basic needs, but not this inner loneliness. It was too strong a word and yet since he was a young boy and his elder brother had died there had been this empty place inside him.

He frowned. It was foolish to think of the past or of the aching regret that still lived with him day and night.

Rupert had work to do and he would do it well, even if it meant risking his life. After all, it hardly mattered if he lived or died.

Chapter One

'There's a ship in trouble in Deacon's Cove.' Morwenna Morgan looked up as her elder brother, Michael, entered the kitchen where she sat with her younger brother, Jacques, and her servant Bess, eating her supper. 'I'm going down to see if I can help the survivors.'

'I'm with you…' Jacques leaped to his feet, closely followed by Morwenna and Bess, and the kitchen became a hive of activity as they gathered ropes, hooks, grappling irons, lanterns and their weapons.

A shipwreck would bring the villagers to the beach and sometimes fights broke out over the spoils. It needed a firm hand to control them and on occasion, Michael had been forced to fire a musket over their heads.

'Not you, Morwenna,' Michael said as she reached for her shawl. 'There's no need for you to come.'

'I shan't be in your way, Michael.'

'Do as you're told,' he snarled. 'Stay here and make yourself useful. We'll need hot food and drinks when we get back.'

Morwenna's hand dropped to her side. She saw Jacques glance at her and smile, giving him a proud look in return. Waiting until the sound of the men's voices had gone, she picked up her shawl and wrapped it over her head.

'Where are you going?' Bess asked. 'You heard what Michael said. He wants you here for when they return.'

'I'll be back in time to help,' Morwenna said. 'I can't just stay here while people out there are in trouble. Michael doesn't own me even if he thinks he does.'

'You know his temper, girl. Your brothers will do all that is necessary.'

Morwenna tossed her head and went out, ignoring the dark look from Bess. It was bitterly cold as she made her way down the cliff towards the cove. She could see that the main beach was teeming with people. A ship had been driven on to the rocks and foundered. She could see figures in the water. Men were swimming out towards the wreck. She knew her brothers would be amongst the first, ropes tied to their waists that were held by others on shore. It was true that she was not needed on the main beach, but, as she knew from experience, sometimes men were carried by the tide round a spur of rock to another smaller cove. Turning aside, she scrambled down a path towards the inlet. As she'd known, no one else had thought of the cove and the tiny beach was deserted…apart from a man stumbling up the beach.

From his manner, she could see that he was injured. As she ran towards him, he fell to the ground and slumped forwards to lay face down on the sand. She threw herself down on her knees and rolled him on to his back. The moon was bright and she could see a nasty gash on his head, which was bleeding. His eyes were closed and for a moment she feared that he might be dead, but then he moaned, his eyelids flicked and he looked up at her.

'Who are you?'

'My name is Morwenna Morgan and I've come to help you,' she said. 'Your ship was wrecked, sir, and the current brought you towards this cove.'

'Mor...' He groaned again. 'My head hurts... I can't...I can't remember...'

His eyes closed and she knew he had lost consciousness again. She would need to get help if she wanted to take him back to the house. Standing, she was preparing to run to the next beach when she saw a man coming towards her and knew it was Jacques.

'I knew you would be here,' he said as he came up to her. 'This is where you found the others. Is he still alive?'

'He was conscious for a moment, but I think he has passed out again.'

Jacques bent over him. 'Help me get him up, Wenna. I'll carry him over my shoulder. Did he have anything with him?'

'Yes, there is a bag just at the water's edge. He must have dropped it,' she said and ran to retrieve what was possibly all that had survived of the stranger's possessions. As she rejoined her brother, she nodded at the unconscious man. 'He's had a nasty bang on the head, Jacques. He will need nursing or he may die.'

'He's lucky you found him then,' her brother said. 'Most of the men they've pulled out are already drowned. One is badly injured and may not last the night—but there were no women or children that we could see. There was some cargo, a few barrels of rum or brandy. The villagers will have them away before the militia gets here. Give me a hand and I'll put him over my shoulder.'

Like her brothers, Morwenna came from strong stock and she helped Jacques to hoist the unconscious man over Jacques's shoulder. Going ahead of them, she held her lantern to show Jacques the way. Because this cove was nearer to the house than the main beach, they would be home in time to have the injured man in bed before the other men returned.

Bess stared at them, shaking her head as they entered.

'Now what have you done, girl?' she muttered. 'There'll be trouble over this, you mark my words.'

'We couldn't leave him to die. We'll take him up to the spare room.'

She followed behind her brother, ignoring Bess's grumbling. The bed was already made up and Morwenna pulled back the clean if slightly shabby sheets.

Jacques soon had the stranger stripped of his wet things and his long boots, while Morwenna hurried back down to the kitchen and helped Bess to boil kettles. The stewpot was always kept bubbling away on nights like this, for they simply added meat and vegetables to what was left of supper to make a nourishing soup.

When Michael came home the soup was ready for him and a couple of the men that crewed his ship; they'd helped on the beach and accompanied him home for some warming food as a reward. Morwenna ladled the nourishing soup into thick earthenware bowls. Served with chunks of bread baked earlier that day, it was a filling meal for men who had fought the sea.

'I found one survivor in the inlet,' Jacques said as he entered the kitchen, giving his sister a warning look. 'He's in the small guestroom upstairs. For the moment he's unconscious, but I think he will recover—unless the fever takes him.'

Michael glared at him. 'What manner of man is he? Did you find anything on him of value—anything to tell you whether he's worth a ransom? Any form of identity?'

'He was wearing good breeches and boots,' Jacques said. 'He had nothing in his breeches pockets and the sea must have taken his coat.

Yet by the look of him I would say he was of good family. If Morwenna nurses him, he will likely pay her well for her trouble.'

Michael glared at him, then turned his dark gaze on her. 'Are you willing, girl?'

'Yes, of course. My mother would never have left anyone to die of neglect, whoever they might be. I care nothing for whether he will pay or not.'

'Then you're a fool. We work hard for what we have, girl, and he should pay if he can. There, I might have known what you would say. Your mother was never one of us,' he muttered. 'I'm not a murderer. I'll allow you to keep your survivor—and don't think I don't know you two were in it together. Nurse him, but be careful. Remember he's a stranger and keep a still tongue in your head. You tell no one anything that is family business. This is important. Listen to me, both of you—make one slip and we may all find ourselves in trouble. It won't be just me they hang, it will be both your brothers, Morwenna—and if they think you're involved you could find yourself in chains and whipped at the cart's tail or in prison.'

'I should never tell anyone even if I knew what you were doing—and I don't,' Morwenna said, a flash of fire in her green eyes. 'You're my brother, Michael. I don't want either of you to hang.'

'Well, remember that when this man starts to recover and becomes curious.'

'I'm not a fool,' she flared back. 'I may have a different mother, but I'm a Morgan the same as you.'

'Just remember that and we shan't fall out.' Michael finished his soup and nodded to Bess. 'Very good. Away to your bed now. You, too, Morwenna—unless you need something for your patient, don't come down again for a while. I've something to say to Jacques and my men, and it's better if you don't know, then you can't tell.'

Morwenna was smarting inside. As if she would tell even if she did know! She didn't answer him, but simply filled a jug with clean water before following Bess from the room. Behind her there was silence. Michael was waiting until she was safely out of earshot before telling his men whatever he did not trust her to hear.

She felt a little resentful and yet she knew that he probably thought he was protecting her. If she could truthfully claim she knew nothing of his darker activities, she might escape should he and the others be caught.

Pray God it would not happen! She did not wish either of her brothers to die a cruel death or the men who sailed Michael's ship—but Jacques was the only one she truly felt close to, the only one who ever took any thought for her. Michael took her service for granted, forgetting that she should have been waited on instead of waiting on them.

She thrust the thought of Michael's secrets to a tiny corner of her mind as she went into the room in which her patient was lying. He appeared to be peaceful, his eyes still firmly closed. Touching his forehead, she was relieved that he did not appear to be suffering from a fever as yet, though he could of course develop one in the next day or so.

She poured some water into a bowl and dipped a cloth into it, then she bent over her patient and bathed the wound at the side of his head. It had bled quite a bit, but was not deep enough to have opened his skull. He had been lucky, because she'd seen men pulled out from amongst the cruel rocks with their heads cracked open and their brains spilling out. There was never any hope for them and if they still lived Michael despatched them with his knife. It was quick and less painful than seeing fatally injured men suffer a slow death.

'You were lucky,' she said as she bent over him, noticing that he was a fine-looking man. Jacques was right to say he looked like gentry. 'If we had not found you, you might have lain there all night and died of cold.'

For a moment his eyelids flickered, but they did not open. Morwenna poured some of her water into a horn cup and set it on the chest beside the bed. Then she took the salves she had stored in this room and a strip of linen and bound his head. Once again, his eyelids flickered, but did not open.

'You are safe here,' she said, though she was not sure he could hear her. 'My brother Jacques brought you here and Michael has given me permission to nurse you. I'm not sure if you can hear me—but be careful, sir. My brother does not care for strangers. Do not go wandering about the house at night or you may find yourself in trouble.'

The man gave no sign that he'd heard her.

'I shall leave you and return later,' she said. 'I do not know who you are but be careful.'

Leaving him to rest, Morwenna went out and closed the door behind her.

She hoped that Jacques had not helped her carry a spy into her home. It would not be the first time the militia had sent someone to try to discover the truth about her brother's activities. If Michael discovered that this man was one of them, he would not hesitate to kill him—and that would be a shame, as well as dangerous for them all.

Her brother claimed he was not a murderer, but if he acted in defence of his family he would not consider it murder. He had learned to be ruthless since their father died and he'd been forced to seek his living from the sea. Yet at times she could still see in him the brother that had carried her on his shoulder when she was too tired to climb the cliff to their home.

Even so, she would not like anything bad to happen to the stranger.

Morwenna smiled to herself. She was used to the company of strong handsome men, but she liked the look of the stranger and she would not have harm come to him if she could prevent it.

Chapter Two

Morwenna woke as a hand shook her shoulder. She opened her eyes to see that Bess was bending over her and struggled to sit up.

'What is the matter?' she asked groggily. 'Have the Revenue men come?'

'Nay, lass. 'Tis the stranger you brought from the beach. He's burning up and calling out loud enough to waken the dead. 'Tis as well your brothers have not yet returned.'

'Why?' Morwenna leapt out of bed and pulled on a wrapping gown that lay over the chair. 'Michael sleeps like one of the dead and Jacques is the same.'

'Aye, well, best they don't hear what I think I heard him call out.'

Morwenna looked at her curiously. 'He must

have been having a nightmare. What did he call out?'

'Your name and then…' Bess glanced cautiously over her shoulder '…I'm not sure what he said then for 'twas slurred, but I think he said "Nest of traitors," but I can't be certain.'

'If Michael heard that then he would think the worst. Yet on the beach he asked my name and I told him. It might just be that it was all that came to his mind. Mayhap you imagined the rest, Bess.'

'I might have done for 'twas not clear.'

Morwenna went ahead of her servant into the bedchamber where her patient lay. Bess had left a lantern burning and she saw immediately that the man was ill. He had thrown off his covers and she could see his body was covered in a fine layer of sweat. Going to him at once, she touched his forehead.

'He is in a bad fever, Bess.' There was no doubting that he was ill now. 'I must bathe him with cool water. Brew the tisane you use when any of us is ill, please. We'll do our best for him, whoever he is.'

'You'll have to keep him quiet once Michael returns or all your good work will be for nothing.'

Morwenna didn't answer, but a cold shiver ran down her spine as Bess left the chamber. If Michael suspected the man had come here to spy on them he would show no mercy. Gazing down on him as she began to bathe his body with cool water, Morwenna felt something protective stir inside her. She did not know who this man was and he could mean nothing to her, but he was a human soul and entitled to her care whilst ill.

'Morwenna Morgan…no…' he muttered suddenly, flinging his arm out in an arc. 'Jane… please don't leave me…'

'Rest easy, sir. You are safe now,' Morwenna said, stroking his damp hair back from his forehead.

'Nowhere…no place to hide…' the man muttered. 'Alone…she's gone, nothing left… Morwenna…Morwenna…' He cried out in anguish, 'I'm sorry, Mother. I didn't mean to kill him…it wasn't my fault…please…' He was tossing in agony, clearly suffering from the dreams or memories that plagued him. 'Forgive me… forgive me…'

Morwenna's heart wrenched. 'You are forgiven. Hush now.'

'No, no, she will never forgive me.'

Wringing her cloth out, Morwenna bathed his forehead again. She thought he felt a little cooler but it was clear he was still wandering in his mind. Was her name on his lips because she'd told him who she was on the beach? What was it that haunted him so much?

'It's all right,' she whispered softly close to his ear. 'You're safe here with me. Hush now and you will soon feel better.'

His eyes flew open suddenly and for a moment he stared up at her. 'You're beautiful,' he said and leaned forwards, as though he would sit up or touch her. Then his eyes closed and he fell back against the pillows. 'Morwenna... lovely name...'

'Here, my lovely, give him a sip of this.'

Morwenna turned as Bess entered bearing a tankard of hot liquid. It smelled strongly of cinnamon and she knew it contained brandy and the herbs that were effective for fever.

'Help me lift him,' Morwenna said. She took the cup, one arm beneath the man as she and Bess lifted him into a sitting position. 'Open your mouth, sir. This tisane will help you recover.'

She pressed the edge of the tankard to his mouth, unsure that he would respond or could even hear her. Surprisingly, his lips parted and she was able to tip a little of the mixture into his mouth. He coughed and choked, but when she tried again he allowed her to pour some of the mixture into his mouth and this time he swallowed it easily. When she tried again his hand gripped her wrist, pushing her away.

'Enough,' he muttered. 'No, Mother, enough.'

'He must be sick if he thinks you're his mother,' Bess said with a sniff. 'He looks cooler now. He'll probably settle. Go back to your bed, lass.'

'No. If I'd thought he was truly ill I wouldn't have left him last evening. I'll sit with him for a while, Bess. You go to bed. If he is ill for a few days, we'll have to share the nursing and you need your rest too.'

'So do you, miss, but have it your way. Just watch yourself if he starts to fight—and don't let him shout out. Your brothers came in a few minutes ago and they've gone to their beds.'

''Tis nearly morning. Where have they been all this time—and on a night like this?'

'The storm blew itself out a while back,' Bess said. 'The darker the night the better for the "gentlemen".'

'I dare say it was some such business,'

Morwenna said and yawned behind her hand. 'Go to bed, Bess. In a couple of hours it will be time to get up again.'

Morwenna sat in a solid oak-carved chair with a high back. She had made cushions for its seat and the centre splat had horsehair padding covered by tapestry and studded each side to make it comfortable. The first time Morwenna had brought a survivor to this room she'd installed the chair so that she would at least have some comfort as she watched over her patients. Mrs Harding had been very ill, but Morwenna had nursed her back to health and she'd been overwhelmed by gratitude when she was able to return to London and her husband.

'We are cloth merchants, Morwenna,' Mrs Harding had told her as she took an emotional farewell. 'My husband will always be pleased to have you stay with us. If ever you should be in trouble, think of me, my dear, for I would do anything to help you.'

'Thank you.' Morwenna had smiled and kissed her cheek. 'If ever I am in London, I shall seek you out, at least for a visit.'

Morwenna sighed at the memory. It was unlikely she would ever go to London. Her hopes of making a good marriage had gone when her mother died. Since her father's death she had been little more than a servant in her half-brother's house. Michael had resented the woman who had taken his dead mother's place and she suspected that he might resent her, too.

She would not brood on her life no matter how hard or hopeless it might seem at times. While she had Jacques to make her smile she would find the courage to face each day, though there was little else to make her smile in this bleak house at the top of the cliffs.

Sitting down again, she studied the man in the bed. His hair had dried now and she saw it was dark blond. On the beach he'd looked colourless, but now there was a flush in his cheeks. When he'd opened his eyes for a moment she'd seen they were a greenish blue; his nose and forehead had a patrician look, which gave him a slightly forbidding expression, but his mouth was soft and sensual. She felt tempted to kiss him as he lay sleeping, her cheeks growing warm as she realised her own thoughts.

Was she so starved of love that she would consider lying with a stranger? He had beautiful strong limbs and there was not a part of him that she had not seen as she bathed him with the cooling water. A little smile touched her mouth. She'd nursed her brothers before this, so why was she behaving as if she'd never seen a man naked before?

Time passed and she closed her eyes for a while, woke and realised she'd slept, and then she looked at the bed. Her patient was still there, apparently sleeping peacefully. She'd thought he might have disappeared for surely she'd conjured him out of her dreams. Men like this one did not come into her life often. He was every bit as handsome and powerful a man as her brothers, but there was something about him that made her pulses race. Something about his mouth that made her want to kiss it.

Giving herself a mental scolding, Morwenna laughed softly. She was a fool even to consider such a thing—especially if this man had come here to spy on them.

'Why are you laughing?'

Her eyes were drawn to the bed and she saw that he was looking at her. Getting up from her chair, she moved closer to the bed. He seemed to be awake, but was he still feverish? Sometimes patients appeared to be normal, but when you touched them they became violent and tried to fight you. Her brothers had often tried to get out of bed while still too ill to stand and she'd had to fight to keep them there.

'I was thinking foolish thoughts,' she said. 'You were ill and I bathed you to take down the fever. Are you feeling better?'

'I don't know.' He stared at her in bewilderment. 'My head hurts like the devil. I was dreaming…I thought my mother…'

'We carried you here from the beach. Your ship foundered on the rocks, sir. You have a nasty cut on your head.'

'Who are you?'

'Morwenna Morgan. I told you my name when I found you last night. For a moment you were conscious, as you are now, and then you fainted.'

'Did I? I don't recall.' He frowned, his eyes moving about the room as if seeking something familiar. 'I don't remember anything. Where is this place?'

'This is Deacon's House. It belongs to my elder brother, Michael. We live on the Cornish coast. Ships are too often driven in on the cruel rocks in our cove. We do what we can to help the survivors and the villagers bury the dead.'

'And then take what you can scavenge from

the wreck—is that not the custom in these parts?' He wrinkled his brow. 'I do not know why I should remember that but nothing else.'

'You cannot recall even your name?'

'No.' He drew a hand over his forehead, as if it pained him. 'Is that usual after being washed up from the sea?'

'Perhaps, though I have not known it to happen before,' Morwenna said. 'It may be the bang to your head. Have you truly no memory, sir—or any idea why you came here?'

'I can't remember anything.'

'You must surely remember your own name? You called out things in your fever, personal things concerning your mother and other things that I couldn't quite make out.'

'Did I? If they haunted me, then they have left me now. Was there no clue to my identity?'

'None. My brother found nothing in your clothing. Your coat was gone, abandoned or cast off perhaps as you tried to swim for the shore. You can recall nothing of the storm or how you came to our cove?'

'No. My mind is a blank, there is nothing but the sea raging about me and then I opened my eyes and saw a beautiful face. She said her name was Morwenna Morgan…was that you?'

'Yes, sir. It was. I found you in the inlet, which is away from the main beach. My brother Jacques helped me bring you here.' Morwenna placed a hand on his forehead. He was still warm but cooler than before.

He threw back the covers, as if he would get up, then glanced down at himself, realising that he was naked. 'My clothes?'

'What's left of them—your breeches and boots—are drying in the kitchen. Your shirt and coat were, I fear, lost to the sea—and there was nothing to identify you, no papers or even a ring on your hand. Your baggage must have been lost with the ship, but there was one small bag I found near where you lay. It is lying here on the window seat.'

'Please bring it here,' he said and made an effort to sit up but fell back with a moan. 'My blasted head. Please open the bag for me and see what is inside. It may tell us something of who I am.'

Morwenna fetched the bag and brought it to the bed. Opening it, she found brushes, crayons, bottles of powder in different colours and some soggy boards that she knew might be used by an artist. There was also a small leather purse that felt quite heavy. She tipped the contents on to the bed and twenty gold coins tumbled out.

'It would seem that you have some money and perhaps you are an artist, for these things must belong to an artist.'

'Yes, so it would seem.' He frowned. 'Is there nothing else that bears my name?'

'I don't believe so.' Morwenna felt something in a side pocket and inserted her fingers, drawing out a small metal token. It had writing on one side. She read the lettering and frowned. 'I think you must be a gambler, sir, for this is a token from what would appear to be a gaming house in London.'

'Let me see, please.' He took the little token and studied it. It bore the words Harlands of London and was a token for five guineas. 'It would seem that I have recently been in London, would it not?'

'Yes, I think you must have been,' she said. 'Perhaps you won the money there at this place? There are no clues to your identity, but if you returned to London and asked someone might know you at this place.'

'Yes, thank you,' he said and closed his fingers over it with a kind of desperation. 'I must hope that someone will tell me who I am.'

'Do not despair just yet, sir,' she said and smiled at him. Now that she suspected he might be an artist she was no longer afraid that he had been sent to spy on her brothers. 'You had a nasty bang on your head and the loss of your memory may be temporary. In time it will return to you.'

'Perhaps. You are good to be concerned for a stranger.'

'I have helped others in similar circumstances, sir. I am glad to have been of service to you.'

'Yet I should go,' he said. 'I must not be a burden on you. Pray turn your back, Mistress Morgan. Preferably leave the room. I need to relieve myself.'

'Lie still and I shall bring you the chamberpot, sir.'

'Turn away for your modesty.' He put his legs over the side of the bed, touched the floor with his feet, then moaned and fell back. 'Damn it, I'm as weak as a kitten.'

'You have been shipwrecked, sir, and your head bled from the blow you received. You will feel dizzy at first. Lie back and I'll give you the pot.'

Morwenna reached beneath the bed and

brought out the chamberpot. She handed it to him and retreated to the other side of the room to gaze out of the window. The sun was coming up over the sea, turning it pink and orange; this morning it would be as if the storm had never been except for the wreckage on the beach and the man in her bed.

'Have it your own way.'

The sounds of him using the pot kept Morwenna looking out to sea until he had done. She turned as she heard him place it on the chest beside the bed with a grunt, then returned to take it by the handle.

'I am used to nursing my brothers, sir. Please do not be embarrassed. Someone will need to care for you while you are forced to stay in bed.'

His gaze narrowed. 'Have you no servants to do the menial tasks?'

'How do you know I am not a servant here?' she challenged.

'You spoke of living here with your brothers—besides, you are too proud a wench to be in service, methinks.'

Morwenna laughed. 'At least then I should be paid for my work. My mother was a lady and my father called himself gentry, though he had rough country ways. However, they are both

dead and we have little money. I do have one
servant. Bess was our nurse and she helps me
now that we have no other servants.'

'Where are you going?'

'To empty this, sir. If you wish for it, I could
bring you something to eat. There is a tisane by
your bed. It must be cold now, but it will still
taste good. I shall return soon with food and
more drink.'

'It is not fitting that you should wait on me
or do these things for me. Send your servant instead, Mistress Morgan.'

'Bess is asleep and I shall not wake her.'

'I am grateful for all you have done, Mistress
Morgan, but I feel it wrong that a young woman
of your breeding should do such things for me.'

'You are no different to me than my brothers,' Morwenna lied. 'As soon as you feel able
to leave your bed you would do best to leave us,
sir—but until then I shall help you as best I can.'

She went out before he could answer her,
pride and temper carrying her down the stairs.
Who did he imagine he was to tell her what was
right and proper? She was accustomed to doing
much as she pleased, for even Michael did not
interfere unless it suited his purpose.

It was awkward that the stranger had lost his

memory. Michael would want to know who he was and why he was here—he suspected any stranger that came to their village. Morwenna would not have him mistreating the stranger. She must find a way to keep him safe until he was well enough to leave them.

It might be best to tell her brothers that he was an artist—and if necessary she could invent a name for him. Better that than leave Michael suspecting the worst about the stranger in their midst.

The stranger smiled as the door closed with a little snap. The fire in Morwenna's eyes as he'd told her it was not fitting that a woman of her breeding should care for him had amused him. She was proud and beautiful and it seemed that she had compassion, for she'd taken him in without knowing who he was or where he came from. His smile faded as he tried to remember who he was and why he was here in Cornwall.

The token in his bag suggested he'd once been in London. Why had he left town to come to a part of the country that most thought of as God-forsaken?

Someone had said that recently. At least, the phrase had come easily to his mind. He seemed to recall that he found the Cornish coast rugged but beautiful—that he had either painted it before or was looking forward to painting it in the future.

Perhaps that was his reason for being here. If this bag belonged to him, he must be an artist. Was he a successful one? Did he have money—more than the few gold coins lying on the bed by his side?

Something was not quite right. He felt that there was more to his life than that of an itinerant artist, moving from place to place to earn a living as best he could.

Was he a gambler down on his luck? Did he have a family and where did he belong?

Something told him that he was not married. He had a feeling that he was a lonely person and that there was an empty place inside him.

Now why did he feel that? For a moment a feeling of panic swept over him. Why could he not recall even his name? Supposing he never did?

Fighting his panic, he focused on the girl who had just left the room. She was right to suggest that he must seek his identity in London. Whatever his reason for being here, he must return to town and try to discover his name and family.

Once again a smile touched his mouth as he thought of Morwenna. She and her brother had carried him to their house and the girl had nursed him through the night. He dimly recalled feeling very ill and crying out as he tossed and turned, but whatever had haunted him then had gone, lost in the mists of amnesia. When he'd woken he'd seen the girl sitting in her chair near the bed. She was laughing to herself...at her own thoughts. The look on her face had intrigued him. What was she thinking? She might almost have been dreaming of her lover.

Something in him had rebelled at the thought of her with a lover. Perhaps he'd spoken out of turn, telling her that it was not fitting for her to do what she'd done. Had she left him on the beach he might have been killed, though the villagers would find little profit in robbing him for he wore no jewellery—at least he wore none now. Could the girl or her brother have taken it?

No, that was an unworthy thought! Had she been a thief she would have taken the money from his bag. If he wore no jewellery, he could not be anyone in particular—a gentleman often wore a signet ring with a crest, but he did not.

Yet instinctively he knew he was of gentle birth. Perhaps he came from an impoverished family and had chosen to make his living from his talent, if he had talent? He was still not certain that the bag belonged to him. Other men would have been on the ship that went down.

One of the first things he must do when he felt able to get up was to find something to draw on and then he might discover if he could be a painter. Until then he could only surmise that he was an artist.

He would have liked to get up, but for the moment he felt too ill. He must just lie here until his strength returned. Since he had nothing more to occupy his mind, he would think of Morwenna and that look in her eyes...

'Will you take this tray up to him?' Morwenna asked when Bess entered the kitchen. She had prepared a plate of hot crispy bacon with eggs and bread fried in the fat, also a mug of grog made from ale spiced with cinnamon and a dash of brandy. 'He was awake and he may be hungry or thirsty.'

'This is food for a hearty appetite,' Bess observed. 'If he is sick he needs porridge or gruel to ease his hunger.'

'I think he would throw it at you. He cannot yet leave his bed for he is dizzy, but there is little wrong with him—though he claims he does not know his own name or from whence he came.'

'You think he lies?'

'I don't know. Michael mustn't suspect it or you know what will happen—but he ought to leave this house as soon as he is able to walk.'

'Aye, I know it. Give me the tray. I'll ask if he wishes for anything more.'

'I emptied the pot and will bring it up with a can of water. It's my day for cleaning the bed-chambers, though my brothers will sleep clear through the morning if I know them.'

'Least said the better, lass. They were out helping to rescue men from the sea last night. No need to say more.'

Morwenna nodded as Bess picked up the tray and went out. She cut a slice of cold ham, placed it between a thick slice of bread and munched it as she waited for the water to boil. A part of her was eager to see the stranger again, though her common sense told her she would be best to let Bess care for him. By his manner and his look he was gentry, though perhaps like her he had little money. Why would he make his living as an artist if he were wealthy?

She shook her head. It was unlikely—though, sometimes, rich aristocrats spent time sketching simply to amuse themselves, of course. Twenty gold coins were not a fortune, but it was more than Morwenna had ever owned in her life.

A little smile touched her lips as she thought how handsome he was, but she shook her head almost at once. She was a fool to daydream over a stranger. She could not deny the instant attraction she'd felt, but he was unlikely to have felt the same.

It was because she seldom saw anyone other than her brothers, of course. Morwenna had no life of her own, nor any amusement or pleasures outside of what she made for herself.

Bess was always telling her to go to her mother's sister in London, but she knew her aunt to be an unkind, bitter woman. She'd buried two husbands and she had money to spare, but she was unlikely to spend it on the daughter of a man she despised.

'My sister, Agnes, never forgave me for marrying your father,' Morwenna's mother had told her when she was ill. 'She warned me that he would break my heart or drive me to an early grave. It is not your father's fault that I am sick, dear heart. I was always sickly, which was why my sister warned me against marriage to a man like William Morgan. I needed a gentle, kind man, but I loved him and I followed my heart. I do not regret it, though the bitter winds here have been my undoing.'

Morwenna had mourned her mother more than her father, though she knew that he, too, had grieved deeply, and despite his denials it was love of his dead wife that had caused him to neglect his own health and die of an infected boil on his neck. Morwenna would have cleansed it and bound it for him, but he would not let her touch him. At the end the physician told her that the poison had seeped into his blood and led to the fever that ended his life— but perhaps he had not wanted to live. He had quarrelled fiercely and often with his eldest son and ruined the family with his gambling and bad investments, though no man could govern the weather and a risky cargo lost at sea was the undoing of more than one merchant adventurer.

Her father had been given to risky ventures, but he had always been loyal to Queen Bess in her time and the King, even if he disliked his politics. It had been on a visit to court after his first wife died that he'd met and married Morwenna's mother, bringing her back to this house at the edge of the cliff. Jenna Morgan had always dreamed of taking her lovely daughter to court, but the girl's father had forbidden it.

'No good giving the girl ideas above her station. She'll marry a local man and do what I think best for her,' he'd declared, but he'd never bothered to find her a husband and Michael was too wrapped up in his work to think of such a thing.

Carrying the empty pot in one hand and a pewter can of warm water in the other, Morwenna started up the stairs. Pausing outside the door of the guest chamber, she heard a curse and then a muffled laugh.

'Damn you, old mother,' the stranger muttered. 'Have it your own way, crone. I'll suffer you to help me since I cannot do it myself.'

Opening the door, she went in and saw that her patient had managed to struggle into the hose and breeches he'd been wearing when she found him. Bess had provided him with one of her father's best shirts and a doublet of well-worn leather. He was now lying on the bed, propped up against the pillows. She noticed that he had eaten the food and had the tankard of warmed ale and cinnamon in his right hand. His gaze fell on her as she entered and he frowned.

'I brought you some water to wash, but it seems you forestalled me.'

'I used the cold water in the jug, with Bess's help,' he said and made a wry face. 'Did I not tell you it is not fitting for you to wait on me, Mistress Morgan?'

'You'll tell her until you be blue in the face.' Bess chuckled. 'Mistress Morwenna be a law unto herself, sir. She never minds me nor yet Master Michael, though sometimes we all have to take care for he has a rare temper.'

'Bess, do you not have something to do downstairs?' Morwenna asked. 'Take the tray down. I've work to do up here but we'll start the baking when I come down.'

She turned to the door when the stranger spoke. 'I've decided you should call me Adam, mistress. 'Tis not my name, but it will do as well as any until I know my own name.'

She stopped, turned to look at him. 'Adam was tempted by Eve and thrown out of the Garden of Eden for his sins. This house is not Eden, sir—but you should think of leaving as soon as you can walk. My brother does not care for strangers in the house.'

'What does he have to hide?'

Morwenna's eyes narrowed in suspicion.

'You should not ask. Believe me—you would not like to see my brother in a temper.'

'Does he treat you ill?'

'He shouts at me and orders me to do his bidding, but I keep a still tongue and then do as I please. I am his sister and Jacques would stop him if he lifted a hand to me. Besides, I am useful. Michael knows that I would leave this house if he once struck me.'

'Where would you go?'

'I do not know. Perhaps to my aunt's in London.'

'If she would take you in, you should go. A house like this is not fitting for a woman like you.'

'Indeed? What do you know of this house or my family?'

'Only what you have told me. Forgive me, mistress. I dare say you think me arrogant, but I am grateful for your help. Let me give you some of this money to start a new life somewhere else.'

'You presume too much, sir. I need no help from you nor anyone else. If I needed to, I could find my own way in the world. I am strong and I can work.'

'You might find it harder on your own than

you think,' he replied. 'The world is a wicked place, Mistress Morwenna. You need someone to protect you when you leave—your aunt or—'

A look from Morwenna silenced him. Once again he looked rueful.

'I have said too much. Away to your work, mistress. I thank you for the food and your kindness. As soon as I am able I shall leave this house, but I shall not forget you.'

'I pray that you recover your memory soon, sir. I need no thanks or recompense for the little I did—but 'tis for your own sake that I tell you to leave as soon as you are able. Michael does not care overmuch for strangers in his house.'

He inclined his head, but said no more. Morwenna left him and went slowly along the narrow passage to her own room. She would clean her chamber and Bess's, leaving her brothers' bedchambers until later when they were out about their own business.

She had warned the stranger to leave for his own good, but knew she would regret it when he had gone. Yet she could expect nothing from this chance encounter. Her life would be the same when he had gone. If she wanted more, then she must either go to her aunt or look for a husband nearer to home.

There was only one man who would ask her to marry him, but she disliked the man who was in charge of the local militia. Captain Bird was waiting for his chance to ask for her hand, but she would rather be single all her life.

Captain Bird was a Revenue Officer, but he had struck up an odd relationship with Michael. Although he told her nothing, Morwenna knew that her brother was involved in smuggling goods from France. The local gentry paid him well for brandy and silks that had never paid a penny in tax. That alone would see Michael hang if he were ever taken, but somehow he always seemed to know when the soldiers were coming and he was never in the house. It was Morwenna who had to fend off their questions—and yet Captain Bird never made more than a perfunctory search of the house before leaving them in peace.

Why should he be so accommodating? Did he and Michael have some understanding?

It would not be unusual for money to change hands in such business. If Captain Bird took bribes, he was little better than the smugglers he was supposed to arrest when he found them.

Morwenna was frowning as she began to rub beeswax perfumed with lavender oils into the solid oak furniture. She had drifted from one day to the next, vaguely unsatisfied with her life, but unsure of what to do to change it. Now she was aware of feeling restless. Unless she went to live with her aunt she really had little choice, for she knew that it wasn't enough to be willing to work hard. She wasn't as innocent as the stranger imagined and knew what might await her if she went to London or one of the big cities to ask for work. She would find herself being forced into a profession that would shame her.

Chapter Three

'He says he feels much better,' Bess said when she entered the kitchen later that day carrying a tray. The food had been cleared from the pewter platter and the tankard was empty. 'He asks your indulgence for one more night and says he will go in the morning.'

Morwenna hunched her shoulder, feigning indifference. 'He must stay until he is better. I would not grudge him a bed or food.'

'I've told him so, my lovely. Jacques went in to see him before he left to go fishing. Michael asked me about him and I said he was still tied to his bed. He went off on some business of his own before you finished cleaning upstairs.'

'We must hope the stranger is well enough

to leave soon—before Michael decides to throw him out.'

'Your brother said he might be away for some days.'

'Michael has gone away—to France?'

Morwenna knew that from time to time her brother had some business in France. Whatever he did there was secret. He did not even tell Jacques what he did when he was away for days at a time. She supposed he must be dealing with merchants or some such thing, but when she'd asked once he'd flown into a temper and told her to mind her tongue.

'He did not tell me. He said only that I should tell you not to expect him home until you see him.'

'Then he has gone somewhere on his own business. It is useless to ask for he tells us nothing.' Morwenna felt the relief sweep over her. 'If Michael has gone, we need not be too anxious, Bess. Jacques will not mind the stranger resting here for a while. He has his own work with the fishing fleet and only answers Michael's call when he must.'

'Jacques speaks of leaving Cornwall and finding a new life elsewhere. I think he does not like what his brother does.'

'He should go sooner rather than later. I sometimes fear that Michael will bring trouble on us all and I would not have Jacques hang as a smuggler.'

'And where would that leave you? You wouldn't live here with Michael without him.'

'No, I should go away.'

'You would be best with your aunt. I've told you so a hundred...'

Morwenna put a warning finger to her lips and then went to the door, wrenching it open swiftly. As she had suspected, the stranger was standing there.

'How long have you been there? Were you listening, hoping to learn something?'

'Why should I spy on you, mistress?'

Morwenna felt her cheeks heating. 'Forgive me, sir. I should not have accused you.'

'I heard nothing. I came to speak with your brother Michael—is he here?'

'No, he has gone away. Jacques is out fishing with other men from the village. What did you wish to speak with Michael about, sir?'

'I thought I might hire a horse somewhere.' He frowned. 'Will Michael be long?'

'He has gone away on personal business for

a few days. I do not know why. He does not discuss his affairs with us, sir.'

'Will you not call me Adam, as I suggested?'

'It is not your name, so why should we?'

'So you prefer sir?' He smiled oddly. 'Have it your way, mistress. Since your brothers are not here perhaps you would show me the way down to the inlet where you found me—if you have the time?'

'Why did you wish to go there? You have no need to leave for a day or so. With Michael away no one else will bother you.'

'I think I shall go straight to London when I leave here. However, would you allow me to stay here a little longer? I'd like to try my hand at some painting, perhaps it will help me to recover my memory. I can repay you from the money you found in my bag and still have sufficient for my journey.'

'Have I asked for money?'

'No, you have not. I would like to explore the inlet. If I can find anything that belongs to me there I might recall my name at least, and then I might find a way to be of assistance to you.'

'I told you earlier, I need no help from anyone. However, I'll take you down there myself. The way is steep, but it's easy enough once you

know how. I doubt you'll find anything. If the
sea brings anything of value ashore the villagers take it. The living is hard here, sir. You cannot blame them, for they live by the bounty of
the sea. There is little work other than on the
land or in the mines, but they often close if the
copper runs out.'

'Do they not have silver or gold in their
mines?'

'Very seldom and only in small amounts. No,
the living comes mostly from the sea for local
people. They may have some sheep on the common or a cow, but little else. What comes to
them from a shipwreck is seen as a gift of God.'

'Perhaps it is—but not if they lure ships in
to their doom.'

'Do you think that is what happened to your
ship? I should be sorry to think it. My father
was always against it and so are my brothers.
My father was seen as the law in these parts
and he would have punished anyone who was
caught wrecking.'

'I am glad to hear it, Mistress Morwenna.'

Morwenna looked at him proudly, then
reached for her shawl and pulled it around her
shoulders. The storm might have blown itself

out, but it could be cold on this part of the coast, especially now it was autumn.

'Follow me, but tread carefully,' she instructed as she went out. 'In the dark the path is difficult to find unless you know it, but it is easy enough to follow in daylight.'

The stranger followed behind her, though she did not turn her head to look at him. 'What made you think of looking in the inlet when everyone else was on the main beach?'

'I found some survivors there after a different ship was wrecked last year and took them to the house. It was a woman and child. We cared for them until they were well enough to leave us—but she knew who she was.'

'How fortunate for her.'

Morwenna concentrated on the descent, resisting the urge to glance back at him. He made her angry and yet he intrigued her. Something in his manner told her that he must be more than the itinerant artist she had thought him for at times he was arrogant, as if used to being obeyed.

Who was he really and why was he here? Had he truly lost his memory?

The inlet was tiny and belonged to Michael, though it was no use for anything and normally the sole province of sea birds and small crabs that lived in the shallow pools and were not nice to eat. Sometimes the villagers took mussels or limpets from the rocks. Michael allowed them to take what little harvest there was, because he and Jacques set their lobster pots out further in the bay. They normally caught enough fish to sell in the village or further inland, besides what they brought to the house for use at table.

Apart from a few pieces of driftwood the beach looked clear. Obviously, someone had been here before them and it was unlikely that her guest would find his possessions even if anything else had been there to find. He walked down to the water's edge and stood looking at some rocks, then, seeing something in the water, bent down and picked out a piece of drift wood.

'Have you found anything interesting?'

'It looks as if it came from a rowing boat,' he said and showed her what was in his hand. 'The tide must have dashed it against the rocks.'

'A rowing boat?' She saw some lettering on the wood, though not enough remained for her to be able to read the name. 'It must have broken free of the ship when it foundered. I doubt anyone would have been foolish enough to try to come inshore in a small boat last night. It was obvious what would happen; he wouldn't have stood a chance.'

'No, I'm sure you're right,' he replied and smiled. 'There is nothing to see here. Thank you for showing me the way. I can find my own way back if you have something else to do?'

'I've done most of my work for the day.' Morwenna shaded her eyes and looked out to sea. 'There's a ship out there. It's safe enough on a day like this. I wonder what it is waiting for?'

'What makes you think it is waiting for anything?'

'Well, it appears to have anchored. I don't think it's moving, do you?'

He looked towards the horizon. 'I expect they just want to admire the view for a while.'

'It can't be fishermen. I cannot imagine that a merchant vessel would anchor off shore just to admire the view.'

'Perhaps it is a spy waiting for dusk,' he said, a teasing note in his voice.

'Or waiting to take a spy off again once he's done his business.' Morwenna threw an accusing look at him. 'Just why did you come here?'

'The sea brought me,' he replied. 'What would a spy want with you or your family,

Mistress Morgan—unless you have something
to hide?'

She turned from him. 'I have nothing to hide
and my brothers, well, they can speak for themselves. If you question them you may wish you
hadn't, sir. If you're at all worried, I advise you
to leave now before you wish you had not become involved.'

'If only I could.'

'What do you mean?'

'I do not know where to go,' he said. 'What
else should I mean? Since it is obvious I shall
learn nothing here I may as well return to the
house.'

'No, stay and search for whatever you hope
to find. Sometimes things get caught there.' She
pointed to the jutting rock. 'There is a little pool
round the bend and the tide takes things there.
It's slippery, so take care, but the villagers do
not bother to look there because the tide can
be treacherous. You might find what you seek.'

'Thank you for the advice. The name of the
ship might help me—should I find the rest of
this.' He indicated the piece of driftwood, which
must have come from a rowing boat.

He walked away across the beach in the direction she had indicated. Morwenna watched

for a moment, then began the steep ascent back to her home.

Had he truly lost his memory? Could she believe him? Or was he here for the reason she dreaded? Michael might have a terrible temper, but he was her brother and she did not wish him to come to harm. She ought to send the stranger away before he could discover something that might lead to her family's destruction.

If only the look in the stranger's eyes did not make her feel as if she wanted to melt into his arms.

Adam walked the length of the beach, searching for anything that might have been washed ashore at the same time as the sea drove him this way. There was nothing to see. The villagers must have taken even the driftwood to keep their fires going through the winter. He could understand their need, yet felt a sweeping despair that he would find no clues here to help him rediscover his life.

It seemed that he must return to London as soon as he was able to travel and hope to trace his last movements at the gaming hall. He could not even be sure that he had meant to come here—his ship might have been driven off course by the storm.

Had he been travelling on his own ship? He was not sure why the thought should occur to him, but the sight of that ship out in the bay had made him wonder if at some time he'd been the owner of a vessel similar to the one they'd seen.

It was no use. Try as he might, he could not lift the curtain of mist in his mind.

He should return to the house, discover the nearest hostelry and hire a horse. There was no help for him here and yet he had a feeling that he had indeed come here for a reason. Besides, he was oddly reluctant to leave this place too soon.

Why? Surely he could not be thinking of remaining here longer because of Morwenna?

True, she was beautiful. Even her name sounded like music on his lips. He felt something each time he saw her, but could not place what emotion was uppermost in his mind. She infuriated him with her accusations. Clearly, her brothers were involved in some kind of nefarious business. Smuggling was rife on this coast and it was likely Michael Morgan was off on some such business—if nothing more serious.

Now where had that thought come from? What else might Michael Morgan be doing?

He shook his head. It was as if he were reaching for something—an important fact that lay just behind that damned curtain.

No, he should not speculate. It was not his business and yet something was nagging at him, telling him he should use the time while Michael was away to discover all he could.

Discover what? It was no good, his mind was confused—blank at times and at others teeming with pictures that did not make sense. Faces flitted through his mind. An older woman and another, pretty, but not his wife or his lover. Who were they?

Morwenna had said he'd cried out thinking her his mother when in his fever. Was his mother still living? Did he also have a sister?

Somehow that seemed right. He felt instinctively without knowing that he had a family, but no wife. Were his family worried about him?

He shook his head and pushed the thought away. It was not his family that taunted him, trying to burst through the fog in his mind. For the moment something else was more important, but he did not know what it was.

He turned back towards the path that led up the cliff. He would be wiser to leave and return to London, but something was holding him here. There was something about the wild-eyed Cornish woman, something that turned his guts soft and made him burn with a need he recognised. His memory might be missing, but his instincts were intact. He wanted to lie with her. He wanted to know her body, to touch that soft white flesh and kiss those full lips. Whether she knew it or not she had a pure, clear sensuality that called to a man of his nature, arousing the hunting instinct. He wanted her and knew he would stay until she sent him away. Perhaps he might persuade her to go with him. She obviously did not have much of a life here.

She was a fool to let the stranger get beneath the guard she normally kept on her senses. Morwenna frowned as she chopped roots and onions to add to the stewpot. It had been simmering for two days now, fresh meat and vegetables added each day so that the gravy was very thick and the flavour intense. Morwenna had cooked oatcakes, fresh bread that was flat and hard on the outside, soft within. She had butter, pickles, cheese and cold ham as well as a dish of neeps and a large piggy pie that Bess had made to an old Cornish recipe.

It was a hearty meal, the kind her brothers relished, but the stranger was to join them at table that night and she wondered if he would think it plain fare. Neither of her brothers had a sweet tooth and though she liked curds and custards herself, she scarcely ever bothered to make them. Michael called them pap and turned his nose up at such trifles. Yet if the stranger were an aristocrat, as she suspected, he would be used to finer dishes.

After his return from the beach she'd asked if he would join them in the kitchen for supper. He'd hesitated for a moment, then inclined his head. Something told her that he was not used to eating in a kitchen with the servants, but she had no time to set out the huge table in the large hall. It was seldom used these days and her brother Jacques would have thought she'd gone mad had she done so. Her father and mother had held dinners and feasts there for special occasions, but Michael did not bother. Often enough the brothers ate at different times, coming in to the kitchen to snatch what they could find before disappearing again. She hoped that Jacques would sit down with them that night, but there was no telling what time he would return from his fishing trip.

* * *

As the church bell tolled the hour of six down in the village, her brother entered the kitchen. She was pleased to see that Jacques had made an effort to dress as befitted a gentleman's son instead of his usual jerkin and breeches.

However, she frowned at him as he snatched at one of the freshly baked rolls and began to eat.

'You might wait for our guest,' she reprimanded.

'You can't make a silk purse out of a sow's ear,' Jacques said with a grin. 'Your guest will have to take us as we are, dear heart. It's too late to change us now.'

'Mother would turn in her grave if she could see you…' Morwenna began, the words dying on her lips as the kitchen door opened and the stranger entered. He was wearing the clothes she'd given him, but somehow he made Jacques look disreputable. He wore his pride like a velvet cloak, so obviously a gentleman that she felt a moment of shame for the way her brothers usually behaved at table.

'Forgive me for being late to table,' he said. 'The food smells good, Mistress Morgan. I believe I am hungry.'

'You spent a long time walking on the cliffs and in the village today,' Jacques said. 'What were you looking for?'

'I was admiring the scenery,' he replied. 'It appeals to my senses. I think I may be an artist, for my fingers wished for some charcoal that I might sketch what I saw.'

'An artist, are you?'

'If you would permit, I could try my hand after supper. I might sketch Morwenna—or any of you if you care for it. At least we would know if I have any talent.'

'A bang on the head often renders the mind hazy for a while,' Jacques observed. 'If you feel you can draw a person's likeness, your memory may be returning.'

'Yes, perhaps,' he said and his eyes moved to Morwenna. 'I must have had a reason for coming here, though as yet I cannot recall it, or my own name. I have asked that I be called Adam for the time being.'

'As you wish, Adam. What will you do next?' Jacques asked. 'You can stay here until you feel able to leave, but Michael would not be pleased to find you still here when he returns.'

'Your elder brother is averse to strangers?' The stranger looked up as Morwenna ladled stew into the bowl in front of him. 'Thank you, mistress. I am sure it will taste as good as it smells.'

'Morwenna is a good cook. She needs a husband, someone to keep her in the manner to which she is accustomed,' Jacques quipped, but his smile faded as his sister glared at him. 'Sorry, I know you shouldn't be waiting on us the way you do. It was merely a jest, dear heart.'

Morwenna made no reply. She finished serving the others and then took her own place at the far end of the table.

'I think I shall find somewhere else to stay tomorrow,' the stranger said. 'I wonder if I should stay here in the cove for a while in case someone comes to look for me. News of the shipwreck will have reached London by now, I dare say, and my family—if I have one—may look for me here.'

'What makes you think they will hear of the wreck? Do you come from London, then?' Jacques asked, his gaze narrowed.

'I do not know if I have a family, but I must have friends, people who know me. I think it is in London that ships are registered when they founder. I feel that I may have come from there—just as I feel I may be an artist. I can-

not know anything for sure, which is why I perhaps ought to stay close until someone comes
who can tell me who I am and whence I came.'

'There is no need to leave for a few days.
Michael will not return for a while. Stay here
in case your fever returns. He has no need to
leave, has he, Morwenna?'

'He may stay until Michael returns if he
pleases.' She kept her gaze lowered. 'It is no
trouble to feed an extra man.'

'That is kind. It would suit me to stay—if I
may?'

'We shall not hear of your leaving for a few
days, until we are sure you have recovered,'
Jacques said. ''Tis a pity the sea took your papers, for you might have known where to begin
your search. If you feel you came from town,
why not return to London when you are completely well and be seen there? If you are known,
someone will hail you and you may find your
family sooner.'

'That was my first thought.' The stranger
glanced at Morwenna. 'I feel I owe your family something, because your sister saved my life.
Once I regain my memory I may be able to
repay her in some way.'

'Morwenna wants for nothing. She does not need your money, sir.'

'Perhaps there are other things more important to Mistress Morgan. I may know people who would sponsor her in town so that she could find a husband best suited to her needs.'

'She has a suitor if she wants one.' Jacques threw him a challenging look. 'Captain Bird would be happy to oblige, would he not, Morwenna?'

'I will thank you not to discuss me at table—any of you.' She glared at her brother and then at the stranger, surprising a look that might have been concern or sympathy in his eyes.

'Help yourselves to bread and cheeses and the oatcakes. There's honey if you want it, sir. I'm going up to my room. I'll come back later to clear up, Bess.'

She rose from her chair and walked from the room, her back very straight. Behind her there was silence until Jacques laughed.

'I fear I have offended Morwenna,' he said. 'It was a mere jest, of course. Morwenna wouldn't have that militiaman if he paid her his weight in gold.'

Hearing the stranger laugh in response to Jacques, Morwenna smarted with anger and humiliation. How dared the brother she loved and trusted discuss her in front of a stranger? How dared the stranger suggest that if he regained his memory he might know someone who would sponsor her—as if she were in need of his pity or compassion!

She had been shocked to learn that he planned to leave the next day and felt a sense of loss until Jacques invited him to stay—but after that remark she would be glad to see the last of him. The last thing she needed from anyone was pity!

Turning away from the stairs, she went outside into the cold night air. She was suddenly weary of her life and the duties she performed every day, rebelling as she realised that nothing was likely to change for her unless she made it change herself.

It seemed her only escape was to go to her aunt, but would it be a change for the better or would she be trapped in the house of a bitter old woman?

Tears stinging behind her eyes, she walked up to the top of the cliff and stood looking out to sea. The wind tugged at her gown and pierced her shawl, making her shiver in the cool night air. Autumn would soon be gone and then the winter would be upon them and it would be too dangerous to stand at the edge of the cliffs lest the lashing rain had made the soil loose. For a moment her eyes were blinded with tears, but then she saw a light flash from somewhere out at sea. She thought someone must be signalling with a lantern. As she stood, her nerves tingling, she saw a light from the shore, which appeared to be answering the ship. Was it the stranger? Was he indeed a spy and was he signalling to the ship in the bay?

Even as the thought came into her mind, she heard a sound behind her and turned to see a man walking towards her. It was the stranger and he did not carry a lantern. So it could not have been him on the beach.

'I thought you would be here,' he said. 'I'm sorry if what I said at table upset you, Mistress Morwenna.'

'It wasn't your fault. My brothers think it is a great joke because Captain Bird makes no secret of his hopes.'

Since he wasn't the one signalling to the ship, it must be someone else—and that person was likely to be Michael, who might not have gone abroad after all. If he was arranging for contraband to come ashore, it would be best the stranger did not see it. She moved towards him, pretending to trip and falling into his arms. He caught her and held her. She looked up at him and the heat in his eyes startled her. A fierce shaft of longing shot through her and she gasped. The next moment he had her pressed hard against his body and his arms were about her. She ought to push him away, but if she did not distract him he might notice the flashing lights.

Now he was bending his head, and his mouth was on hers, taking possession of her lips, exploring her mouth with his tongue, sending little thrills of heat racing through her body. She moaned with pleasure, unable to pull away or tell him to stop. It was as if a sudden fire had begun inside her and she was burning up with the need to allow his kisses and so much more. She wanted him to hold her for ever, to take her down here on these cliffs and kiss her senseless. She wanted to love him, to stand by his side and keep the world at bay.

No, how stupid of her. She was allowing her loneliness and her frustration to take over her mind. To lie with this stranger could lead to only one thing: her ruin. He did not feel as she did, even though his kiss had touched her soul. She must stop this now before it was too late.

'No, you must not,' she cried, though her heart rebelled and her senses screamed to be back in his arms. 'I can't…I can't…'

Wrenching away from him, she ran back down the path to her house, as sure footed in the dark as she was when it was light. She would be a fool to trust a man who claimed not to know his own name. Instinct told her that to let the stranger into her heart could only lead to sorrow.

'Morwenna, please.' She heard his shout, but dared not look back. If she did, she would end by giving in to the need inside her, the need of a lonely girl to be loved.

Chapter Four

'You look like a ghost,' Bess muttered the next morning when Morwenna went into the kitchen. 'Are you sickening for something?'

'I didn't sleep very well last night,' she replied. 'Where is Jacques?'

'He went out this morning early. He didn't tell me where he was going, but said he'd bring me a crab for supper or some fish.'

'Has *he* gone out yet?'

'If you mean "Adam", aye, he's gone to find a hostelry. He gave me a gold coin and thanked me for caring for him and for the food.'

'A gold coin. He was generous, for he has few possessions and only a few coins.'

'He was grateful and insisted that I take it for

my trouble. He said he would like to give you a present, but feared to offend you.'

'I do not want his money.' Morwenna frowned. 'It is odd that the sea did not take everything from him. Unless…'

'What are you thinking?'

'There was driftwood in the cove the next morning—wood that might have come from a long boat. He might have come ashore that way.'

'He did not fake the gash on his head.'

'The rocks are slippery and treacherous when the sea is rough. He could have been washed off by a wave after he'd landed.'

'Only a spy would come in that way.' Bess looked at her. 'If Michael guessed he didn't come from the shipwreck he would find him and kill him. We gave him food and shelter, but if he came here to spy on your brothers…'

'I know.' Morwenna turned away, fighting her feelings. 'I couldn't bear it if anything happened to Jacques or Michael, of course.'

'Well, let's hope he's truly lost his memory.' Bess sent her a pitying look. 'He was a fine strapping man, but I doubt you'll see him again once he leaves these parts. Think of your brothers, girl. That man can never mean anything to you. He's not one of us.'

'I know.' Morwenna blinked away her tears. 'I'd best get on with the baking.'

'We need more butter. Walk down to the farm and fetch some, lovey. I can manage here until you return. There's not much needs doing I can't manage.'

Morwenna nodded and reached for her shawl, wrapping it about herself. She took some coins from the shelf and went out. It was windy again and the door whipped from her grasp and blew shut with a bang. Shivering, she pulled the shawl tighter about her as she set off toward the bottom of the cliffs and then turned away from the beach. The farm was about half a mile further inland, but she was used to the walk and it did not bother her. Bess was right, it would do her good to walk and help her to rid herself of the feeling of restlessness that had been with her for the past few days. Crying herself to sleep had done nothing for her, but the stranger had gone now and she would probably never see him again.

Morwenna was lost in thought as she began her journey back to the house after making her purchases from the farm. When a man approaching on a horse suddenly halted and dismounted in front of her, she was startled until she realised who it was.

'Captain Bird, good morning. I trust you are well.'

'All the better for meeting you, Morwenna.' The militia officer leered at her, his narrow eyes gleaming and his thick lips set in a look of satisfaction.

His manner made her instantly uncomfortable, for he was obviously well pleased at finding her alone. At home she had always felt well able to cope with his official visits, but here alone on this windswept path she felt suddenly vulnerable.

'Excuse me, I must get home for I have much to do.' She attempted to walk on, but he moved to block her way.

'Surely you can spare a little time for me? I thought we were friends. I've turned a blind eye to your brothers' business many times. You might be a little grateful to me.'

Morwenna shuddered inwardly. She lifted her head, giving him a straight look. 'I do not know what you mean, sir. Now, I pray you, let me pass.'

'Give me a kiss for my trouble. I've heard there's folk asking in the village about the

Morgan family. I intended to warn your brother to be careful. I'm not sure what business he's mixed up in now, but it's more dangerous than he realises and folk have become interested in him all of a sudden.'

'What folk?' Her heart raced. 'I do not understand you.'

'Your brother is a smuggler and well you know it. He's escaped the law because I've helped him, but now there's London folk asking about him and I thought he should know.'

'London folk? How do you know they come from London?'

'Because they came on official business, that's why, mistress—and I can't tell you more, except that Michael may be in trouble if he doesn't watch his step. You tell him he owes me a debt for sending them on a false trail. He knows what I want from him.'

Something in his eyes made her shiver and feel suddenly afraid. Had Michael promised him something—and did it concern her?

'As you wish.'

'You know I would not see you or your family come to harm, Morwenna.'

'I thank you for your good intentions.'

Once again she tried to pass, but he caught

hold of her. His fingers dug into the soft flesh of her arm, but she did not cry out, merely lifting her head to look at him proudly. 'Not so fast, sweet mistress. I deserve a kiss and I intend to have it.'

'No! I do not wish for your kisses.' She thrust him away, kicking his shin as he tried to hold on to her.

'You little hellcat. I ought to teach you a lesson.'

Morwenna screamed, though there was no one to hear her. 'Lay a hand on me and you will be sorry.'

'Michael told me I need only ask if I wanted you. I'll marry you, Morwenna. You know I care.'

'No, leave me alone. I don't want you to touch me. Let me go.'

'I should do as the lady asks if I were you, sir.'

Morwenna was startled. She turned her head and saw the stranger from the sea glaring at her. Where had he come from? She had not seen him approach.

'And who the hell are you?' Captain Bird demanded, bristling at his interference. 'This is between me and Mistress Morgan. Stay out of my business.'

'Forgive me, but when I see a lady being molested it becomes my business.' The stranger glared at him. 'I suggest you get on your horse and leave now—before I teach you a lesson you'll regret.'

Captain Bird stared at him, then looked at Morwenna resentfully. 'I don't know who he is, but your brother has promised me I can have you if I can get you and you'll be sorry for this.'

'Michael would never force me to wed you or anyone else.' Morwenna lifted her head proudly.

His face a mask of fury, Captain Bird walked to his horse, mounted, then rode off without glancing back. Morwenna breathed deeply, shaking and clearly distressed until the stranger put out his hand to touch her. She flinched away, as if she'd been stung.

'I'm not going to seduce you,' he said, smiling wryly. 'I'm not like that insensitive oaf. Last night I was tempted, though, when you fell into my arms.'

'I tripped.'

'Did you? Yes, I suppose you did, though it seemed to me that you were not exactly averse to finding yourself there.'

'It was foolish of me. I was upset and…I shan't deny I liked being kissed by you,' she said, putting her chin up. 'It gets lonely here when I hardly ever see anyone other than my brothers. Perhaps I shall go to my aunt—though she may not welcome me. She was not kind to my mother.'

'If I could help you, Morwenna.' He moved closer to her, his eyes intent on her face. 'Believe me, I am not your enemy. If ever I could be of service to you I would—without asking for anything in return.'

'I'm not sure that would work,' she replied, but she was smiling now, because there was something about him that reached out to her. 'I think you know I like you more than I ought.'

'Believe me, I like you too, far more than is good for me. I shouldn't let my feelings interfere with my search.' He hesitated, then, 'I need to discover who I am and why I came to this part of the Cornish coast.'

Morwenna looked at him intently. 'You gave Bess a gold coin…there was no need. You should keep what you have until you know where you came from. That money may be all you have in the world.'

'I dare say I can earn my living with my paints and crayons.'

'Are you're certain you can draw now?'

'I proved it last night. I drew pictures of your brother and Bess. My work made them smile and Jacques has asked me to draw a picture of a house in the village as a gift for a friend. I am going to meet him and the owner now.'

'I'll walk a part of the way with you,' she said and wondered why she was so pleased to meet him like this. It wasn't just because he'd saved her from an unpleasant incident with Captain Bird. She ought to ignore him, to do all she could to make him move on, leave her house and the district, but somehow, all she wanted was to be with him. The memory of his kiss was melting her insides, making her long to be back in his arms. Yet she recalled Captain Bird's warning about strangers from London—could this man be one of those sent to investigate Michael Morgan?

And what was Michael doing that the militiaman thought so dangerous? What business other than smuggling was her elder brother engaged in now?

She had known for a while that Michael was hiding something from them. He had always been secretive, but mostly the smuggling was an open secret within the house—this other work was different.

Could it have something to do with the signals on the beach the previous night? And where had her brother gone?

'I'll be travelling to London in a few days,' the stranger said, breaking into her thoughts. 'If you wanted, I would take you with me. You'd be safer travelling with me than alone and I could take you to your aunt's house. If you stay here, your amorous friend might try to seduce you again and next time you may not have anyone around to help.'

'He wouldn't hurt me. Michael would kill him first.' Morwenna turned her thoughtful gaze on him. 'Why should you do that for me? Take me with you to London? I might be a burden to you, if you are still searching for your own life, your memories.'

'You saved my life. If escorting you to London would help you, I should be happy to be of service, Morwenna.'

The way he spoke her name sent little spirals of sensation winging through her body. She turned her face aside, not wanting him to see how he affected her, because her need mustn't show. It was a chance for a different life and something told her if she accepted his offer she would never get to her aunt's house. If she gave into this feeling, this roaring heat she felt between them, she would end by becoming his mistress. She could feel the physical pull between them and knew that he was feeling it too.

Would it be so very bad? At least she would know a little happiness. She might see a different kind of life for a while, but in time he would tire of her and then she would be alone, unable to return to her old life. Her aunt would never take her in if she'd been this man's lover. Yet it might be worth the risk to know what happiness was like just for a while.

'Perhaps,' she said and risked a look at his face. 'I shall think about it.'

'I should like to draw a likeness of you,' he said, surprising her. 'Would you meet me on the cliffs later this afternoon, after I've been to your brother's friend's house?'

'Why on the cliffs?'

'Because it's how I see you, standing there looking out to sea, the wind in your hair and blowing your cloak about you. You are very beautiful, Morwenna—did you know that?' She shook her head and he smiled. 'Given the right clothes you would be a sensation at court.'

'Do you often visit the court?'

'I think perhaps I have in the past,' he replied and his gaze slid away from hers. 'I am beginning to remember a few things. I think my family has a house in the country, but spends time in London—and if they are of any consequence, therefore, at court.'

'You do not seem the kind of man who would come here simply to sketch the views,' Morwenna said. 'I wish I knew who you really were and why you were here.'

'I mean you no harm, believe me.'

She lifted her eyes to his. There was sincerity in his voice but his eyes were shadowed by doubts. She sensed that there were things he would not tell her, things in his past, perhaps, but what of his reason for being here?

'What of my brothers? What do you mean for them?'

'Why do you fear for them? Why should you think I might seek to harm them?'

'What makes you think I do?'

'You are defensive about them, as though you think they may be in trouble—or danger.

I believe you care for them and particularly Jacques?'

'Jacques is the closest to me, but I would not see harm come to Michael. He is not always kind, but he is my brother—at least, my half-brother. My father married again after his first wife died and I sometimes think that Michael resents me because of it.'

'But you are close to Jacques?'

'Jacques is my full brother and loves me— even though he teases me at times.'

'As last night?'

'Yes. I was foolish to be upset. He said nothing that mattered.'

'Yet you fear for him—for both of them.'

'I could not bear it if Jacques…' She shook her head, trying to clear the memory of the militiaman's malicious hints that her elder brother was in trouble. 'Captain Bird tried to blackmail me into allowing his kisses. He spoke of danger, particularly to Michael.'

'If your brothers have nothing to hide, they must be safe from whosoever concerns themselves in their business. They are safe from me. Do you imagine I would betray those who had helped me and saved my life?' His eyes were on her now. 'Will you come to meet me later this afternoon?'

'Perhaps.' Morwenna faltered. 'This is where we part. You take the path to the right. I go straight ahead.'

'Please come.'

'Yes, if I can.' She hesitated, then caught at his arm. 'Take care, sir. I would not have harm come to you either. Michael…'

'Are you afraid of him?'

'He has a violent temper. He uses his fists and some of the men he works with are more violent.' She shook her head. 'I shall say no more. I have said too much already.'

'You've told me nothing I had not already guessed, Morwenna. This part of the coast is well known for the smuggling that goes on here. Be at ease, your brothers' secret is safe with me—though they run the risk of trial, imprisonment or death every time they bring in illicit cargo.'

'I know it and I fear it will lead them to trouble. But I suspect there are other things, though I must say no more. Thank you for helping me.' She shook her head and turned away, the sudden tears stinging her eyes as she fought to hold them back.

Climbing the steep path to her house, Morwenna's throat was tight with emotion. She was torn between loyalty to her family and the strange new emotion that had implanted itself in her heart. She was even more certain that he was hiding something from her and her head told her that she must not meet him that afternoon, but something inside—a need so strong that she could not deny it—was telling her that she should go.

Adam walked on towards the village, his thoughts whirling in confusion. His mind was crowded with pictures that made no sense to him and yet the talk of smuggling had triggered a warning bell. He was sure that he had known the Morgan brothers were involved in the illegal carriage of goods that had paid no tax before Morwenna's manner made it so obvious. Was it a part of the reason he had come here to Cornwall?

He tried to tear down the curtain in his mind, but it stubbornly remained, though sometimes now he saw a kaleidoscope of pictures that seemed so clear they must be real. He could see a large country house and a London house; they were both grand houses and he was not sure if he had lived there or merely worked there in his capacity as an artist. Again he'd seen the faces of an older woman and a younger lady—were they his mother and sister? The pictures made him restless, unhappy.

They were a part of his past, but something else burned behind the mist, something important. Whatever it was, it had begun to make him feel uncomfortable. He wished that he could understand the feelings that Morwenna aroused in him. There was a strong physical attraction, a need to touch her and kiss her—to make love to her. She was of good family and yet she had little prospect of marriage.

Would it be a crime to take her from her home and make her his mistress?

Yet something told him that there was a strong reason why he should not become involved with the beautiful Cornish girl. What was her brother's secret—the one that troubled her?

And why should he feel that it might have something to do with his reason for coming to Cornwall? The memory was there just behind the curtain in his mind, but try as he might he could not tear it down.

He must give up all thought of leaving here

until he knew why he had come. Some inner instinct was telling him that it was important he should stay, at least for a while...

'What's the matter with you?' Bess looked at Morwenna as she moved about the kitchen, wiping surfaces she'd already cleaned. 'Why can't you settle? If you're restless, girl, go for a walk.'

Morwenna had almost decided against meeting the stranger and yet every fibre in her body yearned for the sight of him, for the touch of his hand. She knew nothing about him and yet she knew everything she needed to know. His touch and his kisses made her feel more alive than she'd ever been in her life.

'I'll walk to the beach,' she said and reached for her shawl, wrapping it about her shoulders as she went out into the garden. The wind had dropped a little, but there was a hint of rain in the air.

She hesitated at the gate, then, as if her feet had a will of their own, she began to climb upwards, away from the beach. Something was drawing her on, an inner compulsion that made her body tingle with anticipation and her mind sing with joy. It was as if she'd reached a decision, as if a part of her had let go of all the inhibitions and doubts. Her breath came faster as she saw him waiting near the spot where they'd met the previous night, her pulses pounding with excitement. Her heart knew why she had come, though her head told her it was foolish.

Suddenly, she was a woman going to meet her lover and she ran the last few steps towards him. He seemed to sense her mood for he came to meet her, catching her to him and holding her pressed against his body as their lips met in a hungry kiss. She could feel his strength, feel the hardness of his manhood pulsing against her as she melted into him, all caution lost. He was the man she'd longed for all her life, here, holding her, kissing her, and she knew with a bright-white clarity that if she withdrew now she would regret it for the rest of her life.

'Where can we be alone?' he murmured huskily.

'I know of a place.' She took his hand, led him across the plateau, away from the cliff face towards a small cottage. 'This is where the lightkeeper used to live years ago. He would signal to ships at sea that it was dangerous to come in, but when he died no one wanted to live here and so it is empty.'

'I saw it the other day, but thought it might belong to someone.'

'It belongs to Michael, but he never uses it,' she said. 'We shall be out of the rain for I think it will rain very soon.'

'You're certain?' he asked as she found the key under a rock and unlocked the door. 'Your brother will not come here?'

'He never does. Why should he? Besides, he will not be home for some days.'

Unlocking the door, she drew him inside and then locked it again, leaving the key in the door. He stood looking at her, then reached out and drew her against him once more.

'I swear I'll be good to you, Morwenna. When I go I'll take you with me and find you a nice house to live where we can be together.'

She understood what he was saying. He would take care of her, be her protector, but marriage was not being suggested or considered. At the back of her mind a little voice was warning her not to be foolish, but she'd fought the voice before and she knew that this was what she wanted. It was her one chance of happiness. Something she would never find if she stayed at home with her brothers.

'Don't talk, kiss me,' she urged, moving back

into his arms. 'I don't want to think about anything but being with you…'

'You are so beautiful, so passionate,' he said in a voice husky with desire. 'I want you more than I can say.'

Morwenna's lips softened beneath his as he deepened his kiss, her mouth opening, taking him in as his tongue explored and tasted her. She let her fingers explore the back of his neck, stroking the tender flesh at his nape and feeling him shudder as the passion heightened between them. She was so hot, little thrills of anticipation racing through her as he suddenly reached down and lifted her into his arms. Morwenna clung to him as he carried her towards the bed, hardly noticing that it was made up with linens and a thick coverlet. Even when she caught the smell of lavender that she used in the sheets at home it did not register in her mind that the bed linen was fresh and aired rather than damp and musty.

'You lovely, lovely, wild creature,' he muttered close to her ear. His lips caressed her neck, nibbling at her playfully, and his tongue caressed the sensitive skin of her ear. 'Are you virgin, Morwenna? I would not hurt you…if 'tis so, I will go slowly with you.'

'I have lain with no other man,' she murmured as his hand pulled her skirts up and he began to stroke the inside of her thigh. 'I have wanted no other lover.'

'I am honoured to have been chosen to teach you,' he murmured throatily. 'Are you warm enough if I remove some of these clothes?'

'I'm burning up,' she murmured, laughing as she lifted her body to allow him to divest her of needless garments.

When he had her naked and quivering in his arms, he stared at her for so long that she trembled, feeling anxious that he did not like what he saw.

'Do I not please you?'

'You are more beautiful than I could have imagined. Let me get out of my clothes.'

He left her for a moment to strip away his own garments. Morwenna saw the body she'd bathed when he was in a fever, but now his maleness was more apparent, rampant and huge, making her gasp with wonder. As he bent over her, she reached out to stroke down the length of his strong back. His flesh was hot and silky, heating her as it touched, mingling with her own fire. He was so beautiful, so strong and male that she could scarcely breathe, fear of the unknown mixing with a need to discover the pleasure she instinctively knew he could give her. He began to stroke her with hands, lips and tongue, teasing, inviting, lavishing her with sensations she'd never known. Her breath came faster and faster as she touched him, wanting to feel his reactions through her fingers, wanting to appreciate his body as he was worshipping hers.

His kisses began at her lips, traced the line of her white throat to the little hollow at the base. His tongue circled it, teasing her as she arched and moaned. His hand was moving down her body, stroking, bringing her such sweet pleasure as he sought each breast, circling the nipples with his thumb, making her scream as her body became boneless, melting in the heat of passion. His tongue began where his hands had left off, leading her into a maelstrom of emotions so fierce and needy that she just fell apart in his arms, her will subjected to his and the quest for pleasure.

'Yes,' she whispered as his tongue sought the most sensitive areas of her femininity, rousing her to such overwhelming feeling that she gasped and lay quivering beneath his touch, her hips rising to meet him, urging him on to what she did not know.

'You're so hot and wet, my little wanton wench,' he murmured. 'You are ready for me, Morwenna?'

'Yes, yes,' she was begging him to come into her, welcoming the thrust of his huge maleness, even though it stretched and filled her and for one moment she felt a tearing pain that stilled her.

'It will be better in a moment,' he said as he stilled with her and stroked her, bringing her back to that fluid state where she floated in pleasure. 'That's right, sweeting, let yourself go, come to me, come with me, Morwenna.'

And she did, abandoning all thought, all reserve. She gave herself to him body and soul. Their bodies fit together as if it were ordained, moving in a sweet slow rhythm that made her nerves sing with sensation. It seemed for a while that the rain lashing down outside was a part of the wild passion that possessed them as they loved, moving towards a sudden and devastating climax that made her cry out and claw at his shoulders with her nails, while he shuddered and lay on her, slicked with sweat and satiated.

* * *

It was a long time afterwards before either of them spoke, and then his hand caressed the back of her neck.

'You're not sorry?' he asked.

'No, why should I be? It was beautiful.'

'I shall take care of you. Remember that, my sweet love. Whatever happens in the future, I shall make sure you are safe.'

A little tingle at her nape warned Morwenna that something was wrong and yet she did not wish to think or know why there was such an odd note in his voice.

'This bed has been made recently with fresh sheets,' she said, suddenly realising. Her eyes travelled round the room, dwelling on the hearth. 'Someone has laid a fire. I thought Michael had no use for the cottage.'

'Perhaps one of your brothers brings his women here.'

'Michael.' A chilling coldness came over her and she realised what she had done. 'Michael would not bring a woman here, but he might bring others…' Men he wanted to hide from view? 'We should leave. If they came here…'

'No one is coming here on such an afternoon,' he said, holding her to him. 'Listen to the rain. The door is locked. They couldn't get in—and if they tried, we'd make the bed and tell them we sought shelter from the rain.'

'They would know.'

'It won't happen. Besides, I'm taking you with me when I go, Morwenna. You are wasted living here. In London you will be appreciated for your beauty. I shall give you clothes and a house of your own. We shall be together as often as I can get away.'

Morwenna snuggled closer to his body. She could taste the saltiness of his sweat on her lips and she liked the musk of his body. She didn't want to think about what she'd done. Bess would be shocked. Her brothers would be furious with her for throwing away her honour—and Michael would kill the man who had taken it.

She wouldn't tell anyone. It was her secret, a secret to have and to hold. Leaving Jacques would be a wrench, but Michael hardly ever noticed her, except when she served his supper. Bess would miss her and find the work hard, but they would have to hire another servant.

Morwenna wasn't going to think about her family or the future. If she did, she might begin to doubt, to fear. She would hold tight to this moment, to the man lying so close to her. He had promised to take her with him and she believed he meant it. The die was cast. She would not worry about what might happen until it did happen.

'You little witch,' Adam murmured nuzzling against her neck. 'I'm wanting you again already, but I think you may be too sore, because it was your first time. I won't take you again, but that doesn't mean we can't enjoy ourselves. There is a lot more to teach you about loving yet, my love.'

Morwenna smiled and reached up to bring his head down to hers, showing him what she had already learned.

'Teach me everything,' she invited. 'I want to please you as you please me.'

'My sweet, hot, Cornish wench,' he said and stroked the length of her back. 'It shall be my pleasure.'

'Where have you been in this weather?' Bess demanded as Morwenna entered the kitchen. 'I've had all the work to do—and Jacques is back. He wanted to know where you were.'

'I was caught in the rain and decided to shelter in the lightkeeper's cottage,' Morwenna said.

'I'll finish the supper now, Bess. I'm sorry if you've had too much to do.'

'Well, you'd done most of the preparation,' Bess muttered. 'I was worried, that's all. Thought you might have done something silly.'

'Now what should I do?' Morwenna asked, her heart beating madly. Could Bess see a difference in her? Would she know that she'd been in the arms of her lover?

Hugging the excitement and happiness to her as she set about preparing the supper, Morwenna felt a prick of guilt despite her pleasure. It would be hard for Bess when she left with her lover, but her brothers would either have to employ another servant or one of them must marry and bring his wife here.

'Where have you been?'

Hearing Jacques's voice, she turned to look at her younger brother. 'I went for a walk on the cliffs. The storm was sudden and I sheltered in the cottage.'

'You shouldn't have done that, Morwenna. Michael won't like you using it. Stay away from there—do you hear me?'

'Why?' Her breath caught as she saw his angry look. 'I'm sorry, I didn't know you were using it.'

'I'm not, but I know Michael does—and he would be furious if he knew you had been there. It is supposed to be a secret. If you say anything, you could cause trouble for us all.' Jacques glanced at Bess. 'Neither of you should mention that place—especially to the militiamen.'

'I wouldn't betray you,' Morwenna said, but couldn't look at him. In a way she had betrayed him by taking her lover there.

'You know nothing. Let's keep it that way.' Jacques softened his tone. 'Captain Bird was asking for you, Morwenna. He told me he asked you to wed him but you turned him down. He was hinting that he knew something about Michael—something I don't. Be careful what you say to him, he might turn nasty.'

'I'm always careful,' Morwenna said, her head coming up with a snap. 'I wouldn't marry that slimy toad if he were the last man to ask me. He didn't so much ask me to marry him as try to seduce me. He disgusts me. He's sly.'

'Yes, he is. He isn't what I should like for you, dear heart, but I doubt you'll get any better offers here. It may be best for you to stay with Mother's family. If things go wrong, it won't be safe for any of us here.'

'What do you mean?' Morwenna's heart raced. 'Are you in trouble, Jacques?'

'No, but there are things—' He broke off and shook his head. 'It's best you don't know. I think Michael is mixed up in something desperate. At first the smuggling was just a way of making money, but I think it led to other things and now... I'll not tell you so do not ask, but if you won't have Captain Bird you should consider going to our aunt's.'

'Well, perhaps I shall,' she said. 'Please do not worry about me. Are you involved in Michael's schemes?'

'To an extent. He does not tell me everything, but I've guessed at least a part of what he's up to—and it could mean real trouble for us all. You would be safer gone, dearest.'

'Perhaps.'

'At least promise me you won't use the cottage again. If Michael returned, he would be very angry—and you might become involved in something you ought not.'

'Yes, of course I promise,' Morwenna promised and bit her lip as she turned away. She'd promised to meet her lover there the next afternoon, but they could go somewhere else, maybe to a cave where the floor was sandy and dry.

It did not matter where they went, as long as they could be together and alone. She smiled inwardly, hugging her wonderful secret to herself. She had a lover and she was going to London with him very soon.

Chapter Five

'Have you heard from your brother?' The Dowager Marchioness looked at her daughter and frowned. 'Rupert seldom writes to me so it does not surprise me, but I am told he went out of town. Did he say anything to you, May?'

'No, Mother.' May looked anxious. 'I was expecting him to call before this, because it is my birthday tomorrow. It is most unlike him not to bring me a gift.'

'Yes,' the Dowager Marchioness agreed. 'He may not be a good son to me, but he has always been a fond brother. I think it strange that we have not heard from him of late. Richard would never have left it so long before visiting his family.'

'Mother, you are not quite fair. I am sad that

Richard died so tragically, but it was a long time ago. Do you not think you should try to forgive Rupert? It was not his fault that—' May was silenced as her mother's eyes snapped at her.

'What would you recall of it? You were but a child. Rupert pushed his brother into the moat that day. They were fighting as usual despite their father's orders to behave. It was Rupert's fault that Richard became ill and later died. You may forgive him if you choose, but I never shall.'

May made no reply. It was useless to argue with her mother when she was in this mood for she could never win their arguments. The Marchioness had become a cold, proud and bitter woman.

'I wish Rupert would write,' May said, but so softly that her mother did not hear her.

In his sister's opinion it was strange that Rupert had not sent a gift for her birthday and she could not help but wonder if something had happened to him to make him forget.

What was he doing that was so important he could not even send her his good wishes for the day?

'You are so lovely, my darling.' Adam bent to kiss Morwenna's lips, stroking the slightly damp hair from her forehead. 'I cannot tell you how much these meetings have meant to me. I want to be good to you, Morwenna. Promise me you will not lose your courage. You will come with me?'

'Yes, of course.' She smiled up at him, reaching out to trace his mouth. 'I must speak to Jacques before we go. I owe him that at least—but when do you plan to leave?'

'I think I must go soon, the day after tomorrow. Is that enough time for you to make your farewells, see your friends?'

'I have no real friends. Michael did not encourage it.'

'You do not know when he returns?'

'Any time now. He will not send me word, but when he's ready he will simply walk in as if he never went away.'

He nodded, his finger touching the pulse spot at the base of her throat. 'It hardly matters. He cannot stop us, Morwenna. You are mine now and nothing can part us.'

'I love you,' she whispered shyly and waited, but he did not say the words she longed to hear.

Feeling a small hurt that he did not speak of love, she rose from the sandy floor of the cave and brushed at her skirts.

'I should go now. The wind is howling and I think there will be a storm before long.'

'You have many storms on this part of the coast,' he said and rose to look into her face. 'It was on a night like this that I came into your life, Morwenna. Only a few days have passed, but it seems a lifetime—I feel I have known you all my life. Have been waiting for you.'

'As I waited for you.'

'Go home now and I shall follow,' he said, bending his head to brush her lips in a last kiss. 'I have a little business in the village. I must hire horses that will carry us both.'

'Yes.' She stood gazing into his eyes. 'You have still not remembered anything?'

'I have flashes...pictures in my head. My life is there waiting behind a curtain of mist, but I cannot draw it down.'

'What if you never do?'

'Then we shall make a new life together,' he said. 'Go now, Morwenna. I shall see you later.'

'Yes—and soon we shall go away together.'

She smiled and left him, running sure-footedly down the cliff towards her home.

Adam stood watching her for a few minutes, then left the cave and began the descent to the village. Already the rain had begun to make the path wet and slippery and it was growing dusk. His foot slipped on a loose rock and slid from under him, causing him to lose his balance and fall. He hit his head and everything went black.

Morwenna woke and lay for a moment wondering what had disturbed her sleep. She had come to bed late because she wanted to get started preparing her things for her departure. Besides, thoughts of Adam kept her from sleep.

Something had woken her now, but what was it?

Jumping out of bed, she pulled on her clothes and went downstairs. Bess was making up the fire in the kitchen. She turned to look at her, her brow arching.

'Michael came home after you went up. He and Jacques have gone to the beach,' she said. 'It's not like you to sleep through a storm.'

'I must have been tired.' Morwenna's cheeks were pink, because after spending the afternoon in the cave making love with Adam she had slept more deeply than usual. 'I'll go down to the inlet and see what is happening.'

'Michael said I was to tell you not to go out if you woke.'

'Michael is too fond of—' She broke off as

she heard loud popping noises. 'What is that?' she asked, staring at Bess in sudden fright. 'It was like a ship's cannon being fired.'

Without waiting for Bess to answer, she pulled on her cloak and went out, heading for the top of the cliff rather than the beach. A bright moon revealed the scene at sea and on the beach below. Two ships were out in the bay and one had fired on the other. She thought one might belong to the militia, who patrolled the coastline, and the other, if she were not mistaken, was French. Had Michael been down in the bay signalling to the ship? Yet he would not, for on a night like this he would send the signal to say it was not safe. The high winds made it impossible to bring in either boats or the ship and the full moon was the smuggler's enemy.

Looking down at the beach, she saw that another ship had foundered on the rocks. It seemed as if the whole village had turned out and she could see that a large amount of cargo was being washed ashore. She could see one line of men still trying to reach men in the water, but on the beach fighting had broken out.

Not thinking of her own safety, Morwenna ran down the steep path to the inlet. She must make sure no one had been washed to that side of the cliff, because by the look of what was going on the villagers were more interested in grabbing what they could from the water.

She reached the inlet safely, running across the soft sands to the edge of the sea to make certain no one was being crushed against the rocks or lying face down in the shallow water. This time there was no one to be seen, but she caught sight of a small wooden chest bobbing in the water. As she watched, it was beached by the waves. She bent down to pick it up. It was not particularly heavy, but a heavy iron lock, which would not open, secured the lid. Morwenna considered. If she left it lying on the beach, the villagers would take it when they'd finished on the main beach. It might belong to someone who had managed to survive the wreck. Normally she did not take anything she found on the beach, but the chest looked as if it might belong to a woman so she decided to carry it home. If she heard of a survivor, she would enquire if he or she were the owner.

She was startled as she heard shouting and screaming from the beach and the sharp crack of a musket. There must be more trouble on the beach. Had the militia been alerted and arrived on the scene before the villagers dispersed?

Michael would not want her to be involved. She began the climb to her house. Wanting to be home and ready to help if her brothers returned with survivors, she did not look back and was unaware that a man further up the cliff was watching her.

Rupert saw Morwenna make her way back from the cliff path. A sickening horror ran through him as he realised that she was one of the wreckers after all—those ghoulish creatures who lured ships on to the rocks to steal their cargo when it washed ashore—and he'd really felt something for her!

What a damned fool he'd been to get caught up with a Morgan. The knock on the head, as he'd tried to secure his long boat in the inlet on the day of the first storm and been swept on to the rocks, had sent his senses flying. Until that fall on the cliffs some hours earlier he'd known nothing of who he truly was or his reason for being here. Now memories had all come flooding back: his past, the feelings of utter loneliness he'd experienced of late, his mission here and his promise to seek out the nest of traitors that threatened the life of King James I of England. Instead of honouring his promise, he'd spent his time making love to a girl who had lied to protect her traitorous brothers.

When he'd woken from the second bang on the head to find his memory returned, he'd gone straight to the meeting place arranged before he left his ship. Despite the delay of several days, his loyal men had been waiting for him at the inn with clothes, money and his weapons. He knew that his ship was sailing off the coastline, waiting to pick him up if he should wish it, for the ship that was wrecked on the night of his arrival in Deacon's Cove was not the *Sea Raven*.

After consulting with his men on what they had learned while they waited for him, he had been on his way to speak with the local militiamen about the situation here when the church bells started to toll. By the time he'd arrived in Deacon's Cove with some of his men it had been too late to do anything. The sound of firing told him that something unpleasant was happening and, on presentation of his credentials, one of the local militia officers had told him that they'd caught the wreckers actually setting on an unfortunate wretch cast helpless upon the shore.

'They would have killed the poor devil had we not got here in time, my lord. It is a wicked trade and one we are determined to stamp out.'

'You are to be commended for your vigilance. Do you know who is behind this night's work?' Rupert asked.

'I've seen the Morgan brothers on the beach, but I don't know if they were involved. They were fighting with the others—quarrelling over the spoils, I dare say.'

'Like the rats they undoubtedly are.' Rupert looked grim. 'Did you catch any of them?'

'The Morgan brothers got away as usual—but we snatched some of the others. I don't think they're local, but we'll hang the lot of them this time.'

'As they deserve,' Rupert said and left him.

He was unsure what to do for the best. Thoughts of Morwenna's sweetness had flooded back into his mind. She loved her brothers and tried to protect them, but that did not make her a part of this evil work. Despite their trade, Morwenna might still be innocent of any wrongdoing.

In that moment Rupert had known that he could not simply ride away from her without a word. Her brother Michael might be a traitor and it was his duty to do what he could to bring him to justice—but surely he could protect Morwenna. He might also try to keep Jacques out of it if he were sure that he was innocent of treason. He was undoubtedly a smuggler, but that was not Rupert's business. His mission was to discover what he could of the plot to murder the King and he must do what he could to that end, but Morwenna need not suffer. He could still take her away. It was what he wanted.

His steps had turned towards the house on the hill. The rain had stopped by then and the wind was dying. Rupert had almost caught up to her when he saw her enter her house, her shawl over her head. She was carrying something...

As he saw it was a sea chest his heart sank. She had taken goods from the beach like all the others of her kind. She was as bad as her brothers.

For a moment he stood rooted to the spot, the gorge rising in his throat. Should he leave now? Disgust, anger and rising disappointment tore at him and the pain was almost too much to bear. He had thought her different from all the others.

How could she stoop so low? Anger prevented him from simply leaving. He must have this out with her.

As Morwenna entered the kitchen, she discovered that Jacques was there and one of

Michael's crew. Her first glance told her that Benjamin was wounded in the arm. She gave a cry, placed the small chest on the floor by the fireplace and went to him.

'Your arm is bleeding. What happened?'

'Someone in the cove must have lured the ship in. They were strangers, Morwenna—wreckers. Michael told us to drive them off and there was a fight. Then the Revenue ship turned up and started firing on the Frenchie—and then the militia turned up on the beach and set about anyone they could find. Most of our men ran for the caves as usual and will have got away. I'm not sure about your brother. I was set upon by some ruffians and Jacques got me away.'

'I think Michael may have got mixed up with the militia,' Jacques said. 'He was fighting with the wreckers when they poured on to the beach and they probably thought he was one of those that lured the ship in.'

'No, how could they? Everyone knows we don't do that here—the villagers wouldn't dream of it and Michael has forbidden it. He would punish anyone he suspected of such wickedness.' Morwenna felt cold all over. 'Did Michael signal to the French ship to come in?'

'I don't know,' Benjamin said and winced as

Morwenna's brother bound his arm tighter to stop the blood. 'He may have done, but he had nothing to do with the wreckers—you know he didn't, Morwenna. We did what we could to rescue the crew and I think we saved the captain and one of the officers. Three others of the crew were helped by villagers—but the wreckers would have killed them if we hadn't turned up.'

'But if the militia have taken Michael...' Morwenna halted as she saw the look of anxiety in Jacques's eyes. 'It will all be a mistake. When they know who he is they will let him go.'

'Yes, perhaps.' Benjamin stood up. 'I'm going to see what I can find out.' As he took a step forwards, he stumbled and Jacques caught him, forcing him back in his chair.

'Stay where you are. I'll see what I can discover. Give him some brandy, Morwenna, and make him go to bed.'

'Yes, all right,' she said. 'Please take care of yourself.'

'It will be all over by now. I'll go to the village, see if I can find Michael—or anyone else who saw anything—' Jacques broke off as the door was flung open and his elder brother entered.

'I thought the militia had taken you,' Benjamin cried out.

'A trooper had me, but I managed to break free. I think most of the others got to the caves—but I may have been recognised and the militia will be here before morning. We'd best go to the caves, too.'

'Benjamin can't walk,' Morwenna objected. 'Stay here and tell Captain Bird that you were helping the crew, as you always do.'

'There's a new man in charge,' Michael said. 'It wasn't the local militia that came after us, but part of a different regiment. They seemed to know who they wanted and it was almost as if they expected something of the sort.'

'You think we've been betrayed?'

'I've thought for a while there might be an informer.' Michael frowned. 'Something important was meant to happen tonight, but because of the storm it didn't—however, the wreckers were out to make trouble. If they try to blame us...'

'I'll come with you,' Benjamin said. 'You'll have to help me, both of you, but it's best we're not here if they come.'

'Be careful of his arm,' Morwenna said as

the brothers hauled him to his feet and Michael took him over his shoulder.

'We'd best go to our beds and take our time getting up if they come,' Bess said as the door closed firmly behind the men and they were alone in the kitchen. Her gaze fell on the chest Morwenna had rescued. 'What's that?'

'I found it floating in the sea,' Morwenna said. 'I should have left it, but I thought if there were survivors I would be able to return it. If the militia found it here, they would think the worst.'

'Take it and throw it over the cliff.'

'No, that's foolish.' Morwenna picked it up. 'I'll take it to my room. Captain Bird won't try to search my room.'

'Michael said there's a new man in charge.'

'On the beach, but he surely won't come here.' Morwenna was about to pick up the chest when she heard knocking at the door. She pushed the chest into a dark recess, hoping it would not be seen. Then, giving Bess a warning look she went to the door and opened it. A shock ran through her as she saw who stood there.

'You...' she said, the colour draining from her cheeks as she saw his cold expression. This was not the same man she had rescued and come to love, but a stranger. What had happened to him? Had he deceived her all the time? 'Why are you here?'

'To warn you that the militia will be here within the hour. I came ahead of them, but your brothers should hide wherever they usually hide when the militia come looking.'

'You've remembered who you are at last?' Morwenna was shivering because he was no longer wearing the clothes she'd given him and he looked different—sterner and a man of some importance.

'My name is Rupert Melford,' he said. 'It doesn't matter who I am or what I am. Believe me, I would have no harm come to you from this, even though I know you for what you are. That ship was deliberately lured into the cove and to its doom.'

'You can't think that we…' Her throat was tight as she saw the disdain in his eyes. This wasn't the man who had made love to her in the caves and she knew with blinding clarity that she'd never truly known him. 'You lied to me.'

'No, I'd lost my memory, that much is true, Morwenna. When you rescued me I knew nothing.'

'Your memory has returned fully now?'

'Yes, earlier this evening.'

'Why didn't you come and tell me?'

'I had more important things to do.' Morwenna flinched as if he'd struck her. 'I cannot explain, but it doesn't matter now.' His gaze narrowed. 'I saw someone signal to a ship in your cove the first night I stayed here, Morwenna—and I saw you carry that chest back to the house this night. If your family weren't involved, why was someone signalling from the cliffs near your house—and why did you bring that chest from the beach?'

'I thought it might belong to a survivor and I wanted to keep it safe for him or her.'

'I should like to believe you, but it is not easy.' Rupert's lips curved in a sneer. 'So why was your brother signalling?'

'Because it was too dangerous for the—' She broke off, knowing that if she tried to clear her brothers of one crime she would brand them as smugglers and perhaps worse. 'If Michael signaled, it would be to warn a ship the cove was not safe on such a night.'

'I know your brothers are involved in smuggling and perhaps worse. If I could prove they were the traitors I believe them to be, I would show no mercy—but I owe you something for saving my life. Give me the chest and I'll take it to the proper authorities. As for your brothers, they would do better to stick to fishing. You may tell Michael to take great care for he is venturing into dangerous waters.'

'What do you mean? What do you know that I do not?' Her eyes flashed with pride. 'It's the reason you came here, isn't it?'

'I cannot tell you that, Morwenna.'

'You lied to me. You're a spy,' Morwenna accused. 'I loved—' She broke off, turning away to pull out the small chest. 'Take it. I never meant to keep it, whatever you think. Now go away. I never want to see you again.'

'Morwenna…' Rupert hesitated, then his expression hardened. 'I've warned you this time; the debt is paid. Next time your brothers will hang for their crimes against the State.'

'Go away,' she said, her face pale. 'I hate you, do you hear me? I wish I'd never seen you— never brought you here.'

'Your brothers might already be dead if it were not for that,' Rupert said harshly. 'Michael is a fool if he thinks he can get away with being a traitor to his King and country. Tell him that because next time he won't be allowed to slip away.'

Morwenna stared at him, but made no reply. Her throat was tight and her chest was hurting. She felt as if he had thrust a knife into her breast and it was all she could do to keep the tears from falling as he went out.

'I warned you not to trust him,' Bess said as the door closed behind him. 'It's him that's sprung the trap on your brothers, girl.'

'You do not know that for certain,' Morwenna said. 'He came here to warn us. You mustn't tell Michael, please.' Tears were trickling down her cheeks and into her mouth. She could taste their salt. 'I think Michael knows he has a powerful enemy. He will lay low for a while. Besides, it isn't the smuggling…'

'Your brother is a law unto himself,' Bess told her. 'Be careful, my love, or you may lose everything.'

'I'll talk to Michael,' Morwenna said. 'But you mustn't tell him that…Rupert was here this evening. Promise me.'

Rupert Melford! His name was Rupert. It suited him well, better than the name he'd chosen, which she'd known was false. Had he lied to her all the time? Could she believe him when he claimed to have lost his memory for a time?

Did what they'd shared in the caves mean nothing to him?

She wanted to howl and weep with her pain, but held it inside. 'Promise me, Bess.'

'I know when to keep my mouth shut. Michael would blame you for bringing him here. He'll work things out for himself—but 'tis you I'm concerned for. What have you done, girl?'

'What do you mean? I've done nothing,' Morwenna said. Her head was up, her expression proud, but she felt hot all over. Could her friend see the change in her?

Bess had warned her against the stranger, but she'd let her loneliness and her heart rule her head. She had allowed the stranger to seduce her and now he'd shown her what a fool she was to think he cared one jot for her. She'd thrown away her honour and her self-respect for a few hours in his arms.

Rupert Melford—the name was now burned into her mind in letters of fire. He'd known who he was all the time. Surely he must have. He'd lied to her and deceived her—and now she was ruined, but for the moment none of that mattered. She could only pray that Michael's luck would hold and once again her brothers would escape a terrible fate.

* * *

The militiamen came about an hour or so later, hammering at the door as if they would waken the dead. Morwenna took her time getting dressed and went down to the kitchen just as Bess was pulling the bolts, her grey-streaked hair hanging down her back.

'All right, all right,' Bess grumbled. 'It's enough to waken the dead. I'm moving as fast as I can. Dragging a decent body from her bed at this hour of the night…'

'We've come to arrest the Morgan brothers for the crime of wrecking,' an officer Morwenna had never seen before announced. 'They were seen on the beach earlier—and Michael Morgan was seen to signal to a ship in the bay.'

'My brothers are away down the coast fishing,' Morwenna replied, lifting her head high. 'Besides, they would never do such a thing. If they returned to the cove and saw a ship in trouble, they would help save the crew.'

'We intend to search the house, mistress.'

'If that is your wish you may do so, but we are alone here. In case you think to take advantage, I must tell you that Captain Bird knows me and would not take kindly if you abused me or my home.'

'Captain Bird has been relieved of his post. He has failed to stop the rampant smuggling that goes on in this cove. I am in charge here and my name is Captain Richmond.'

'Well, Captain Richmond, you may search my home, but you will not find either contraband or my brothers.'

Morwenna knew that any smuggled brandy Michael might have brought in was well hidden in the deep cellars that ran beneath the house and were impossible for a stranger to find. She nodded to Bess as the old woman looked at her anxiously.

'I think we shall warm a little ale and drink it. Perhaps the men would like a drink, too, for 'tis a cold night?'

'My men do not consort with smugglers and wreckers.'

'You accuse us, but what proof have you?'

'Your brothers were seen at the scene. They were pulling a line in before we arrived.'

'Whoever told you that must know that if they were there they were saving lives. You have only to ask the many men and women we have saved from the sea. I'm sure Sir George Arnley will vouch for us as a family. We saved his son from a shipwreck last winter and there are others who will testify that we do not condone wrecking here. My brothers are fishermen, nothing more.'

Captain Richmond looked uncertain, then glared at her. 'I know my duty, Mistress Morgan. I intend to make a thorough search of the house and if I find anything I shall arrest both you and your brothers.'

'Please search as much as you wish,' Morwenna replied. 'I have nothing to hide.'

He inclined his head and then detailed his men to search the house thoroughly. Morwenna busied herself making hot spiced ale. She saw his men look at it, their faces revealing the longing the aroma set up on their tastebuds. Captain Bird would have let her serve them all warm ale and gone away after a perfunctory search, but she understood that their new captain intended to turn the house upside down.

Ignoring the sounds of the rooms upstairs being turned over, Morwenna concentrated on making the warming drink. She had filled a jug and set out beakers on the table, then she and Bess sat down to drink their own ale. One by one the men drifted back to the kitchen, and after looking over their shoulders, to make sure their zealous captain was not watching, accepted a cup of ale and drank it.

'Tis well known your family are not wreckers,' one of them told her. 'But there were wreckers in the bay this night—strangers, so I've heard, and a French ship out in the bay. I think they may have got away, but the Revenue went after them and the night was too dark to see the outcome.'

'It is surely no crime for a French merchantman to visit these shores?' Morwenna said. 'I fear your information was false and you may be reprimanded from London for causing an incident with a friendly ship.'

'We just obey orders, mistress,' the soldier said and hid his cup behind a pot as Captain Richmond returned.

'There is ale still warming if you've a mind for it, sir.'

The young captain scowled at her. 'You'll go too far one of these days, Mistress Morgan. We know what your brothers get up to and we shall be watching closely in future.'

'I did not know it was a crime to go fishing, sir.'

'Fishing be damned. That Frenchie was bringing in silk and brandywine and if they catch the vessel, we'll have the proof we need. Then we shall be back and we'll arrest the lot of you.'

'I hope you discover your mistake, sir. My brothers are merely fishermen. Occasionally they take their wares and the catch of others to the markets and they may purchase produce to bring back for others, but they are honest men.'

'You're as bad as the rest of them,' the captain said. 'Take care, Mistress Morgan. I do not think you would like a taste of his Majesty's prison.'

Morwenna resisted replying again. She had defended her brothers, as always, but this man was very different from Captain Bird. Instead of admiration there was only scorn in his eyes— the scorn she'd seen earlier in the eyes of Rupert Melford.

Her pain almost overwhelmed her, but she kept her head high until the soldiers had gone. Sitting down at the table, she discovered that she was shaking.

''Tis time Michael changed his arrangements,' Bess said. 'If he continues, he will bring ruin on this family.'

'I do not think it is just the smuggling,' Morwenna said. 'He is mixed up in something worse. I do not know what it may be, but he will not tell me more if I ask.'

She blinked back her tears. Her life here was almost impossible. She would have to go to her aunt's house in London.

'You did well, as always,' Michael said and frowned. 'If they've replaced Captain Bird, they mean business, which means I shall have to be more careful. I intended to change the venue and this makes it imperative.'

'Why do you need to continue with the smuggling?' Morwenna asked. 'You have your ship and could use it for honest trading and Jacques might find other employment if he tried.'

'What of you if we go our separate ways?'

'Perhaps I shall go to my mother's sister.'

'You visited once and came home within a week. What makes you think you would do better this time?' His gaze hardened. 'Bird helped delay them last night to give us time to get away. He met me in the village this morning and told me to be careful for a while. He wants to pay his respects to you, Morwenna. He would marry you if you threw him the occasional smile.'

'I would rather take my chances with my aunt.'

'I've given him my permission to talk to you. I owe him for helping me in the past,' her brother said. 'I'm going away to France and taking Jacques with me. I'll be gone at least three weeks, perhaps more. You have until then to decide. It isn't safe for you here any longer, Sister. When I come back I want an answer. We may have to leave this house quickly and I do not want to be worrying about you.'

'What are you doing, Michael? It isn't just smuggling. It's serious—dangerous.'

'Mayhap. Whatever, it's my business. I've let you have your own way long enough, but I've made up my mind. When I return it's marriage for you—or you'll go to your aunt. The choice is yours.'

Morwenna stared at the door as Michael left. She felt cold all over and yet she had known this was coming soon. The idea of marrying a man she disliked made her feel sick. Besides, Captain Bird wasn't a fool. He would know he'd been cheated of her virginity and she suspected he had a temper if it was roused.

Rupert, as Adam, had promised to take her with him, but he despised her now. She recalled his tenderness as he'd held her in his arms and loved her. She'd known such happiness, but it had all been a lie. He cared nothing for her.

She wanted to go away, somewhere that no one knew her. Yet if she left this house alone she would have to fend for herself. It wouldn't be easy to find work, but she would have to try.

Tears were burning behind her eyes, but her pride would not let them fall. She would not admit that her heart had been broken or wish that she could go back to the night she'd found Rupert Melford on the beach. She had a few days in which to make up her mind, though as far as she could see there was nothing to save her. She could not marry Captain Bird and so she must make up her mind to leave this house, though she was not sure where she would go.

'Walk to the village and fetch me some flour,' Bess said as Morwenna entered the kitchen two days later. 'I need to bake and—' She broke off as they heard someone at the door, looking at each other in dismay. 'Are they here again?'

Morwenna took a deep breath and then went to the door. Opening it, she discovered that Captain Bird had come visiting. He was dressed in a smart scarlet coat and his boots were polished to a high gloss. Realising that he'd come for personal reasons, she hesitated, then stepped back, allowing him to enter the kitchen.

'To what do we owe the pleasure of this visit, sir?'

'I would speak with you alone, Mistress Morgan.'

'I think you may say anything you have to say in front of Bess, Captain.'

'I would prefer to be alone with you.'

'I do not wish it.' Morwenna raised her head. 'Please speak plainly, for I have work to do.'

'Very well, since you will have it—I have come to ask you to be my wife. You know that I care for you. I have long wanted to ask you, but your brother refused me—now he has given his permission.'

'My brother does not own me, sir. I am my own mistress and I have no wish to marry.'

Captain Bird's mouth thinned. 'Yet I think you will change your mind, Morwenna, unless you wish to see your brother hang for treason.'

Morwenna gasped, staring at him in horror. 'What do you mean? What are you accusing Michael of?'

'I know that he is involved with traitors. Michael is too clever to be taken for a smuggler—but I know about the men he smuggled away to France and what they plan,' Captain Bird said. 'Michael is a fool, but his reckless-ness has given me the power I need. You will be mine, Morwenna—or Michael hangs.'

'You wouldn't!'

'Only if you force me to it.'

'I do not believe you. How do I know that what you say is true? You have no proof.'

'I need no proof. Your brother is suspected of treason and if I tell what I know the traitors will all be taken.' He smiled at her. 'Come, give me your promise and we shall forget this con-versation.'

'I do not know.' Morwenna's thoughts whirled in confusion. 'Give me a little time to think.'

'I shall give you until Michael returns from France, where I know him to be consorting with other plotters—and then I shall have your an-swer.'

Unable to speak, Morwenna nodded numbly.

'Remember that you belong to me. I want you and I intend to have you, Morwenna.'

Morwenna felt the gorge rise in her throat as he turned and went out, closing the solid oak door with a resounding bang. Then she dashed to the side door and went out, vomiting in the yard. For a moment she breathed in the cold air and then returned to the kitchen. Bess looked at her, her eyebrows raised.

'He disgusts me,' she said and wiped her mouth with a cloth. 'I can never wed him.'

'Then you must run away.'

'What of Michael? You heard what he threatened.'

'Your brothers are men and can look after themselves. You should go to your aunt while you can, girl.'

'Yes, I fear that is my only choice.' Morwenna turned away to hide the tears that stung her eyes. She had hoped to leave with the man she loved, but that dream was ended. His expression that last night had shown his disgust for the woman that he believed her to be.

No, she would not weep for him, but neither would she marry a man she disliked.

'I will fetch the flour you need,' she said and reached for her shawl from its peg behind the door.

A week later Morwenna was still undecided. What was she going to do? Michael would show no sympathy for her if his own safety was at risk. When he returned Michael would force her to marry Captain Bird. Now that the militiaman was threatening to betray him she would no longer have a choice.

Michael had always been able to escape from the militia by using the caves and tunnels that only he and his men knew of—but if he was mixed up in some kind of plot against the King he would never be able to rest. He could not return to his home and must for ever be a fugitive—and perhaps Jacques, too, would be branded as a traitor.

Morwenna would hate it if she could never see Jacques again. She did not wish either of her brothers to hang, but she could not live as that man Bird's wife. She would rather die.

She must disappear before her brothers returned. Looking about her bedchamber, Morwenna decided to take only what she could carry. She had a little money, which she'd saved from the housekeeping, also a string of pearls her mother had given her and a small ruby ring her father had purchased for her before he died. She would hate to part with either, but if she wanted to try to start a new life in London, perhaps even as a seamstress, she would need money to live on for a while.

The only talent that Morwenna possessed besides her sewing and her cooking was her singing voice. She had sung in the church choir when she was a child, but as she grew up her brother had forbidden her to waste her time in such frivolities.

She would like to sing for her living, but women were forbidden from appearing on the stage and the travelling players used young boys to act the female roles.

If she could not sing on the stage, what else might she do?

Working in a tavern as a chambermaid would be hard and not much of a change from her life here—but she might be forced to accept such work.

With that thought in mind, she decided to travel in one of her plainest working gowns. It would not do to ask for work wearing the silk gown her brother had once given her when he'd done well from his smuggling. Packing her best gown of green velvet into a large satchel, she added some extra shoes and two shifts. Then she took her cloak and slung it over her shoulders; the satchel was slung over her back in a way that prevented it from being easily snatched. Her money and her mother's pearls were in a linen bag sewn inside the skirt of her gown. Morwenna was taking no chances with what little she had, because once she left her home she could never return.

Going down to the kitchen, she saw Bess preparing pies for supper. She took two and wrapped them in clean linen and tied them in a knot that she could slip over her wrist.

'Where are you going?' Bess asked, staring at her in suspicion.

'Please don't ask because I may not tell you—though you can tell my brothers I've gone to my aunt.'

'You foolish girl. Are you running away with that man? He will leave you as soon as he tires of you.'

'He has already left me and I must fend for myself.'

'You'll go to your aunt?' Bess looked at her sorrowfully. 'Please, I beg you, do not simply run away, my love. Jacques will help you when he returns. You have no idea of the wickedness of the world. Anything could happen to you.'

'You must not cry, Bess,' Morwenna said and kissed her cheek. 'You've been a good friend to me—to us all. I have no choice but to leave, for Michael would force me to wed that man—and I cannot.'

'Why do you not let me come with you?'

'Because I cannot afford to keep us both, Bess dearest. You must stay here—what would my brothers do without you?'

'Find another servant,' Bess said sourly. 'I'll not stay long without you, but I know I would be a burden to you.' She embraced the girl. 'I've a few pennies in my pocket if they will help you?'

'Keep your money, Bess. I shall manage. I have some money and my mother's pearls. I will find a way to earn my living.'

'What can you do but cook?'

'Perhaps I shall be a seamstress. You must forget me and think of yourself. If you leave here, make Michael give you something for the future.'

'Aye, well, I've a sister I could go to. She's asked three times since her husband died, but I couldn't desert you.'

'You must go to her now,' Morwenna said and embraced her. 'Farewell, my friend. Please do not weep for me.'

Bess was already sobbing noisily as Morwenna left the kitchen. She paused outside the house and pulled her shawl tighter about her head. She must try to walk as far as she could before nightfall and she would sleep in an empty barn if she came upon one. It would take her

weeks to get to London, even if she were fortunate enough to beg a ride on a carter's wagon,
because she couldn't afford to pay for her fare.
She would try to find work at various stages of
her journey, because otherwise she might spend
all she had before she arrived.

Chapter Six

Morwenna stretched and yawned. She'd slept well enough on a bed of straw in a dry barn, but her pies had been eaten long since. She was hungry and she wanted to wash. She would quench her thirst and wash her face at the first clean stream she came to, but she wasn't sure where to buy food. If she called at a farm, she might be turned away. It might be best to keep walking until she reached Bodmin. There she could buy food from a market stall and no one would notice her. If she were lucky she might find work for a few days—or even a cart heading northwards.

It was a long way to London. The last time she'd visited her aunt her father had sent her in a carriage he'd hired for the purpose with two grooms to take care of her and a maid. A little sigh left her lips as she accepted that those days were long gone. Michael had sold most of the horses and her father had parted with his carriage before Morwenna's mother died. Most of the maids had all been dismissed after her father died and she'd done their work for the past eighteen months. Her hands were no longer those of a lady, which might be a good thing, for had they been white and soft, as they had once been, people would have noticed her more and thought it odd she should be alone. As it was, she was just a working woman of no importance and so far no one had cast more than a glance in her direction.

Shaking her skirts free of the hay she'd slept on, she began to walk, following the road towards the town where she hoped to purchase her breakfast. Apart from a few regrets about leaving Jacques and Bess, she had not allowed her situation to worry her. For the moment she had money and her mother's pearls. The money would last only a few days, but she would try to find work before parting with the pearls.

Perhaps in Bodmin there might be work for her in a tavern or as a kitchen maid. She was not too proud to take menial work, but as soon as she could she would try to earn money from her singing. She was aware that women did not appear on stage, but she'd seen gypsy women singing in the Market Square for a few pennies and did not see why she should not do the same. Perhaps she could not legally appear in a play on the stage, but what was to stop her singing to people as they queued to watch the play inside?

'Lord Henry sent me to ask when you are returning to London.'

Rupert looked at the messenger and frowned, raising his wine cup to sip at the rough red liquor. He did not know why he was not already back at his London house, but something had made him hesitate. What was happening to Morwenna?

When he'd come to Cornwall he'd hoped they might take Michael prisoner and bring him to justice, but somehow the smugglers had escaped again. How? How could they find their way from the beach without using the path, which had been cut off by the soldiers? The water had been far too rough to escape by sea—so there must be a way through the caves. If there were, Rupert had not been able to find it.

'I'm not sure when I shall return to town. I'm

still considering my options,' he said in answer to the courier's question.

'Lord Henry says they have new leads in London and he wants you back, sir. There are whispers of another plot against the King and he needs your help again.'

'I'll come when I'm ready.'

Rupert brooded over his wine as the man turned and left the tavern. He hardly cared whether the Morgan brothers had been stopped or not. There was only one Morgan that mattered to him: Morwenna. Why had he been so unkind to her that night? He'd said terrible things to her—things she did not deserve—but it had angered him to know a ship had been lured into the cove and lives lost needlessly.

He'd been unfair to her. It was unlikely she could have stopped her brother's activities had she tried—and, discovering the chest she'd taken from the beach contained letters and a few small trinkets that clearly belonged to a sailor, Rupert realised that she hadn't stolen anything of worth. Perhaps she had truly meant to return it to the survivor if he came forwards, but there was so little of value that it was unlikely it would ever be claimed.

What shall I do about her? he asked himself. *Ought I to go back and see if she is well?*

They had lain together several times. Supposing she was with child? Supposing she was in trouble with her brother?

Rupert's conscience would not let him rest. He certainly could not think of returning to London until he knew if she was safe.

He'd ridden hard the first day after leaving the area, had been on the point of leaving Cornwall—and then something had made him turn around and head back. He'd stopped at an inn for dinner and a bed for the night, but the next day he would go as far as Bodmin and after that he might ride out to Deacon's Cove and discover what he could of Morwenna's fate.

Morwenna wrapped the bread and cheese she'd purchased from the market in her bundle and slung it over her back again. Then she bit into a crisp apple, enjoying the crunch and the moist sweetness on her tongue. She'd had some water from the fountain in the square, drinking it from her cupped hands.

Feeling better, she began to ask the people she met if they knew of any work in the town. The first woman she asked shook her head and walked away, but the next stopped to consider her for a moment.

'I need a woman to help me at home. You look strong enough, but you're too pretty. My husband would lust after you and I should always be wondering if he had you in the haybarn. Go to the tavern, mistress. I did hear as they wanted a girl to serve in the taproom.'

'Thank you kindly, Goodwife,' Morwenna said and set off across the square to the tavern. The yard was busy with horses and grooms and voices shouting. It was a large inn and looked respectable. Hesitating only for a moment, she went inside and looked for the landlord.

He was busy serving some customers with ale, a large man with a friendly face and a huge belly. Taking a deep breath, Morwenna waited until his customers moved away with their ale and then went up to him.

'Good day to you, sir,' she said politely. 'I have heard you are looking for someone to clean or serve in the taproom.'

He looked at her in surprise and Morwenna's cheeks warmed. She spoke too well to be the kind of girl who would normally work in his inn and his gaze narrowed as he stared at her.

'You're a comely wench and, had you come

an hour ago, I would have given you work—but I hired a girl not thirty minutes past and she's a good worker.'

'I should have been a good worker, too,' Morwenna said. 'But I would not take another girl's work.'

'I am sorry to disappoint you, miss. There will be a hiring fair come next Thursday, if you can wait until then.'

Morwenna thanked him and moved away. She was about to return the way she'd entered when she heard the sound of laughter. Glancing out of the window, she saw that a troupe of players was in the back yard and both men and women had gathered to watch them. Intrigued, she made her way through the open doors to the yard and stood with others, watching the antics of the acrobats and jugglers. A fiddler was playing and two small children were dancing a jig to the amusement of the crowd, who laughed and threw a few groats into the hat a dwarf was passing round.

Hearing a tune she knew, Morwenna moved closer. It was a merry song often sung in the spring. Hardly thinking of what she was doing, Morwenna edged even closer to the fiddler, then she began to sing.

'Twas in the merry month of May he did
come...
With a hey nonny, nonny no...
So sweet and fair was he that he won her
heart
With a hey nonny, nonny...
Yet he was faithless and loved her not
Hey nonny, hey nonny, nonny no...

Morwenna picked up her skirts and did a little dance, pointing her toes as she sang three
verses of the song. When the fiddler stopped
playing the people threw more money.

'You have a fine voice, mistress,' a man
called. 'See that you get your share of the
money.'

The dwarf had collected the money. It belonged to the travelling players and Morwenna
expected none of the coins to come her way, but
as she turned to walk off, her arm was suddenly
caught. She turned to look at the man who had
apprehended her, her heart jumping with fright.

'Be not afraid, mistress,' he said in a deep
resonating voice. 'I am Edward Rawlings, actor
and playwright, and the leader of this troupe.'

'I meant no harm by singing. I have not taken
your money.'

'They gave more generously after you sang,' the man said, his gaze narrow and questing. 'Tell me, mistress, where are you bound and why?'

'I am a widow,' Morwenna improvised. 'I was forced to leave my home and I need to find work.'

'We are travelling to Truro. Indeed, we leave for that town as soon as we have supped. Might I ask if you would care to throw in your lot with us? We are a small band, but we earn enough to keep body and soul together—and we shall be in London by the spring. You would be safer travelling with us. My wife and daughter would welcome you.'

'I would not be a trouble to you, sir.'

'How could you be when you have the voice of an angel?' He beamed at her. 'Women are not allowed to act upon the stage, in the theatre, but sometimes a crowd will listen to a gypsy girl singing in the market place and pay good coin. We could dress you as a Romany and take a chance that your voice will work its magic.

'For myself I think there's no harm in a woman seeking to earn her bread this way, and it has been known before—though I should warn you that in some towns you might find they throw stones at you rather than coins. Many think it a hard life on the roads for we sleep under the stars or in our wagons most nights. Sometimes there is a warm barn to sleep in or occasionally a bed in the inn if we have done well.'

'How kind you are, sir,' said Morwenna, her throat tight. 'If I might travel with you for a while, I should be grateful.'

'Good, good, now tell me your name, mistress.'

'It is Wenna Marlowe,' she improvised, using her mother's maiden name.

'That is as good a name as any,' he said, accepting it without question. 'I was not born a Rawlings, but it has served me well. Now, come with me and meet the others. We shall leave as soon as we have eaten—and with our takings for the day we can afford to eat well.'

'At the inn?'

'No, we shall buy food and take it back to our camp outside the town. The money goes further spent at the market and there are several mouths to feed, for we all have families.'

'I like to cook and I can sew. Perhaps I may be of use in more than one way.'

Morwenna smiled as the other members of

the troupe gathered about her, looking curious but not unfriendly. She believed she was amongst friends and the slight feeling of apprehension that had been with her since leaving home began to melt away. Her life would not be easy, but with friends she would find it less difficult than travelling alone.

It was nearly nightfall when Rupert reached the inn. The market square was empty save for a few townsfolk hurrying home to their beds, the stalls that had crowded it gone now as people locked their doors and windows against the dark humours of the night. As he went into the taproom, Rupert wondered if he would find a bed for the night. This was the best inn in the town, but he was late. His horse had lost a shoe and he'd been forced to lead it to the nearest forge. Had it not been for the delay he might have been here by midday.

Walking into the inn, Rupert hailed the host, a large friendly man who came swiftly to serve him.

'What may I get you, my lord?'

'Supper and some warmed ale, if you please, sir. I would hire a room for the night if it were possible.'

'We can provide supper, but my rooms are all gone, my lord.'

'Then perhaps you will permit me to sleep in your parlour.'

'There may be no need for that,' a voice that Rupert immediately recognised spoke from behind him. 'I should like a private word with you, sir, if you please. If your answer is fair we may share a room this night.'

Rupert turned to look at Jacques Morgan, his brow creasing in a frown. 'I am surprised to see you here, I thought you'd be long gone by now,' he said, lifting his brows. 'How is your sister? Is all well with her?'

'Come, let us speak privately,' Jacques said and moved away to a table in the corner where they could watch the room and not be overheard.

'Has something happened to her?' Rupert was struck by guilt as he saw the other's grim expression and wild thoughts raced through his mind. Had Michael blamed Morwenna for what happened that night? Had he lost his temper and done her harm? 'If your brother has harmed her...'

'Michael gave her an ultimatum. She was to marry Bird or go to live with her aunt in London. When we returned she had gone and...'

He hesitated. 'I am told your name is Melford. Why do you ask about my sister? What is she to you—what has she been to you?'

'Morwenna went to her aunt's?'

'I believe she has other ideas. Bess thinks you were her lover. Is it true?' Jacques gave him such a look that Rupert knew his answer might push the man too far. 'Do not lie, for if you do I shall kill you.'

'I have no intention of lying. Yes, we were lovers. I intended to take her with me to London, to give her a house of her own and—'

'Keep her as your mistress. By God! I should thrash you for the insult.' Jacques clenched his fists. 'She is gentle born even if we have little money. Why did you desert her if that was your intention? Had you no thought for her?'

'I saw the signals that brought the ship to its doom the night of the storm.'

'And you thought it was my brother—that we were wreckers? You thought Morwenna would be a part of something like that—after she saved your life? Good grief, man. You lay with her— did you not know her at all? Did you not see her goodness and her honesty? She has never harmed any, but helped all those she could.'

Rupert looked uncomfortable as he tried to

explain, 'She was carrying a small chest she took from the sea that night. I planned to warn her that the soldiers would search the house that night and when I saw I thought the worst. If I wronged her, I shall apologise...'

'So you did come to spy on us.' Jacques looked at him in disgust. 'Despite her care for you—and her love, for she would not have given herself to you for less—you betrayed us all. You took her sweet innocence and then deserted her. What kind of a man are you, sir?'

'I came looking for a man who plots against his King and Parliament,' Rupert said, his mouth white with stifled pride. 'I misjudged Morwenna—and perhaps you, but your brother is involved with dangerous men. He has helped more than one plotter to escape justice—and there may be more secrets to reveal about his work than smuggled goods.'

Jacques stared at him, rebellion and anger in his eyes, but then he inclined his head. 'I knew there was something. Michael does not tell me all he does. He demands obedience and I give it because he is our brother.'

'A blind obedience that may take you to the gallows?'

Jacques was silent, then, 'I am searching for

Morwenna. When I find her it is my intention to care for her. We shall not return to the house on the cliffs.'

'How do you intend to care for her?'

'I shall find work.'

'Then I shall help you to that end—but first I must make my peace with her and discover what she needs and wants from me. I did—do care for her...'

'I wanted to kill you when I guessed what had happened between you.'

'And now?' Rupert arched his brow.

'We could fight but I dare say you would win, though perhaps not if we wrestled—but I am no murderer. Morwenna comes first. If I throw my life away, she will have no one to protect her.'

'Good thinking.' Rupert laughed softly in his throat. 'I like you better than I did, Jacques Morgan. Are we agreed that whoever finds her first lets the other know? Since we are both of the same mind concerning her welfare we may as well help each other.'

'We shall help each other look for her,' Jacques said. 'But if you think you have my blessing to make her your mistress you are mistaken. I shall do my best to persuade her that it would be foolish. I am not sure you are to be trusted.'

Rupert winced for he deserved the other's censure. 'You speak truly and your words are sharp, but, believe me, she will come to no harm in my care. So we are of one mind?'

'Aye. We'll share a room this night and continue the search in the morning. She cannot have gone so very far on foot and will, I believe, try for London—though she has little money and may look for work.'

'I will try the inns and towns if you take the farms and villages. Her looks are distinctive and if anyone has seen her they are not like to forget.'

'I spoke to the innkeeper earlier. He told me of a woman who may have been Morwenna. She asked for work, but he had none and he did not see her leave for he was busy. I have searched the town, but no one seems to have seen her. The market was here today and she might have found work with a farmer's wife. Tomorrow I shall seek out anyone who hired a new female servant.'

'It is not fitting that she should do menial work. Your brother should be ashamed of himself for bringing her to that state when she was born a lady.'

'Do not be so swift to blame, sir. Michael has some cause for what he does. Had he done nothing we should have lost even the house.'

'I am sorry for it. I would not condemn him for the smuggling despite he breaks the law—but this plotting against the King is evil and I must do all I can to prevent it.'

'I know nothing of any plot against the King. I'm not sure what my brother knows. Michael has spoken of dangerous times, but he tells me only what he needs me to do. I fear my brother may end at the rope's end if he continues his foolish work.'

'You should warn him to mend his ways.'

'He would not heed me.'

'You still intend to strike out alone?'

'My father told me to do so and I should have done it long ago had it not been for Morwenna. I had to stay to protect her.'

'She is fortunate to have such a brother.'

'She would not thank me for saying it. Morwenna believes she can look after herself and needs no help from anyone.'

'She will find it harder now that she is alone and without friends.'

'Yes…' Jacques shuddered. 'She has never been much into the world. I fear for her if she should fall into the hands of rogues.'

'We must find her before that happens. As you said, she cannot have gone far as yet.'

'We have covered several leagues this afternoon,' Morwenna said, to the woman who was driving the covered wagon. The players had taken her in and Sylvania had offered to give her a place to sleep and a seat on her wagon. 'Alone, I could never have travelled so far.'

'The horses do not tire as easily as we.' Sylvania had dark flashing eyes and hair as black as night. Once she must have been very beautiful and even now in her middle age she was still a sensuous woman who oozed charm and warmth. 'It was Edward's good fortune that you chose to sing with us today. Your voice is pleasant. You will draw people to us, though we must be careful for the law is against women actors. Although it has been known, it is illegal for a woman to act upon the stage. We use a young boy to play the female parts.'

'I saw the mummers and the juggling. Do you give plays as well?' Morwenna looked at her, feeling excited by the idea. 'I have never seen a miracle play, though I know the players come to Bodmin at Christ's mass.'

'We have performed such pieces at the feast of Christ,' Sylvania agreed, 'but Edward hath a clever mind and he devises plays of his own contriving. We shall be performing at an inn in Truro.'

'I thought I might sing, but a play...' Morwenna felt a tingle of excitement. 'How wonderful it would be to act upon the stage.'

'You must not think of it. I have told you, it is not legal. I too should like to play great parts for Edward says I have talent and I read the parts he writes for all the actors to help them learn. Yet I know my place. I sew costumes and help with rehearsals, but I may not act. And nor may you.'

'That is so unfair,' Morwenna objected. 'You have a way of holding your head and speaking and would make a fine actor—and Master Rawlings is very clever to devise such things.' She sighed. 'My father had few books, but Mama read much as a child and she told me stories of history. She had a book of love stories, which I have still, and she taught me to read herself. My father did not believe in schooling a girl, but Mama said it was important that I should know a little of the world.'

Sylvania nodded and smiled. 'You will learn more of the world with us, Wenna. We travel from place to place and you will see things, as you have never seen them before.'

'Yes, I am sure I shall,' Morwenna said. 'It was fortunate for me that I met Master Rawlings.'

'Edward is a good man and you may trust him,' Sylvania told her. 'But be careful of Peacock Henry. He is a vain spiteful man and if you fall foul of his tongue he will show no mercy.'

'Is he the one that wears such very bright colours?'

'Yes.' Sylvania laughed. 'It is why we call him a peacock. He likes to strut about in fine clothes and thinks himself a great actor—but Edward gives him only easy parts, for he forgets his lines. He is fond of pinching and touching us when he thinks he can get away with it, so be warned.'

'I shall.' Morwenna smiled, keeping her sigh inside.

She was not sure how long she could stay with her new friends. In the country she might sometimes be allowed to sing in a public place, but in London she would be forbidden from performing at the theatre. She might sew or cook for the players, but there must be something more worthwhile she could do with her life.

It was unfair that she was not permitted to seek her fortune on the stage, but there were many things forbidden to her sex and she must simply accept it. A woman's lot in life was to marry and provide heirs for her husband, but she would never find a husband now for she was ruined.

For a moment she thought of Rupert and the pleasure she'd found lying in his arms. Where was he and did he ever think of her? It was unlikely that she would see him again, for he must surely have forgotten her.

'That was a deep sigh,' Sylvania said and looked at her. 'Were you thinking of your husband, or your lover?'

Morwenna met the older woman's knowing eyes, a flush in her cheeks. 'I must forget him,' she said. 'He does not think of me and I shall not think of him.'

'Men were ever deceivers,' Sylvania said and then laughed. 'I must remember that line, for Edward will put it in a play. Forget him if he is faithless, Wenna. You have friends now and we shall look after you.'

Morwenna thanked her. Because of her new friends she was in no immediate danger of starving or falling prey to robbers and evil men, but her heart still ached when she thought of Rupert Melford. She could not stop loving him just because he had betrayed her and left her to her fate.

'I shall never see him again,' she said and made herself smile. 'Besides, I am looking forward to my new life with you and the others.'

It could be a good life for her—once she could put her heartache to one side. She thought she would not love again, but life went on and so must she.

Chapter Seven

'I was busy that morning,' the landlord told Rupert the next day. 'She might have been the lady you seek, my lord, for she was beautiful and she spoke well. Her hair was the colour of ripe damson plums in the sunlight. I seem to recall she went out into the yard.'

'We had players here yesterday morning,' his wife reminded him. She had been listening while her husband answered their questions and now came forwards to offer her information. 'I think she sang in the yard and she might have gone off with the leader of the troupe.'

'She went with the troupe of travelling players?' Rupert's gaze narrowed, his hands clenching at the thought of Morwenna in such company. They might be thieves and rogues for all he knew. 'Are you certain?'

'I cannot be certain, my lord—but I did see her talking with Edward Rawlings. His people have performed here before. They travel up and down the country and sometimes overseas, I think. They have never made trouble here and so we allow them to come when they will.'

'I thank you for the information, Goodwife,' Rupert said and held out a small gold coin to her. 'Have you any notion of where they meant to perform next?'

'I think someone mentioned Truro, but I do not know for sure,' the woman told him and slipped the coin in her pocket. 'I noticed the girl, for she was pretty—and I thought her bold to sing and flaunt herself in the inn yard.'

There was a hint of disapproval in her voice, as there might well be. Rupert frowned. Had Morwenna no idea of the risk she ran by flaunting the law? She could well be arrested as a vagrant if nothing more. He must find her soon, before she brought trouble on herself.

'They were headed for Truro?'

'I cannot be sure, my lord but I heard some mention of a performance to be given in the yard of the Black Cockerel Inn.'

'Thank you. Perhaps I shall find the lady I seek there.'

He was thoughtful as he left the inn and went out to the stables, where the lad had his horse ready and waiting. He was not sure what he would do if he found Morwenna at the inn. Would she be willing to come with him after the way he had treated her or would she tell him to go away and leave her alone?

He could not force her to be his mistress, but he was determined he would not simply walk away and abandon her. It behoved him to make sure she was safe and to look after her, at least until her brother came to claim her.

Thoughtful and uneasy, Rupert mounted his horse. It seemed he might discover Morwenna within a short time, but something was telling him that the path ahead was not smooth for them. If he could go back to the beginning and start again…yet what would he do differently?

Had they met at another place and another time…

What was he thinking? Surely not of marriage! It would not do. His family were proud of their service to the King and to bring the sister of a traitor who would likely hang for his misdeeds into their midst would be shocking.

Besides, he had no desire to wed. He had supposed that one day he must get an heir, for he had promised his mother he would do so, but for the time being he had no thought of it. The idea of marriage to his Cornish wench was ridiculous.

It was true that Morwenna had been virgin when she came to him, but he had not forced her. She had come to him willingly, their loving spontaneous and by mutual desire.

She was the loveliest creature he had ever known. The scent of her filled his senses, haunting him both waking and sleeping. The feel of her in his arms and the touch of her lips lived in his memory, hovering at the back of his mind. He smiled at the memory of their first loving. It had been so very sweet that it touched something within him, a place that had been empty for so many years.

He had wished a thousand times since regaining his memory that things had been different—but the facts remained. Michael was a dangerous conspirator and, when the plotters were taken, he would either be killed or brought to trial and hung.

Morwenna might hate him if she knew that he was one of those determined to bring her brother and his fellow plotters to justice. He smiled ruefully. Knowing her, she might even take a knife to his throat herself.

No, no, he wronged her. She was fiery and passionate—and he wanted her back in his arms and his bed.

Morwenna looked down at the costume she was wearing. It was bright, the skirt very full like the Romany women wore. The colour was green and suited her well, her hair hanging loose on her shoulder and topped by a cap of gold thread and false jewels that nevertheless gave her a queenly look.

'You will do well as our Queen of the Gypsies,' Sylvania said as she finished arranging her costume. 'You know you are to sing and then introduce the first scene? Then you must leave at once. Do not linger a moment longer.'

'Yes, I know.' Morwenna smiled. 'It is such a lovely story. A knight is wandering in the forest, lost and wounded after a defeat in battle. He lies close to death and is awakened by a beautiful woman, but she is a wicked elfin and will lead him a merry dance before she breaks his heart. At the end Edward will read the moral of his tale aloud.'

'Which is that beauty be not everything and we should not be led astray when our hearts are down, but uplift them and look to God for our salvation.'

'It is a sombre piece, for the sad knight dies,' Morwenna said. 'I prefer the merry scenes where the fool plays his jests and they all dance and sing.'

'Most people we play to are simple souls,' Sylvania told her. 'They love a jest, music and dancing, but when it comes to a play they demand high drama, tragedy and a moral ending. It is because Edward makes his tales moral that we are allowed to practise in peace. If we were licentious and encouraged immorality, we should be tried by the church, beaten and driven out of town at the tail of a cart.'

Morwenna looked at her in horror. 'Are people so cruel to you?'

'Sometimes, when times are bad, they drive us away rather than let us perform, but at other times they are pleased to see us.'

'It must be a hard life for you.'

'Yes, but I would have it no other way. I enjoy the travelling and the excitement of never knowing where we shall be the next day.'

Morwenna was silent as she followed her new

friend from the caravan where they had changed their clothes. She was enjoying the company and in summer or even autumn, as now, the life was good, but in winter she thought she might find it hard.

'Remember, Wenna, you must sing your song, then announce the play starts and run behind the stage. It is not your place to be a part of the play itself.'

Morwenna nodded. It had been easy enough to sing in the inn yard in Bodmin, but that had been an impulse and the simple folk there had been in a good mood that day, but this was different. They had set up a stage in the inn yard and people had paid to see the performance. It had, in fact, become an outdoor theatre and as such it was forbidden to her to play upon the stage. Edward had told her that to do so was illegal and punishable by imprisonment or a fine, but said that it had been known for a woman to impersonate a man in order to deceive; though, if discovered, the woman would be taken for a wanton and punished for her boldness.

Morwenna felt nervous as she went round to the front of the stage. A few cheers greeted her appearance and then some whistling and jeering, as the men in the audience realised that she was a woman and not a man dressed as a woman.

Opening her mouth, Morwenna began to sing. Her throat was dry and she found she could not make the words come. Someone called out an insult from the crowd and another spoke of wanting their money back. Forcing herself to stand her ground, she lifted her head proudly and suddenly her voice was there. Her song was pure and as the notes rose clear and sweet the crowd fell silent.

After her song was done silence fell and then there was some desultory cheering and clapping, though some called out insults.

'It is now my duty to tell you of the play,' Morwenna announced lifting her head proudly. ''Tis of a knight bewitched by a lady who is a wicked elfin and will lead him to his death...'

'Witch!' someone cried out in the crowd. 'Wanton whore. Get you from the stage or face the punishment you deserve.'

'Nay, her song was sweet,' a man cried.

'The wanton breaks the law...'

Morwenna realised she had outstayed her welcome and ran behind the curtain. What had made her speak of the story? All she'd been meant to do was hold out her hand and say, 'Now the play begins.'

Sylvania looked at her oddly as she came off the stage.

'What made you speak of the play? You were told to sing and run behind the curtain.'

'Forgive me, I was excited and forgot. I said but a few words more, that's all.'

'Yes, but…' Sylvania shook her head. 'I wish you had stuck to Edward's instructions. I fear they took against you. It was a big enough risk to let you sing.'

'I'm sorry. I meant nothing wrong.'

'People are righteous and superstitious. I told you that they sometimes drive us away with stones.' Sylvania shook her head. 'Someone called you a wanton and a witch. If they truly think it, it could be dangerous for you—for all of us.'

'Surely not?' A cold shiver ran down Morwenna's spine as she saw her friend's anxious look. 'It is just a few words. They could not think…'

'It was the manner of your speech.' Sylvania shook her head and tried to smile. 'I dare say I am foolish. You meant no harm. Edward calls for me. I must go. Be careful, Wenna, and stay hidden.'

Morwenna waited behind the screen. The play had begun and the actor playing the part of the Faery Queen had found the knight asleep. Morwenna heard a hissing sound as Peacock Henry bent over the sleeping knight to whisper words of seduction into his ear.

'Another witch! 'Tis a mortal sin to watch such wickedness as this!' a voice called out from the crowd. 'Are we so lost to morality that we allow such evil beings in our town? God is watching. Fear for your immortal souls, my friends—or the fires of hell await you.'

Peeping round the curtain Edward had erected, Morwenna sought for the source of the trouble and saw a man dressed in the robes of a priest. He was haranguing the crowd, some of whom now seemed more interested in listening to him than the play.

Some voices in the crowd told him to go away and shouted that it was naught but a play, but he continued to drone on about sin and the fires of hell and it was clear his preaching had made their audience uneasy.

'Damn his sour tongue,' Edward said and Morwenna turned to look at him. 'You were magnificent out there, Wenna—but I fear our audience is lost. They are drifting away. I must call the others back, for I think the mood grows angry.'

Edward beckoned to his actors, then brought the curtain down quickly. Some cries of disappointment came from the front and there were the sounds of a few scuffles, but no one stormed the stage or attacked the actors as they left it.

'We had them until that priest began to preach of hellfire and damnation,' Sylvania said. 'Perhaps if we gave a show of dancing and buffoonery it might serve.'

'That priest has stirred up bad elements within the crowd.' Edward said. 'It may be best if we leave before night. If they have a chance to drink and—' He broke off as someone pushed aside the curtain and came through. 'What do you want, sir? We do not look for trouble and Wenna is no witch nor a wanton…'

'I am Lord Melford and I mean no harm to Morwenna.' Rupert looked at her as she stood silent. 'It is as well I found you. There are some out there that would drag you before the priest and put you to the test as a witch. What possessed you to sing upon the stage and then speak of witchery?'

'She is one of us and spoke the words I gave her...well, mostly.' Edward looked from one to the other, noting Morwenna's pale face. 'I warn you, sir. I shall protect her with my life.'

'No, sir, you mistake him,' Morwenna said, finding her words at last. 'He thinks to protect me, do you not, my lord?'

'Of course. Your brother Jacques is looking for you, but I was lucky enough to find you first. Will you let me take you away?'

Morwenna hesitated. The players had gathered to look at her, their faces registering different emotions.

'Take her, for she is naught but bad luck for us,' Peacock Henry said spitefully. 'We might have earned good coin here today had it not been for her pride.'

'Forgive me, Mr Rawlings.' Morwenna ignored the spiteful taunt. 'I think it may be best if I do leave you. I did not realise what effect my performance would have.'

''Tis these country folk. They are superstitious fools.'

Sylvania looked grave. 'I am sorry for it, Morwenna, but I think you should go. Your lover has come for you, be glad of it and may good fortune shine on you.'

'I do not wish to bring trouble on you.' Morwenna glanced at Rupert, then quickly away, shivering as she saw his frown. 'If you will wait while I change into my own things.'

'Be quick, then. I do not wish to tarry.'

'Forgive me.' Blinking back her tears, Morwenna left the troupe of players, hurrying to the changing area at the back of the stage. She pulled off the bright clothes of the gypsy queen and pulled on her own dark gown. She felt humiliated and distressed, for she had spoiled what had promised to be a good day's takings for her friends who, she sensed, no longer wished her to be one of them.

Returning to the wings, she found Rupert in conversation with Mr Rawlings and saw some coins change hands. The other players had gone as she walked up to the two men.

'You are in safe hands,' Edward said and pocketed the gold. 'I am sorry you are no longer to be one of us, but no harm has been done. May good fortune go with you, Wenna.'

He walked away and she turned to look at Rupert. 'Did you pay him for his losses?'

'It was but a few silver pence and of no consequence.' Rupert frowned at her. 'You are ready to leave? I think we should go quickly, for that priest may yet make trouble.'

'Why must people be so cruel and so ready to condemn? Why is it so wrong for a woman to play upon the stage?'

'It is the law and those that flaunt it risk punishment. You are not the first to risk it, Morwenna, but until the law is changed 'tis a dangerous profession. People are superstitious. Have you not heard of the Witchfinder? Women have been put to the test for less, Morwenna.'

Morwenna shivered. 'I had no idea they would think the story true—'twas merely a play and I said so little.'

'Have you no idea how magnificent you looked? Your words had me shivering in my boots. For a woman to sing in a public place was seen as a moral outrage—though I doubt not the day will come when the law will change and women will take their place on the stage without fear of the law, even if they have to play youth's parts.'

'I am glad you gave the players money. They were kind to me and I meant no harm.'

Morwenna felt close to tears as Rupert took her arm, pushing her out into the inn yard.

Holding her tight, he led her to where his horse stood waiting.

'You must ride with me. We have no other choice.'

'I know how to ride. My father taught me.'

'We will buy you a horse, but not from here. I do not wish to spend more time here than necessary. That priest is stirring them up and I would not have them come after you, Morwenna. Even I could not be sure of holding a mob if they hunted a witch.'

She was pale and silent as he put her up and then jumped into the saddle, but his arms went round her, holding her, comforting her, and she felt the ice melting about her heart. How could she be angry with him when he had come to her rescue?

'We shall be in England soon. I shall take you to my home first and then we'll go to London.'

Morwenna made no reply. She was uncertain what else she might do, though she could not forget the words he had spoken to her on the night of the wrecking. If he thought her a merciless creature that would lure men to their death to steal their goods, why had he bothered to come in search of her? Yet she must be grateful for his arrival, for had he not come in time she might have had to leave her friends and strike out alone once more—and had the crowd turned nasty… A shiver ran through her at the thought for she had heard vague tales of women being put to the test, though it had never happened in her village.

Rupert's arms tightened about her. 'You are safe now, Morwenna. I shall not let those fools hurt you. I am sorry for the things I said to you the night of the storm. I saw dead men in the water and it made me angry, but I should have known that you had played no part in luring that ship to its doom.'

'Nor were my brothers to blame. Michael would punish the culprits if he found them, but they may have been strangers. We might be smugglers, but we are not wreckers.'

'Jacques told me the same and I believed him. Think no more of it, my love. I have regretted that night a thousand times. We are together now and if I have my way nothing shall part us. I have vowed to care for you and I shall do so if you let me.'

Morwenna was silent. With all her being she longed to be with him, to be his mistress and give him all the love that was in her, but was she wise to do so?

Yet if she found a way to leave him, she would be alone and that morning had taught her that the world was a more dangerous place than she had guessed in her father's house.

Morwenna looked at the house before them. They had left Truro two days previously and now they were in England, on the borders of the Welsh Marches. It was not a huge house Rupert had brought her to, not the kind of dwelling she would expect a lord to live in, but she sensed it meant something to him. She felt a response in him as they approached, as if he felt at home here.

'What is this place?'

'It is my retreat,' he said and smiled as he lifted her down into his arms. 'My family came from these parts before my father was made a marquis. My great-great-grandfather bought the estate. It was only when the family became very rich and acquired larger estates that they moved to the castle.'

'You are a marquis and live in a castle?'

'I inherited the title from my father. Sometimes I live in the castle, but not often. My father died three years since, but my mother and sister live in the castle still. I visit from time to time, but I am often at court in London and when I have leisure I come here to Melford.'

'It is a lovely house,' she said. 'The stone is mellowed by time and it looks golden in the sunshine.'

'Yes, I like it here. The people who care for it are simple folk. We shall not share a bed here, Morwenna. The servants must be allowed to believe you are a distant cousin fallen on hard times and that I have brought you here for your safety.'

Morwenna felt the hot blush sweep up her cheeks. 'Are you ashamed of me? Why do you not take me to the nearest town and leave me? I can make my own way to London.'

'Who will you fall in with next?' he asked, an odd smile on his lips. 'If you do not wish to stay with me when we get to London, I will take you to your aunt's house and you can send word to Jacques.'

'I do not wish to go to my aunt's house. She is a sour, cold woman and would make my life a misery once she knew—' She broke off, feeling hot all over.

'Knew what, Morwenna?' Rupert looked down at her. She turned her head away, but he caught her chin and made her look at him. 'That you had been my lover?'

She would not look at him as she said, 'You need not feel responsible. I was willing enough.'

'You were virgin when we loved. I took your innocence and must take care of you. For though you have a rascal for a brother I know you to be honest.'

'Even so, I am capable of looking after myself.'

'Indeed? You will allow me to be the judge, Mistress Morgan. I found you in some difficulty, you may recall.' He turned away to greet the elderly man and woman who came out into the yard to welcome them. 'Tomas and Anne—I would have you be kind to my cousin, Mistress Morwenna Morgan. Her family has fallen on hard times and I have brought her here so that I may protect her. We shall go to London in a few days, but for now I want her to rest and recover her spirits.'

'Welcome, Mistress Morgan. It is good to see you, milord,' the old man said. 'All is well here, as always. My son sees to the land and we care for the house. Come in, for your chamber is always ready and the guest chamber will take but a moment to prepare.'

'We shall have food and wine in the parlour, Tomas. My cousin has few belongings. I shall supply her lack before we leave for town.'

'There are trunks of silks and good wool cloths in the store chambers, my lord,' the elderly woman said and curtsied to Morwenna. 'For such a beautiful lady I would advise the silks be made up by the seamstress. I will send for her today, should you wish.'

'I can help to sew the garments,' Morwenna said and then blushed as the woman looked at her curiously. 'I do not wish to be a trouble to you.'

'I have told you that my home is yours, Morwenna. My people will be glad to work for you.' Rupert took her arm, looking at her sternly. 'Come, I shall show you my house.'

Morwenna made no reply. Tears were stinging behind her eyes as he took her inside the beautiful old manor house. Although very old and built in the fourteenth century, it had been kept in good repair and the inside was well furnished with both ancient oak and more modern walnut pieces with twisty legs and splats in the back of the elbow chairs. There were carpets on the floors and some of the walls had been recently panelled with light oak to make it warmer. Bright cushions in jewel-like colours were placed on carved benches and the smell of rose petals was everywhere. It was the house of a wealthy man and one that cared for his home.

'Someone is industrious here,' Morwenna said as she looked about her. 'This is a lovely home.'

She sighed, for even when her mother lived the house in Cornwall had never been this comfortable or so well appointed. After her parents died, Morwenna had struggled to keep it clean and the little touches that made a house a home had been forgotten.

Seeing the smiling maid, busy with her beeswax, and the potboy come up from the kitchen in his coarse apron to look at her, she smiled. Clearly the people here were curious about her and she wondered if this was the first time Rupert had brought a lady to his home. One or two other servants had drifted into the hall, eager smiles on their faces as they looked at their lord and his guest and then at each other.

They imagined her to be their lord's intended. Morwenna's throat caught as she thought how happy she would be if that were the case, but Rupert had made her position clear. His servants were to believe that she was a poor relation he had taken pity on—and in a way that was true. He had rescued her from an unpleasant incident that might have turned nasty and because she'd been virgin when he seduced her, he believed it was his duty to care for her.

For a moment fierce regret swept through her. If she had not lain with him she would not be in this awkward position. Rupert did not truly love her, though he called her his love and spoke of sharing a bed. She would be his mistress while he wanted her and then he would send her away, no doubt with sufficient money to live in comfort somewhere in obscurity, especially if they should have a child.

She shook her head because it was not a future she cared to see. Her pride would carry her through these next few days, because these people were good honest folk and clearly thought much of their lord. She would not make a fuss or deviate from the story he chose, but once they left here she would find a way to slip off and make her own way to London.

Yet it broke her heart to think of leaving him. Why should she leave him? There was nothing in life for her without him.

Chapter Eight

'Do not look as if you were a trapped fawn,'
Rupert said as the door closed behind them and
they were alone in his parlour. 'Eat some of this
good food. I dare say you have not tasted as
good since you left home.'

Morwenna picked up a piece of fresh bread,
spread it with pale butter and added cheese to
it, chewing with some relish. Rupert had taken
it on himself to fill her plate with slices of ham,
relishes and a slice of piggy pie.

'I am not sure if the pie is as good as you
make, but I think you will find it has its own
taste.'

Morwenna nibbled at a tiny slice and smiled.
'It has a distinctive taste, very different to the

recipe that Bess makes. She would be curious and I think she would like this…'

'What happened to her? Is she still at the house?'

'No, she was to go to her sister. Michael must find a new servant, I think.'

'Your brothers may soon find themselves eating prison swill if they do not mend their ways.'

Morwenna's eyes flashed fire as she looked at him. 'Why do you say that? What harm did they do to you?'

'It is the harm they may do to others that matters here. Jacques says Michael tells him only what he needs him to do—is that the truth?'

'Yes, why?'

'It may save his life if it is accepted at their trial.'

'You would see my brothers ruined? You would see them broken on the rack and hanged?' A sob rose to her lips, but she denied it.

'It is not my wish, Morwenna. Jacques is determined never to return to that house and may escape Michael's fate. I think he might like to come here as my steward—do you think such a position would suit him?'

Her eyes opened wide. 'It is exactly what

Jacques would like—but are you sure? Why should you do something like that for him?'

'I trust him now I know he isn't involved in the plot to murder the King and destroy our constitution—and my steward ages. He will need help as the years pass.'

'You think my eldest brother is involved in this treason?'

'I have been told that there is proof of involvement with known Jesuits and Catholic troublemakers. We suspect that a plot is being hatched—and the men involved have been seen with Michael. One of them was arrested. He escaped and was followed to your village and then disappeared before the militia could deal him with.'

'You think Michael helped him get away to France on his ship?'

'I am certain he did and I think it was not the first time it has happened. Your brother is deeply involved with the plotters.'

'If you will excuse me, I shall go to my chamber...'

Morwenna turned away, but he caught her arm, refusing to allow her to leave him. 'Not so fast. I know now that neither you nor Jacques was involved in these plots. I may keep you both

safe if I can but unless Michael mends his ways
he will be taken and punished.'

'Why do you say these things to me? Do you
wish to torment me? To punish me?'

'Why should I punish you?' His hand reached
out and caressed her cheek. 'Surely you know
I care for you, Morwenna? I must tell you the
truth, for I would have no more lies between
us. Had I not lost my memory I might never
have known you, for I came in search of a traitor and you were his sister. For all I knew you
were involved in their plotting, but my memory had gone and I found you lovely. As sweet
and warm as you were honest. Can you blame
me for what I did? The feeling between us was
mutual, I think.'

Morwenna's stomach clenched as she tried
to control the heat that raced through her at his
touch. Her lips parted on a ragged breath. She
caught back a sob.

'I know what my brother does is wrong—
but Michael lost so much when Father died and
we realised we had nothing left but the house.
The woman he was to have married was forced
to marry another.' She sighed and her protest
died away. 'I know that does not excuse what
he does, but he is still my brother.'

'And your caring does you credit,' Rupert said, smiling. 'Yet he has chosen his own way and will not heed you. You must put the past behind you and think of the future.'

'Yes, I know.' She caught back a sighing breath. 'I am but a woman and can do nothing.'

'Come now, eat your food and then Mistress Anne will show you to your chamber, where you may rest. She may have found you a clean gown that will do until we can have more made.'

Morwenna nodded, trying to banish the threatening tears and to swallow food that seemed to stick in her throat. It was foolish to be so emotional.

Rupert was being kind to her, but she wanted more. She wanted so much more than he was willing to give. He had never promised her marriage. It was her fault for falling in love with him.

Morwenna must accept what he offered or find a way to escape him.

'Do you play an instrument?' Rupert asked when they were alone in the parlour that evening.

'My mother had fine instruments and she taught me to play the virginals and the harp.

My father destroyed them after she died, for he could not bear to look at them, but had I an instrument I would play it.'

'I think my sister had a harp, but she did not play the virginals. When we are in London I shall buy instruments for you. I sometimes play the flute and I like to sing. Even though you may not sing upon the stage, Morwenna, our friends will enjoy your voice.'

'Shall we have friends if I am—?' She broke off and blushed as he looked at her.

'Most of my friends have a mistress,' Rupert said. 'We shall entertain them and they will ask us to their houses. You must not think I mean to hide you away.'

'Oh.' Morwenna looked away from him. She was not sure what it was to be a man's mistress. Her family would think it shameful, but great men had different ways and if it was accepted in London amongst his friends then perhaps it would not seem so very wrong. She must accept her fate, for to leave him now would surely break her heart. Besides, her reputation had been lost when she ran away from home. 'I see. I was not perfectly sure.'

Rupert moved towards her. He took her hand and kissed it.

'I care for you, Morwenna. We shall have a good life together and you will find no shame in being my lover, I promise you. I shall never cast you off or hurt you and if we part it will be because we no longer wish to be together. Even then I shall offer you my friendship and protection.'

'I thank you.'

She stumbled over the words, for the tears burned behind her eyelids. Rupert was a man of honour and generous, but he did not love her as she loved him. He had no idea that he was breaking her heart or that she might one day be forced to leave him because the hurt simply became too much to bear.

She would hide her pain behind a smile, because there was nothing else she could do.

'Have you enjoyed your stay here, Morwenna?' Rupert came upon her in the gardens of his home as she bent her head to sniff at a beautiful white rose that had somehow escaped the frosts of autumn. 'I know you like to walk, for you rise early every morning. What else do you enjoy?'

'Is this not a beautiful rose?' Morwenna asked, smiling at him. 'It has a delicate perfume. Mama tried to grow roses, but the winds were too cold for them and they withered. Shall we have a rose garden, Rupert?'

'Yes, of course, if you wish it. I remember there was once a beautiful red rose that grew here in a sheltered spot. Its perfume was matched only by the deep crimson of its petals. You must tell me what you like and I shall try to provide the things you need.'

'My needs are not great,' she said. 'I like to talk and laugh and to walk or ride. I think it would be pleasant to have dogs if one lived in the countryside.'

'I thought we might live in London, but I dare say we could spend time in the country if it suited you,' he said, a slight frown creasing his brow. 'Do you like to embroider? Shall I buy you silks and a frame for your pleasure?'

'That would be pleasant. I could make shirts for you and embroider your initials on your nightgown.' She saw the laughter in his eyes and her colour rose. 'What have I said to amuse you?'

'I sleep naked, Morwenna, just as I was when you nursed me and bathed my heated body.'

'Oh.' She turned away hastily lest he should

see her embarrassment. It was true that she had thought him beautiful when she cooled his fever.

Was it because she had done those things for him that he thought she had no shame? Did he think her wanton or unworthy in some way? He spoke of caring for her, but he had never once suggested marriage.

Why? Was there some reason why he could not wed her—or was it simply that he thought her the sister of a traitor, unworthy of his name?

The thought struck her to the heart, but she thrust it from her mind as he held out his hand to her.

'Come, Morwenna. I shall show you my favourite places. The trees I liked to climb and the stream I fished in as a boy.'

Morwenna took his hand. Sometimes in this beautiful place she could almost believe she was his wife and loved.

'That colour becomes you well, Mistress Morwenna,' the old woman said as she fastened the ties at the back of the beautiful green silk gown. It had a squared neckline with a broad band of embroidery, a narrow stomacher, which was embroidered with beads and silk, and a full skirt that gathered into a little train at the back.

''Tis a shame you have no jewels to wear for the gown deserves them.'

'I do have some pearls my mother left me,' Morwenna said and went to the coffer she had been given for her use. She lifted the lid and took out the little pouch that contained the precious necklet. The pearls were small and misshapen, but precious to her because they had been her mother's. She put them around her neck, slipping the clasp into place. 'There, will they do?'

'They look well enough,' Anne said, but there was a note of reserve in her voice. Clearly she thought Morwenna should wear something more in keeping with the status of her protector's family. 'I dare say my lord will present you with jewels worthy of you soon enough.'

A protest rose to Morwenna's lips, but she held it inside. It had become obvious to her these past few days that Rupert's servants believed she would be their new mistress. She would not disillusion them, for they would learn the truth soon enough.

Leaving her chamber, she went down the stairs to the parlour. As she paused outside, she heard voices. Resisting the temptation to listen, she turned away and went out into the garden. If

Rupert wished her to meet his guest, he would come in search of her.

Her time had passed pleasantly since they'd arrived at the manor, for she had been allowed to do exactly as she pleased. Rupert had been busy with his steward and his agents, riding his acres and making decisions that would be carried out to the letter. She had seen for herself that the land was in good heart and everything was well ordered. Rupert might not come often to this house, but his servants were industrious even when their master was not at home.

How she would love to live in this house as its mistress! Morwenna sighed deeply, for she knew such a dream was impossible. Rupert had promised to look after her, but she would be his mistress and see him only when he had the time to spare. She would not be a part of his family and but a small part of his life.

Her throat was tight and she fought the tears, pulling her cloak tighter about her as she shivered in the cool breeze. Soon now the autumn would be over and they would be deep in winter.

She had her back turned to him when she heard Rupert's approach and turned slowly to face him.

'Forgive me if I have neglected you,' he said, his eyes moving over her with warm admiration. 'Your new gown becomes you, Morwenna. Are you satisfied with it?'

'Yes, perfectly. The silk is finer than I have possessed before.'

'I am pleased if it finds favour in your eyes.'

Morwenna smiled, but made no reply. Fine gowns were all very well, but what she needed was a sign that she truly meant something to him. Since their arrival he'd kept his distance, never approaching her when they might be in seclusion. She'd had plenty to keep her busy, but she enjoyed the short time they spent together in the evenings when they supped and spoke of their day before parting each to their own bedchamber.

Rupert had been scrupulous, treating her exactly as he would a spinster lady of his family. He was courteous and respectful, but sometimes she saw a spark of fire in his eyes and believed he was thinking of what it might be like if she lay in his bed each night. If only they could spend every night and the better part of their day together. She would then have all she could ever want.

'Did you have a visitor earlier? I heard voices

when I came to your chamber, but I turned away for I did not wish to intrude.'

'It was merely a messenger from London. I am instructed to return as soon as possible. We shall leave here the day after tomorrow.'

'Must we?' Morwenna sighed for she had felt happy here and wished they might stay a little longer.

His brows arched as he caught her sigh. 'You like it here so much?'

'I have never known a home like this,' she replied honestly. 'I could wish that it were mine, but I know that is impossible. Your plans for me do not include taking me into your home. I have felt a sense of belonging, but of course I do not belong here.'

'Do you not?' Rupert's gaze narrowed and she saw an odd expression in his eyes. For a moment he looked so bleak that she wondered at the memories behind that look. 'We must see how we go on, Morwenna. My business takes me to London, but…' He shook his head as if gathering his scattered thoughts. 'I should tell you that there is more information concerning the plotters. If Michael is involved, I shall not be able to save him.'

'My brother is a law unto himself. If Michael

is the traitor you think him, then he must take the consequences. However, I would plead for mercy for Jacques. Michael tells him what to do and he does it, but he is not wicked.'

'Why does Jacques not press him for answers if he doubts him?'

'Michael is the head of the house…' She faltered and looked away, then, 'Jacques told you he would no longer be a part of Michael's plans?'

'If he keeps to his word, he is safe.'

'Thank you.' Tears stung her throat. 'You must think us a troublesome family.'

'Perhaps.' Rupert smiled. 'I, too, long for adventure at times, which is why I became involved in this business. I understand your brothers more than you might imagine. I will help them if I can, but Michael holds his own fate in his hands.'

'Yes, I understand.'

Morwenna turned away, tears stinging her eyes. Rupert reached out and caught her wrist, holding her so firmly that she looked back at him, her throat tight.

'You know that I care for you?'

'Yes.' Her voice was tremulous, uncertain. 'You told me when we lay together. I was not sure you meant it. You were so angry the night the wreckers came. You thought me one of them.'

'I have wished my cruel words unsaid a thousand times.' He drew her closer so that she was but a breath away from his body, gazing down at her. 'If I kiss you now, I shall take you to my chamber and make love to you. Since I do not wish to ruin your reputation and shock my staff, I shall keep my distance until we leave this house.' His eyes caressed her, hot and needy. 'I want you so much and I shall always take care of you and, if we should have children, they will not want. You need not fear for the future, Morwenna. As soon as we reach London I shall find a suitable house where we can be together. You will have servants to care for you and many more fine gowns, jewels and horses. I shall spend as much time with you as I can. It will be a good life. I hope it will content you?'

'Yes, I think I shall be happy when we are settled.'

What alternative did she have? Alone and friendless, she would end up in some menial position if he abandoned her. Morwenna must take what he offered and make the most of what he gave.

He moved closer still, eyes seeming to scorch her as he looked into her face. She felt the heat of his passion engulf her like a flame, setting her on fire. How could she ever leave him when she wanted to be in his arms so much? Her thoughts of running away were wild and foolish—she wanted to lie with him in scented sheets as they had that first night in the cottage at the top of the cliffs. A part of her said it was not enough and yet her heart cried out that it would break if she left him.

'You'd best go into the house,' Rupert said at last. 'If we stay here longer, I shall carry you into a secret place and ravish you. For the sake of my people and your reputation, I shall wait until we are in London and no one knows us or cares what we do. My friends have their mistresses and you will be welcomed by them all.'

Once again her throat felt tight and tears pricked, but she held them back and smiled. What more could she expect? She was a lady born, but she had given herself to him like a wanton. She could expect nothing more than he was offering her. No man would ever wish to wed her now.

Turning away so that he should not see her tears, she went into the house with her head held high. One day he would tire of her, but she knew he would not simply cast her off. She would be provided for even though he looked elsewhere for his pleasure. In the meantime she must make the most of what he offered.

Rupert watched her walk into the house. She had the poise and bearing of a queen. He knew that, had her circumstances been other than they were, he would not have been offering to make her his mistress. She was all fire and passion, but she was a lady and she deserved more than he could give her.

Yet he could not wed the sister of a man who was likely to be taken for treason, tried and executed. As his mistress, she would be hidden away and no one would connect her with Michael Morgan, but if he were to marry her, her name and family must be known.

What was he thinking of? Marriage was out of the question. He owed too much to his family name and tradition. No, it was impossible. His father would stir in his grave and his mother would weep and beg him to think of her before allying himself with the sister of a traitor. She would remind him of his promise and of other things, using all her strength to punish him.

Rupert was his father's second son. His brother Richard should have inherited most of what was his, but an accident when they were playing as boys had lead to a terrible tragedy. Richard had fallen into the moat when they were fighting on the steep banks. He had been the elder and stronger, but though they fought in jest and laughed, his foot had slipped when Rupert pushed him. In falling into the icy water of the deep moat that surrounded the castle he'd struck his head, going down like a stone beneath the murky water. Rupert's screams had brought men rushing to his rescue, but though alive when dragged from the water, he'd died of the resulting fever some days later.

Rupert's father had understood it was an accident, but his mother—his mother had never forgiven him. She blamed Rupert for the loss of her favourite son. Indeed, he thought she hated him, insisting that it was his fault, though Richard had begun the game.

'You should not have been fighting near the moat,' the Dower Marchioness had told him many times. 'If you'd obeyed your father, my son would still be alive.'

Rupert's pride prevented him from begging for understanding. He'd begged her pardon, but her cold eyes told him that his sin would never be forgiven. She would never accept Morwenna Morgan as his wife and the future mother of his heirs. Even though he found the idea appealing, he knew it could not be. His proud mother would not have it and he'd promised her grandsons she could love.

No, no, such an alliance was not to be thought of. Indeed, Rupert had not thought of marriage for some time. Not since his betrothed died of that terrible fever. He had been devastated by her sudden and fatal illness and since then he'd taken his pleasures lightly, never considering a relationship that would touch his heart. If he had not lost his memory, he might not have fallen for Morwenna's sweetness so easily.

She deserved so much more than he could give her.

No other woman had come close to touching his inner citadel, but, he realised now, Morwenna had broken down his defences. He would not wish to part with her. She had become more to him than he'd ever intended.

He would do his best to make her happy. It was natural that she should be a little uneasy after the way he'd raged at her and then walked away. She needed time to come to trust him and that was one of the reasons why he'd brought her here, to a place where he knew he could not indulge his own needs, his own passions. Rupert wanted her in his bed. He wanted to make love to her all the time, to see that drowsy satiated expression in her beautiful eyes when they lay together in the candlelight. If he'd cared only for himself, he would have found an inn and taken her to bed the first night, but he wanted her to be ready. To welcome him without doubt or fear in her eyes.

In London he would give her all the things she'd never had, lavish her with love and affection and the luxuries his money could buy. Surely then, when she saw how he cared for her safety and her pleasure, she would be ready to become the passionate mistress he needed?

'Come back to us soon, my lord,' Mistress Anne said as she and the steward accompanied them out to the courtyard. Morwenna was to ride a fine, milk-white palfrey, which stood waiting for her docilely as she made her farewells. 'And bring Mistress Morwenna with you, for she brings sunshine to us all.'

'Thank you for looking after me,' Morwenna said and pressed a small coin into her hand.

The old woman shook her head, but Morwenna closed her fingers over it. 'For your grandchildren if you wish it so.'

'For the children, mistress. It has been a pleasure to look after you these past few days.'

Morwenna kissed her cheek, then turned away. A groom helped her to mount her horse as Rupert took his last farewell. Then they were moving out of the courtyard. She looked back once, noting the way the old stone walls glowed in the late autumn sun. The best of the year had gone now and soon it would be winter. Here it had seemed as warm as summer these past few days, but she knew it was but an illusion, just as the peace and serenity of the old house was merely a dream. Life was never this sweet in reality. If they had stayed longer she would have seen the truth soon enough, but it was a pleasant memory to take with her and something she would never forget.

Rupert brought his horse alongside hers, his smile seeming to ask a question. 'You will be happy in London, I promise you.'

'Yes, I'm sure I shall.' She threw him a gallant smile. 'How long shall we be on the road?'

'A few days,' he replied. 'Impatient, Morwenna? You need not be. I shall come to your bed this night!'

Her heart fluttered like a trapped moth against a windowpane, her throat closing as she raised her head and gave him a proud look. She wanted to be in his arms again, wanted it badly, but she needed so much more than he was prepared to give.

She wanted his love. Yet she dared not express her own.

It was late when they finally reached the inn that night. A thick fog had sprung up on the way, cutting their sight of the road off for hours at a time and causing delay. Had they passed another inn they might have taken a room, but none had been found and it was not until it began to rain that the mist cleared and they were at last able to find the right road and complete their journey.

'I took only one room here for I planned on spending the night together,' Rupert said as he helped her dismount. 'I know it is late and you are tired. I will ask if there is another room.'

'No need,' she said in a small whisper. 'I would rather you stayed with me. I shall feel more comfortable if you are by my side.'

'The inn is respectable, though a little noisy,' Rupert said as the light spilled out into the courtyard and there was laughter and shouting from inside the taproom. 'The host's wife will take you straight up. I shall bespoke supper for us and we will have it in our chamber.'

'Thank you. I am not very hungry, but perhaps some warmed ale and bread or scones with preserves.'

'I shall order a selection and you may eat what you wish. If you are tired, rest on the bed. I shall not disturb you should you fall asleep.'

Morwenna nodded, but she was not in the least tired, her nerves stretched and tingling as she thought of his coming to her later.

She was taken up to a large comfortable chamber where a fire burned. Warm water in pewter jugs was waiting for her, together with cloths for washing and drying.

'If there is anything more, my lady, you have only to ask and I shall send one of the girls up with it.'

'You seem to have thought of everything, ma'am. I thank you for your kindness.'

'Nothing is too much trouble for his lordship's lady.'

Morwenna felt a warm flush in her cheeks.

Did the woman think she was Rupert's wife—or merely his mistress?

She had not removed her mother's ring which she wore on her left hand. It had served her when she posed as a widow and would serve her now—yet she knew the truth and a part of her mind felt shamed.

When she'd gone to him on the cliffs that night, she'd seen herself as his lover—seen them as being true lovers and thought no further. Now it was coming to her that she was a kept woman, a scarlet woman. She had forfeited her modesty and her respectability for love—but did Rupert understand why she had abandoned her modesty that day? Or did he think her a wanton who would lie with one man as easily as another?

That thought was distressing and she thrust it from her immediately. Rupert had taken her virginity—and he claimed to care for her.

She must not regret what had gone, but welcome the future.

Chapter Nine

Rupert and their supper arrived at the same moment. The serving wenches laid out the various dishes on a trestle table in front of the dormer window, then accepted a small coin from Rupert's hand and departed.

'You have ordered so much,' Morwenna said as she took her seat and saw the array of foods. There was a rich stew that smelled of onions and beef, also cold chicken, relishes, cheese, bread, butter and preserves and a sweet dish of honey and curds. 'I could not eat so much, especially when we are about to go to bed.' She blushed as she spoke and saw him smile.

'Our journey was made longer by the mist, as you are aware. We are both tired and hungry. Eat as much as you wish. I shall make no demands on you this night.'

'I wasn't meaning…' Morwenna's stomach rumbled and she blushed and then laughed. 'Perhaps I am hungry after all.'

'We should have eaten long since,' he said. 'Our host has no spare rooms, but I can sit by the fire and sleep. It would not be the first time I've passed the night in such a way.'

'Please do not be foolish.' She yawned and then took a sip of ale. 'I dare say I may fall asleep as soon as my head touches the pillow, but there is no reason why you should not lie beside me. You will find it more comfortable than that chair.'

'Yes, I should,' he agreed. 'Very well. You may trust me—I shall not take advantage as you sleep.'

'Why should you? We have all the time in the world once we find a place to stay.'

'How sensible of you, Morwenna.'

She looked at him, sensing that he was laughing. 'Please do not mock me. It is the truth, is it not?'

'I was not mocking you and it is the truth,' he replied with a smile. 'Eat some of this excellent stew. I promise you that it is very good.'

'I could not at this hour, but the rolls and preserves are very good and so is the curd. I seldom have such sweet treats, though I like them.'

'Yes, I have noticed,' Rupert said. 'I think at
home you cooked for your brothers rather than
yourself, is that not so?'

'Yes, it was easier,' Morwenna said. 'It
seemed a waste to prepare such dishes just for
me, because even Bess was not partial to them.'

'I enjoy sweetmeats sometimes. We shall
have them when we dine together, but your cook
will prepare them,' Rupert said. 'Your hands
are not so sore now, I think. In time they will
be white again.'

'Yes, perhaps, though I am not sure they will
ever be as soft as they once were.'

'I shall buy you lotions and salves that will
help.' Rupert lifted her right hand and kissed
the palm. 'I intend to spoil you, my love. You
shall have all you desire.'

All I want is your love.

The words were in her mind, but she did not
speak them. She could not ask for more than he
wished to give. She had agreed to be his mistress and she must not demand more.

Rupert lay looking down at her as she slept.
Her skin was softly flushed, her hair spread on

the pillow. She had been very tired, falling into a deep sleep almost as soon as they lay down. He, too, had slept, but his habit was to wake early, for he needed very little sleep and so he had been lying watching her for some time.

The temptation to touch her hair and kiss her lips was strong, but he had promised not to take advantage. He must wait until she woke, until she was ready to let him make love to her as they had in the cave that last time.

She'd given herself so sweetly, holding nothing back. He wanted her to be that way again, which was why he'd waited for so many days, tormented by need, but afraid of appearing too demanding. This must be strange and a little frightening for her. She did not know where they were going or what she would find there— nor was she certain of his affection. It was strong. Perhaps stronger than either of them yet knew, but even so he could not offer what she deserved. He ought in all honour to offer marriage, but it was not possible and yet...

'Rupert?' She opened her eyes and looked up at him and then smiled. 'I thought I was dreaming. I thought you had gone and that I should never see you again, but you're here.'

'Yes, I'm here, dearest,' he murmured huskily

as he bent his head to caress her lips with his own. She opened to him as his tongue danced along her mouth and their tongues met in a delicious duel of love. 'You still taste of honey. I've never know a woman to taste that way first thing in the morning.'

'It was such delicious honey,' she murmured and ran her pink tongue over her lips. 'I was greedy and ate too much.'

'I like the taste on you,' he said, 'but you always taste sweet. I think it is your own taste and owes nothing to the landlord's honey.'

Rupert kissed her long and hard, his hand stroking the length of her down to her thigh. His tongue flicked at her mouth, then moved lower, moving aside the soft material of her night chemise, laving the sweet valley between her breasts and circling her nipples until she arched and cried out in need. His hand caressed her breasts, cupping and squeezing gently before moving slowly down to the warm moistness between her thighs.

'You smell good, too,' he murmured, bending his head to inhale the perfume of her musk. He kissed her mound of soft curls and threaded his fingers through them, before slipping his hand between her thighs. His finger sought and stroked the nub of her femininity, making the moisture run as she spilled her essence over his fingers and arched into him, mewing like a kitten.

'Not yet, my sweet,' he murmured throatily. 'I'm starving.'

'After all that supper?'

'I wasn't speaking of food. It's you I want, Morwenna. You I need now.'

'I want you, too,' she breathed as he lowered himself over her, his heat burning her as he moved against her and she felt the soft skin of his huge male organ between her thighs. 'Oh, yes…yes…'

Her legs opened wider for him as he sought entrance. He found her moist opening, easing his huge sex inside her and letting her settle about him before he thrust up into her silken sheath. She fit him perfectly, accommodating his length and thickness with ease.

Together they moved as one, relishing the sweetness of this early morning loving. His hands continued to stroke and caress her, squeezing her buttocks as she lifted herself towards him so that he could plunge deeper and deeper inside her.

Rupert took his time, easing himself in and out, pausing to kiss and tease her with his tongue, so that the anticipation was sharpened and their loving continued on and on rather than coming to a frantic end.

Morwenna's nails were scraping his shoulders as she clung to him, her breath coming in little panting cries that grew louder as the sensation of pleasure mounted, until at the last she screamed his name and dug her nails into his flesh, her body trembling and jerking as something gave way inside her and she came and came again in waves of mind-rending pleasure. His seed spilled inside her and then he lay still, his face buried in her hair, sated and content.

They lay entwined for some time until Rupert rolled away, taking her with him so that they were still joined together by tangled limbs, but his weight no longer lay full on her.

'Are you content?' he asked as she sighed against his shoulder.

'Very content.'

'Good.' He kissed her hair. 'We shall do well together, Morwenna. Now, I should get up before the chambermaid brings water. We shall leave as soon as we've broken our fast.'

'How many more days must we spend on the road?'

'Three or four, perhaps,' he replied. 'It will pass, my love. When we are in town you may stay in bed all day if you wish.'

'Only when you are in it,' she said. She sat up and looked at him, sudden excitement in her face. 'I want to explore London, see the palaces and the Tower and everything of interest.'

'What of the shops? Do you not want to visit the silk merchants and purchase all manner of trifles? I shall give you money of your own so you may shop to your heart's content.'

'Yes, I should like that, for I have seldom had the chance to choose what I like,' she said and laughed, giving him a naughty look. 'Do you mean to spoil me, Rupert?'

'Yes, of course. What else should I do with my mistress? Especially if she pleases me the way you please me.'

Rupert rolled away from her and pulled on his hose and breeches. He did not notice her smile dim or see the look of hurt in her eyes.

He thought of her as his mistress, a woman his money could buy. For a moment she was swamped by humiliation. Did he not know that she had given herself to him because she loved him, that she would never love another man this way?

The words built inside her, wanting to boil over in a hot torrent of regret and reproach. She was not a whore, even though she had thrown away any claim to reputation or modesty. She gave because she loved and thought nothing of jewels or money she might receive in return. Surely he must know? Yet it seemed he did not.

'I shall go for a ride before breakfast,' Rupert called over his shoulder as he dressed. 'Stay in bed for a while longer. I will order the food to be brought up to us on my return.'

Morwenna did not answer him and then he was gone, the door closing with snap behind him. For a moment the angry tears stung her eyes and for two pins she would have thrown on her clothes and left the inn to find her own way to London.

Yet what good would that do her now? She'd given her innocence and her heart to a man who seemed not to realise it. In time he would no doubt cast her aside in pursuit of another love, but she would stay with him until the moment he broke her heart.

Yet she had no wish to stay in bed. Flinging aside the covers, she got up and dressed. It was cool out for the month was drawing to its close and soon winter would be upon them.

Remembering the wild waves that raged about the cliffs below her home in mid-winter and the strong winds that had almost swept her off her feet, Morwenna felt a swathe of regret for her lost family. She would not mind if she did not see Michael much in future, but she was going to miss Jacques and Bess, too.

The inn yard was empty save for some ostlers sweeping debris from the cobbles and a dog nosing at a pile of straw. Leaving the inn yard, Morwenna walked into a little lane behind it and strolled towards a small wood. The birds were singing as they perched on branches above her head and it was a peaceful morning. Some of the pain Rupert's careless words had inflicted eased away as she walked. Nothing was lost for, she'd known from the start that he would never offer her marriage.

She could run now while he was out riding, but if she did she would be alone and her heartbreak would begin immediately. No, she must take what she could from this relationship, even if her head was telling her she was a fool.

'Are you telling me she is with you at the inn?' Jacques looked at the other man, relief washing over him. 'Thank God! At least I know she is not lying at the side of some road with her throat cut.'

'I told you I would find her and I shall protect her—you, too, if you will give me your word that you will not become involved in your brother's schemes.'

Jacques looked uncomfortable, then, 'I've seen Michael. He was furious that Morwenna had gone off and he blames you. For a moment I thought he would kill me, but it seems you are the one he intends to kill when he finds you.'

'He may certainly try. I dare say I might feel the same in his shoes.'

'What are your intentions towards my sister?'

'I shall not desert her. She will be well cared for. I give you my word on it.'

'You will not marry her?'

'My family would not welcome the sister of a traitor. Had your brother not been on the verge of committing treason, it might have been different.'

Jacques cursed. 'I could kill him myself for ruining her life.'

'Morwenna is happy with our arrangement. She could never have expected to be the wife of a marquis, I think.'

Jacques glared at him. 'She would never have looked so high, but she might have wed a good country squire had my father not lost his money.'

'She will have everything my wife would have other than my name.'

'What is all the rest worth without it? Morwenna imagines herself in love with you, Melford. She may be happy enough now, but what of the day you tire of her? How will she feel when you take a wife, as you surely must in time?'

Rupert frowned. 'I have cousins enough to take my place. I had thought of marrying to get an heir, but it is different now.'

Jacques narrowed his gaze. 'Do you care for her truly?'

'As much as I have cared for any woman,' Rupert admitted. 'I can see no future in these discussions. The die is cast. It was in my mind to offer you a position should you wish to take it.'

'Are you bribing me to go away and leave my sister to you?'

'If that were my intention, I need not have told you that she was here. Come to the inn.

Have breakfast with us, unless you feel she has shamed you too much?'

'I am not such a jackanapes. Morwenna is my sister. I love her. I would never censure her. If she is with you, it is because you make her happy.'

'That is my intention.' Rupert ran long fingers through his hair, which had blown into a tangle as he rode. 'Michael told you nothing of his plans, I suppose?'

'Nothing except that he seemed unusually on edge. I think he brought in a special cargo recently, for he warned me not to visit the caves. He impressed on me that it might be dangerous, though he would not say more.'

'Dangerous?' Rupert frowned. 'It sounds to me that something is being prepared. Something that may cause much harm to others.'

'I would like the position you spoke of,' Jacques said. 'But I must earn it first. Michael spoke of moving the goods. He also mentioned London, for he said it was his intention to search for Morwenna once his business was done. Do you know where you will be staying in London?'

'Do you wish to tell him?'

'I thought that I might follow him, try to discover what his dangerous cargo is and what he and the others plan.'

'Spy on your brother?' Rupert looked at him hard. 'Why would you do that?'

'If I could bring you news that enabled you to catch the plotters before they can cause this harm, would you give me your word that Morwenna shall have a house of her own and money if you part with her?'

'She would have all that and more in any case. I shall provide for her and our children should we have them. You need not betray your brother for her sake. I have given her my word and I do not break it lightly.'

'Something might happen to you and your family might cast her out. Secure property and money to her now, while it is in your mind, and I will try to discover what they plot.'

'Very well, if it will ease your mind.' Rupert was thoughtful. 'You may succeed where others have failed. You may always get word to me at my house in Westminster. Now come and eat breakfast with us and I shall give you my direction.'

'Yes, I shall, for I should like to see Morwenna.'

'To make certain she has not been forced into

a position of shame.' Rupert smiled wryly. 'She shall not lose by it, Jacques. I shall make her my wife in all but name.'

Jacques nodded, but the doubts remained in his eyes. Morwenna had given up so much for this man, though he seemed to think it nothing to lose reputation and family. He would speak to her, make certain she was happy, and then he would embark on the most dangerous work of his life. If Michael suspected him of spying, he would not hesitate to kill him.

Morwenna was returning to the inn when she saw the two men talking. Her heart jerked and then raced wildly. For a moment she wanted to turn and walk away so that they did not see her, then, as her brother turned his head and smiled, she knew it was too late. Lifting her head proudly, she walked to meet them.

'Have you come looking for me?'

'Why did you go off that way? You must have known I would help you when I returned. I would never have let Captain Bird force you into marriage.'

'I suppose I lost my nerve,' Morwenna admitted. 'Forgive me for not waiting, Jacques. As you see, all has turned out well. Rupert found me and I am quite safe.'

'This is what you want—to be with him?'

'Yes, of course. I was in some trouble and he rescued me, but if I had not wished to be with him I might have gone on alone. I had the chance this morning when he was out riding.'

'I should have pursued you. A woman alone is prey to all kinds of rogues,' Rupert said. 'Your brother is to break his fast with us. He will take up his position as my steward next month, but we shall see him in London before that, I believe.'

'You may count on it,' Jacques said, his mouth set in a determined line.

Rupert walked into the inn ahead of them, leaving them to talk alone for a few moments while he ordered their food.

Jacques looked into her face. 'Unless you would prefer to come with me, Morwenna? We could go to France or wherever you wish.'

'I am where I want to be.' Morwenna lifted her head, giving him a proud look. Her walk had cleared the doubts and she had come to terms with herself. 'Can you forgive me and love me still as your sister despite what I am?'

'Of course.' Jacques smiled and reached for

her hand. 'I love you, Morwenna, and always shall. I've warned that rogue to be good to you. If he fails, I shall thrash him or die in the attempt.'

Morwenna nodded, her lips trembling in a shaky laugh. 'I know you would do what you thought right for my sake, but the last thing I desire is for you to fight over me, Jacques. I am here of my own free will. If we are honest, we both know that any chance I had of a good marriage vanished long ago.'

'Yes, perhaps a marriage you would wish for, I dare say. Melford would never have come your way in the normal way of things, Morwenna. His family is too high for us.'

'Fate threw us together. I know she is a fickle mistress, but I have decided to make the best of my life while I can. I love him, Jacques. I love him more than my life.'

'You are not the first woman to be the mistress of such a man and some would think no shame to it,' Jacques said. 'I think he cares for you, as much as he knows how.'

'Yes, I believe it. I think he does not know what love is, Jacques.'

'Then you must teach him,' her brother said and took her hand. 'You have so much love to give, Morwenna. Perhaps he may come to see that your birth matters less than what you are. In time he may marry you. It has happened before—important men have married their mistress years later when they have their heirs.'

'I do not think it,' she said and laughed. 'Father married two women and was faithful to neither, though he mourned them deeply when they died. Are all men faithless, Jacques?'

'If I loved, I should not be so,' he said. 'Yet a wife may seek consolation from property and status.'

'Rupert would not see me starve. He will not desert me.'

'Then I can leave you with him and do what I must.'

'What must you do? I thought you were to work for Rupert?'

'Aye, but I would earn my place. There is something I may be able to do for him and for all of us.'

Morwenna shivered as she saw the grim set of his mouth. 'This concerns Michael, does it not?'

'Our brother is set on his own death,' Jacques told her. 'He will listen to no one and he will not deviate, but I do not see why he should take others down with him. He must be stopped from what he plans, Morwenna.'

'Be careful, Jacques. If Michael thought you had betrayed him, you know what he would do.'

'Yes, I know, but I cannot allow him to go unchecked. If he does he will bring us all down and, perhaps, even Rupert.'

'Rupert?' Her eyes widened. 'Through association with me and you? Yes, I see.'

'Nor can I condone what he does, Morwenna. I did not mind the smuggling but I think Michael and his fellow plotters plan something much worse. I heard him speak of a man called Guy Fawkes—a man who has agreed to undertake a dangerous mission.'

'Do you know this man?'

'No. I have not met him, but Michael seemed to think him very brave. I mean to discover more of this man and what it is that makes my brother have nightmares and call out in his sleep.'

Morwenna frowned. 'I think he has become involved in something terrible without realising what he did and now he is in too deep to withdraw.'

'Do not underestimate our brother. He hates King James with a passion and all those close to him. Michael would bring back the old faith to England if he could and he is merciless. You did not see the way he treated Captain Bird. Though he lives, he will not dare to speak out against Michael again.'

'I did not wish it so! Please be careful,' Morwenna begged and shivered. 'You frighten me, Jacques.'

'Do not fear for me. Michael would never suspect one of us. The other men are too lazy to defy him; they take his orders and his money, but I have had enough of such work. I want honest employment and a chance to be happy.'

'Yes, I know. It is what you should have done long since, Jacques.' She smiled at him. 'I know you stayed for me.'

'I could not desert you, dear heart.'

Morwenna nodded, slipping her hand in his as they went into the inn to join Rupert for breakfast.

Chapter Ten

'Will this content you?' Rupert asked as he took her inside the house. It was a double-storey building with overhanging windows, built of red brick with timber boarding on the upper storey and dormer windows with leaded glass. 'It is not huge, for there are but five bedrooms and the servants' quarters, but I shall look for a larger one in time if we should have children.'

Morwenna looked about her at the large front parlour, which ran the length of the house. It had oak panels on the walls and a wooden floor covered here and there with bright rugs of an eastern design in patterns of red, gold and blue. The furniture was a mixture of good solid oak and the newer mahogany pieces with legs like sticks of barley sugar.

'It is beautiful,' she breathed. 'I do not wish for larger, unless...' Her heart leaped in her breast, for to talk of the children they might have was to give a kind of permanence to their relationship and she hardly dared to believe it.

'This house is yours,' Rupert told her with a smile. 'You may change the furniture to your own choice if you wish. Some of the oak came from my own house, but the other is new. You will have an allowance for your own use and may do as you wish with it.'

Morwenna clapped her hands, her eyes lighting with pleasure. 'I have never been able to do just as I wish with a house,' she said and looked up at him. 'You are too good to me, Rupert. I do not know if I deserve so much.'

'You deserve more, much more,' he said and bent his head to brush his lips over hers. 'I have only just begun to spoil you, Morwenna. We shall go shopping this afternoon and buy your clothes and I shall have a present for you later.'

'You are not leaving me so soon?'

Fear clutched at her as she saw him turn towards the door. They had been in London two days, staying at an inn, and he had gone out for the better part of each day, coming back to dine with her and take her to bed at night.

'I have business that takes me from you,' he said. 'You will do well enough here. You have a housekeeper and a lackey to do your bidding. Once you know your way about London, you may take a sedan chair and visit the emporiums alone. Send your accounts to me, though once we have filled your clothes' chests you must learn to live on your allowance.'

'I am sure I could if you tell me what it is.'

'For the moment the accounts will come to me. I want to spoil you and to show you where it is best to shop. There are many silk merchants in Cheapside but some are rogues and sell inferior goods.'

'You will take me out this afternoon?'

'Yes, and we shall go to a theatre this evening. I have arranged for a boat to take us across the river to Southwark. You will need a domino and a mask. No decent woman attends the theatre unmasked.'

'Am I a decent woman?'

'Of course you are,' Rupert replied, looking annoyed. 'You do not behave in a lewd manner and ogle the gallants. I am your protector, but ours is a discreet arrangement. You are not a whore to be passed from one man to another. I do not wish rogues or rakes to look upon your beauty so you will go masked.'

'Thank you.' Morwenna's heart caught at his mark of respect. Sometimes when he looked at her in the way he looked now, she felt that he loved her as she loved him—that she was special to him. 'How long will you be gone?'

'Perhaps three hours or so, perhaps more,' Rupert said. 'Surely you can find something to do here?'

'Yes, of course. I want to rearrange things and I think I saw an embroidery frame.'

'You will discover a chest with silks and all you need for your industry,' he said and bent to kiss her softly on the lips. 'We shall be together soon, my love. I shall not desert you, so do not fear it.'

Morwenna nodded, her throat tight. He called her his love, but was she really? He had told her he cared for her but she was not sure how much she meant to him. Rupert did not think of her as a whore though she was a kept woman, but so, too, were wives—at least those that brought little or no dowry with them.

What could she do to please Rupert? To give back a little of what he had given her?

Her mind sought for the one thing she could

give him other than her body and that was food. At least she could make sure that her cook prepared the dishes he liked best and did them well.

How often would he dine with her? She did not know, but suspected he was a busy man. He was wealthy and rich men had business to attend. Morwenna must become accustomed to seeing him leave her in the mornings, and perhaps he would leave their bed at night after he had loved her.

Had she been his wife, she would have had friends to entertain. Would Rupert bring his friends here or would he be ashamed of her?

The thoughts tortured her when she allowed them, but she was often able to banish them for hours at a time. They usually returned when Rupert left her, but this far she had managed to keep them from spoiling her happiness.

Pushing the doubt to the back of her mind, she looked about her. The furniture could be so much better placed, but was too heavy for her. The lackey Rupert had employed was a man of advancing years, but kindly and respectful, and still strong enough to make the changes she required.

She would summon him and make a start on ordering her new home as she liked it. It was as she approached the door to call for help that she heard the knocker sound and hesitated. Who would call on her here? She had no friends in London.

'Where is she? I demand to see her!'

Hearing a harsh voice she recognised, Morwenna drew back into the front parlour, her heart beating wildly. She would have had the lackey deny him, except that she knew Benson would be unable to keep out the force that was her brother Michael, especially when he was angry.

She moved to the window and stood looking out, trying to master her nerves. How had he found her so easily? What would he say to her?

'So, there you are, Sister.' Michael's tone was accusing and furious. 'I could not believe it when I saw him bring you here. Are you so lost to modesty that you would live here in his house openly?'

'The house is mine,' Morwenna said, turning to look at her brother. He was glaring at her, his eyes dark with temper. 'I may have lost my modesty, but I have gained so much more.'

'Had you waited I should have provided you with a dowry in time. Why do you imagine I have risked everything, if not for my family?'

'I thought you did it for yourself, because you were angry that Father had left you nothing but the house. I asked you for nothing, Michael, and I ask for nothing now except that you should go away and leave me to live as I wish.'

'I have no intention of allowing you to shame me,' Michael raged at her. He reached for her wrist, his fingers closing about it, digging into her flesh so that she cried out in pain. 'You are coming with me. My business is done here and I leave for France tomorrow.'

'What do you mean your business is done?'

'I have played my part. The rest is up to others. I am for France and the others will come with me if they choose. There is little left for us here. I have been well paid and we may start a new life amongst strangers who will know nothing of your disgrace.'

'Let go of me, Michael,' Morwenna said, lifting her head proudly. 'I do not wish to go with you. I do not know what you have done, nor do I wish to know, but I was not involved and I have no intention of running away.'

She got no further for he struck her across the face, making her jerk back and cry out. The taste of blood was on her lips and she put her free hand up to her mouth, feeling the split.

'Are you proud of yourself?' she asked. 'Have you forgotten I am your sister? Or are you so lost to decency that you would strike a woman and not regard it?'

'You should not speak to me of decency,' Michael said, giving her a look so fearful that she shrank away from him. 'You are that rogue's mistress. Do not try to deny it, because I know this is his house. I came here to confront him and saw you enter with him.'

'You do not understand, Michael. I am committed to him and he cares for me. He has provided for all my needs.'

'You stupid fool!' Michael cursed and struck her again, making her scream out in fright as she saw the look he gave her. 'I shall teach you to wish you had never seen his face, girl.'

Morwenna screamed again as the door opened and a man rushed in. She hoped it was Rupert, but instead it was Jacques. He threw himself at Michael and wrenched him away from her. The next moment they were exchanging blows, hitting each other in a way that spoke of anger and resentment that had little to do with her.

'Leave her alone, damn you,' Jacques grunted. 'She has the right to live as she pleases.

You have done little enough for her. When you became a traitor you forfeited your right to tell any of us what to do.'

'Damn you, whelp,' Michael said and went for him with renewed fury. 'Keep your snout out of my business or I'll kill you.'

Perhaps because his anger lent him strength, Jacques landed a punch that sent his elder brother to his knees. He stood glowering down at him as Michael clutched at himself and a trickle of blood oozed from his mouth.

'If you hurt her again, I shall kill you,' Jacques said. 'You deserve what's coming to you, Michael—and I shall not lift a finger to save you when they discover what you're up to.'

'I'll kill you now and save myself the trouble.' Michael lifted his fist only to discover that Jacques was holding a knife with a wickedly long blade. 'You wouldn't dare.'

'Come near Morwenna again and I shall kill you. I could have done so any time these past two days.'

'You've been following me?'

'Yes, and not just now. I've followed you in the past. You are a fool, Michael. These men are dangerous traitors. They have used you and if anything goes wrong you will be the one that hangs. Take my advice and leave the country now before the whole thing blows up in your face.'

'Blows up?' Michael looked stunned. 'How much do you know?'

'Perhaps more than you think, Brother. I know that the dangerous stuff you spoke of was gunpowder. There was enough to blow half of London apart in those caves.'

Michael stared at him for a moment, then his frown cleared. 'You don't know anything,' he said and laughed, clearly relieved. 'You are not as clever as you think yourself, Brother. Had you kept your mouth shut…but now I'll make sure I'm not involved in the last bit of the plot. You will never guess where those barrels are to be placed very soon now. I'll take your advice and leave at once. I was going anyway once I had her. I've told the men to bring my ship to Greenwich and then we're for France and a new life.'

'If I were you, I wouldn't wait for the ship,' Jacques said. 'If I can discover what you're up to, others will know more. I was not the only one following you.'

'Thank you for the information, little whelp,' Michael said nastily. 'I'll change my habits and be away before your friends can stop me, but watch your back. One of these days you'll find a knife in it.' He turned his bitter gaze on Morwenna. 'You will rue the day you took sides against me, girl. Your mother was a wanton bitch, for she lay with my father before she wed him and it seems you are of the same stock.'

He flung from the room, leaving silence behind him. Morwenna sat down in one of the chairs. Jacques came to her. He knelt by her side and took her hand, looking up at her as he took a square of white cloth from his coat pocket and dabbed at the side of her mouth.

'This wants cold water and a salve,' he said. 'I should have killed him for what he did to you, Morwenna.'

'It does not matter.' She glanced round as her servant entered.

'Are you hurt, mistress?'

'Bring cold water and salves,' Jacques told her. 'Your mistress has been attacked. If that man comes again, deny him access.'

'Mercy on us,' the woman cried. 'The wicked brute for attacking you. I'll tend to your hurts, mistress.'

As she hurried away to fetch what was needed, Jacques stood up and walked over to the window. 'If they catch him, Michael will hang,' he said. 'They have gunpowder—more than I've ever seen, though God knows what use they mean to make of it, for I could not discover it.'

'You must tell Rupert—' She broke off as someone entered and then gave a glad cry as she saw him. 'You are back so soon.'

'I forgot something,' Rupert said, frowning as he looked at her. 'You are hurt. What has happened here?'

'Michael came looking for you,' Jacques told him. 'He beat Morwenna and threatened her when she would not go with him. I told him that he should flee to France, for he is in trouble. He and his friends must be stopped, Rupert. They have a huge quantity of gunpowder and whatever it is they mean to do they intend to use it soon.'

'This much we know,' Rupert said. 'You are not the only one who has been following your brother. He was allowed enough rope, for we hoped to find the other plotters. Now he will be arrested as soon as he is found again.'

'Where do they mean to use so much gunpowder? It would be enough to blow half of the city apart.'

'If I knew, I could not tell you,' Rupert said with a frown. He turned as the servant entered with a bowl of water and salves. 'Thank you, mistress. Leave them and go.'

'Yes, my lord.'

The woman put down the pewter bowl, her linen and her pots and departed. Jacques moved forwards, but Rupert waved him back. He took a cloth, dipped it in the water and applied it to the cut on Morwenna's mouth, frowning as she winced.

'If I see Michael again, I shall kill him,' he said coldly. 'The man is a selfish brute and deserves no less.'

'Let him be tried for his crimes,' Morwenna said. 'I would not have you do murder for my sake.'

'Believe me, it would be merciful,' Rupert replied grimly. 'Have you any idea what they would do to him if he were taken and tried for treason? He will be tortured to reveal the names of his friends. If he meets death at the point of my sword, he should thank me.'

Morwenna gave a little sob, for the idea of her brother fighting her lover appalled her. 'What of you? Michael is skilled with the use of swords and other weapons. He might kill you. He has sworn it.'

'He is welcome to try.' Rupert's expression was grim. 'I show no mercy to traitors.'

Tears filled her eyes and one trickled down her cheek. He wiped it away with his fingers.

'Your pardon,' Rupert said. 'Do I hurt you, Morwenna?'

She shook her head. 'It is no matter. If you will excuse me, I shall go to my room and finish this myself.' She took the bowl and the salves on the tray and walked from the room.

'Morwenna is in shock,' Jacques said. 'I came in time to save her from worse, but the brute hurt her. We fought, but I should have killed him.'

'It is as well you did not. He will be followed and if he thinks they are in danger of being discovered he may contact others amongst the plotters.'

'I doubt it. He was amused, for I let slip that I had no idea what they planned to do. It will be shocking, I know that, something terrible indeed.'

'You do not need to know more. You should keep out of this affair now for the retribution will be swift and bloody. Go to my house and take up the position of steward. I cannot tell you, but I know that information has been received. A letter of warning was sent to someone and we believe we may know what these evil men intend. God willing we shall apprehend the plotters before they can carry out their wicked purpose.'

'Why do you not arrest them at once if you know?'

'It has been agreed to wait until we have all the rats in the trap. I pray for your brother's sake that he is out of it. If he has any sense, he will leave for France before it is too late. Once they have the ringleaders they will round up the others and they have no mercy. I pity those that live beyond this night, for they will wish they had died.'

Michael fumed as he walked away from the house in which his sister now practised as a whore. Had that interfering whelp not arrived he would have had her away. She was his sister and she had shamed him. He would not allow her to continue as that man's mistress.

He knew that he should get away now before it was too late, but he could not go without Morwenna. If he left her behind as that rogue's mistress, he would have failed in all he had tried to do. He had risked so much for his family and, had he stuck to smuggling, might still have been risking his life to give them all that had been taken from them, but he had been tempted into dangerous waters.

He knew that he'd been a fool, but it was too late to go back now. He must begin a new life in France and he was determined that he would take his sister with him. Besides, he had lied to Morwenna before—he had not yet been paid for his work. Michael had risked so much, thrown away the easy trade that had caused him little trouble for the sake of all that was promised him. To run now without payment would ruin his plans for the future. One day he would be rich, a gentleman again, and he would force Morwenna to marry well and restore their reputation.

It was just a matter of waiting until the time was right. In the meantime he must find somewhere new to hide.

'Are you sure you feel able to go shopping?' Rupert asked when Morwenna came down wearing a cloak over her gown a little later. 'We could leave it until another day if you prefer?'

'I should like to go,' she said. 'Forgive me if I do not smile at you. My mouth feels sore and stiff. I think I must look terrible.'

'You are always beautiful to me,' Rupert said. 'Forgive me for allowing him near you. I did not think he would dare to molest you in this house.'

'Michael said it is your house—is that true?'

'It was mine, but is now yours,' he replied, a serious expression in his eyes. 'My family has a much larger house in London, which is my mother's for the moment. She lives there with my sister when she is not at the castle.'

'Why did you have another house if your family has a home here? Was it to house a former mistress?'

Rupert glanced at her, seeing the shadow in her face. 'I had a mistress. I shall not deny it, though I have parted with her on good terms. No, she never lived here. I bought the house so that I could be alone. I do not always wish to be in my mother's pocket. We do not always agree and I find it more comfortable to live alone. I am not my mother's favourite person.'

'I see.' Morwenna forced a smile, though it hurt and not just because Michael had hit her. 'Where are we going this afternoon?'

'To Spitalfields to the silk weavers there and

perhaps Cheapside. There is a goldsmith's that I would visit. I have commissioned gifts from him before and I wish to buy you something— perhaps a necklet or something for your hair.'

'You mean to spoil me,' Morwenna said, eyes very bright.

'You are worth spoiling. As far as I am concerned we shall be together for a long time, Morwenna. No man can promise a lifetime, for none of us know what awaits around the next corner, but you are the woman I wish to spend my life with.'

'Is that truly so?' Her heart caught, then soared with sudden hope. If he loved her, a wedding ring did not matter so very much.

Morwenna looked at him as he smiled. 'Aye, my love. Do not question my feelings for you. You have all I have to give of myself, though it may not be all you wish for.'

'If you truly care for me, it is enough,' she said and held back her sigh.

'You are not ill? That brute did not harm you?'

'No, though he might have, had Jacques not come when he did. Michael would have forced me to go with him.'

Rupert cursed, his look as black as thunder. 'Had I heard that he might not have lived.'

'Forget him,' Morwenna said and held his arm tighter. 'I am looking forward to seeing the silk merchants and this goldsmith you spoke of visiting.'

His expression lightened and she was relieved. Even though Michael had hurt her, he was still her brother. She would prefer that neither man harmed the other.

She prayed that Michael had got away to France. If Rupert was forced to kill him, it might sour things between them. Far better that her brother should leave England while he had the chance.

'Mother, you cannot be sure,' the girl said, looking uncertainly at the older woman. 'If Rupert were in town, would he not call for politeness' sake if nothing more?'

'Your brother is an unnatural son,' the Dowager Marchioness of Melford said sharply. 'We quarrelled when last we met and I think this is his way of punishing me. To be told that Rupert is in town by another when I had no knowledge of it is humiliating. It is all of a piece, I dare say. He loses no opportunity to insult me.'

'I do not believe my brother would deliberately insult you, Mother.' May looked at her doubtfully. 'I have not heard from him for some weeks. I feared he must be ill.'

'If he has not written to you, then something must be going on,' the Dowager Marchioness said thoughtfully. 'Depend upon it, May, there is some mystery here. Your brother is hiding something from us.'

'Rupert is a man grown, not a child,' May said. 'If he has a secret, he is entitled to keep it.'

'I am his mother and if he is keeping something from us it is because he fears my anger. I am determined to discover what he is doing, May. I will not have your brother bring disgrace upon us all.'

'Mother, you should not suspect him of ill doing.'

'He delights in thwarting me.' The Dowager Marchioness glared at her. 'If you hear from Rupert, you will tell me immediately, do you hear me?'

'As you wish, Mother. May we not speak of other things? I believe we are to go to court this evening?'

'Indeed we are, Daughter, and you must look your best. It is time we were thinking of your marriage.'

May sighed inwardly. She had drawn her mother's fire upon herself to deflect her thoughts, but now she would have to endure another lecture for the Dowager Marchioness had a sharp tongue and used it often on her children. May did not blame her brother for staying away. If she had her choice, she would leave too, but she must wait until she received a proposal of marriage. Since she would have little choice in the matter, she hoped that she could like the man her mother chose for her—although Rupert was the head of the family and could make his wishes known if he chose.

As yet, there had been no offers and May had not met anyone she would care to wed. Perhaps when Rupert decided to visit she would ask him to find her a husband. He would be kinder in his choice than her mother.

Just what was her brother doing and why had he stopped writing to her for so many weeks?

'You are certain they know nothing, Morgan?' the man with the dark swarthy face asked.

'You should have slit your brother's throat. If he guesses what we mean to do, we'll all die.'

Michael glared at him. 'Jacques knows we transported a large amount of gunpowder, but he has no idea what we intend to do with it.'

'If our plans are thwarted because of your carelessness, I'll kill you myself,' the man muttered. 'We have not plotted for months to have that young puppy destroy us at the last.'

'I tell you, he knows nothing. If I thought he had the least idea that we intend to blow up the King and Parliament when they sit together, I would kill him rather than let him speak.'

'Hush. Never speak the words aloud. We have come so far. Tomorrow we shall be rid of that tyrant for good.'

'Amen to that! May God go with you. You are a brave man, Guy. That amount of powder is unpredictable. Make sure your fuse is long enough or you will die as the roof of the tunnel falls in on you.'

'We have made our calculations. I shall take my chances and trust in Providence. If it is my destiny to die in such a cause, then I die willingly. What would rot my soul is if we were discovered before I can set the fuse.'

'If that happens I pity you, my friend. They will show you no mercy.'

'As I show none to them. If the tyrant and his lapdogs are to be destroyed, we must be decisive. One bold step and the future is ours.'

'May God be with you.' The two men clasped hands.

'What of you? Are you for France?'

'In good time. I have something to do first,' Michael said and his eyes gleamed. 'I am owed money and there is a score to be settled.'

Chapter Eleven

'Kiss me,' Morwenna said as she snuggled against Rupert in the large tester bed with its deep feather mattress. They had left the curtains open and the moonlight peeped in through the small window. 'If you are careful it will not hurt too much.'

'My sweet love.' Rupert held her to him, one hand smoothing down the satin arch of her back. His lips against her hair, he murmured words of such tenderness that Morwenna pressed closer, her body trembling with need as she gave herself to him. 'You are so beautiful. You know that I care for you so much. If anything should happen to me, I have made certain that you will be provided for. As I told you, the house is yours and my lawyer has money put aside for you. He would make sure you had all you need, even if my family objected. My sister would not—bless her, for she loves me—but my mother is another matter. However, I have signed the deed and my lawyer is a good honest man.'

'Do not speak of such things. I want only you,' Morwenna said lifting her face for his kiss. 'I pray you will not speak of death or loss.'

'I did not mean to worry, merely to reassure you, my love. There are things I must do and any man is vulnerable. Yet I do not foresee it.'

Morwenna trembled as he bent his head, circling her nipples with the tip of his tongue. The heat was building inside her as she ran her nails lightly down his back and felt his shudder. All conversation was suspended as they explored each other, discovering new delights with each caress and touch, their passion white hot as they came together at the last in an explosion of desire and need.

Afterwards, they lay together, sated and content, drifting into sleep.

It was early morning when Morwenna woke and heard something that disturbed her. What was that noise within the house? Rupert still lay beside her and she knew he slept.

She was certain she had heard something. Touching Rupert's shoulder, she tried to wake him, but he was soundly asleep and did not stir. Smiling, she slipped from the bed and pulled on a wrapping gown of silk, tying the sash about her waist and slipping her feet into soft-soled slippers.

Leaving Rupert to slumber on, she walked down the stairs to the hall below. Where had the sound come from? It might have been the kitchen. Perhaps the housekeeper had risen early to prepare for baking or some such task. She turned towards the back of the house and stood at the top of the staircase leading down.

'Are you there, Mistress Janet?' she called. 'Does something ail you? Do you need my help?'

Morwenna had not brought a candle with her for it was dawn and the light was beginning to shine through the windows. She hesitated, about to descend to the kitchen when she heard a slight noise behind her and half-turned just as the blanket was thrown over her head.

'No!' she screamed out. 'Rupert! Help me. Rupert...'

'Be quiet, you little fool,' a voice she knew only too well instructed. 'If he hears you and comes I'll kill him—and you if you cause me too much trouble. Be quiet and no one will be hurt.'

'Let me go!' Morwenna struggled and protested, but she knew the sound of her voice would be muffled by the blanket and her brother had hold of her in a strong grip that prevented her from breaking away from him. Besides, Rupert was sound asleep. 'Please, let me go,' she sobbed, but knew he would not listen to her.

Her struggles were in vain as he carried her from the house and then dumped her unceremoniously across his horse. Her head dangling against the beast's neck, Morwenna was jolted over cobblestones as her brother put his mount to a fast trot, carrying her away from Rupert.

'Lie still and you will not be harmed,' Michael told her. 'You've put me to trouble enough, wench. Cause me worse and I'll make you sorry you were born. You are my sister and I shall not let you shame me with that rogue. Had I not feared to raise the house, I should have killed him.'

Rupert would look for her and not find her. He might think she had run away and left him. Tears trickled down her cheeks beneath the blanket. She loved Rupert so very much, but she was afraid she might not see him again.

'Where are you taking me? Why are you doing this? What do you mean to do with me?'

The questions tumbled in her mind, but were lost in the thickness of the blanket. Would Rupert come to look for her again? He had found her once, but this time it might be too late.

Rupert roused, thinking he heard a cry. His hand slid across the bed, searching for Morwenna. Her side of the bed was still warm, though she was not there.

'Morwenna?' he asked, still half-asleep. 'Are you well?'

The silence was somehow menacing. His spine prickled and some inner instinct warned him that all was not as it should be. Cursing, he left the bed, pulled on his breeches and shirt and went downstairs, his feet still bare. It was almost light now and he could hear a shutter banging somewhere to the rear of the house. Perhaps that had woken him.

'Morwenna? Where are you?'

The silence was frightening him. She ought to have heard him by now. She should be answering him, coming to find him. Damn it!

Why had she left him sleeping? Had she gone to the kitchens in search of a drink?

He turned towards the back of the house and then saw something at the head of the stairs leading down into the kitchen. It was a slipper, Morwenna's slipper. Now the chills were chasing down his spine and he was fully alert. Had she turned dizzy and fallen down the stairs?

'Morwenna,' he shouted and ran down them. 'Morwenna—where are you?'

The kitchen was empty save for a cat purring on a rush mat before the stove, which was still warm from the previous night.

'What is it, my lord?' The footman came stumbling into the room, half-asleep, still pulling on his coat. 'I thought I heard something. Is anything amiss?'

Rupert showed him the slipper. 'Your mistress may have been abducted. Raise Mistress Janet and search the house.'

'The lady gone?' John the footman stared at him. 'The house was locked last night, my lord.'

'I heard a shutter banging.'

'There is one that does not fasten properly in the back lobby.'

'Show me,' Rupert commanded. 'If someone

entered that way, they came for her. I can only
think of one man who would dare so much.'

He followed his servant to the back of the
house, where, sure enough, the shutter was
hanging. The hinge had been forced and it hung
loosely, swinging in the breeze that swept in
from the river that lay behind the house. The
gate was opened, its lock broken. Running out
into the lane, Rupert saw fresh horse droppings
and then a short distance further along the road
another slipper to match the one he still held.

His horse was in the mews, too far away
to fetch it and still have hope of catching her.
Morwenna had been snatched while he lay
sleeping. He could only think that her brother
had done this, but why? Was it merely that it offended his pride to think of his sister as Rupert's
mistress—or something more sinister?

Cursing himself for being a fool, Rupert returned to the house. He wanted to set off in
pursuit, but which way to turn? Where would
Michael take her?

He was at fault. Had he taken Morwenna to
his home and left her in the care of his mother
she would have been safe, but he knew that
the Dowager Marchioness would not have accepted the woman he loved. This house with

just two servants was not properly protected. It had suited him well enough when he stayed here alone or with friends, but he should have realised that Morwenna might be in danger from her brother.

What were Michael's intentions? Did he mean to flee to France and take his sister with him or was he looking for revenge?

Rupert's thoughts were whirling as he returned to the house. He had only himself to blame for this mess. Had he married Morwenna, her brother would not have snatched her away. Yet was it his honour Michael meant to avenge or something else?

Rupert knew that certain things had been afoot the previous night. After the letter to William Parker, 4th Baron Monteagle, warning him not to attend the State Opening of Parliament, certain measures had been put into place. For months now the men whose task it was to protect the King and his ministers had been aware of plotters who wished to sweep away the King and place his Catholic daughter Elizabeth on the throne in his place. Rumours of a revolt had reached the ears of important men, but it was not until recently that they had realised to what lengths these desperate men might go. Rupert was aware that it had been Lord Henry's intention to search the cellars beneath the Houses of Parliament. Had something been discovered? Had the plotters been taken or disturbed at their work?

'Is there any sign of her, my lord?' the footman asked as he returned. 'She is nowhere in the house.'

'I think her brother may have taken her,' Rupert said, raking his hair back with frantic fingers. 'For what reason I cannot be sure. Unless he means to lure me into a trap.'

'What may I do to help you, sir?'

'You may go to the mews, saddle my horse and have Mistress Janet put me up a change of clothing. I may have to leave town.'

'Yes, my lord. I am sorry. I should have had that shutter mended.'

'Yes, you should, but I should never have brought her here.'

Rupert took the stairs two at a time. For days now he had been haunted by indecision. His affair with Morwenna had started lightly. He had hardly thought where their relationship was going for his family would not accept a marriage with the sister of a traitor. Michael Morgan might be only a small part of the conspiracy, perhaps no more than a tool for obtaining the gunpowder and spiriting away men who might otherwise have been caught and punished by the law.

Rupert was well aware of the unrest in various parts of the country. Catholics of all walks of life were dissatisfied with the religious intolerance under King James's rule. He had friends who met and spoke of change, but most were hopeful that it could be brought about in a peaceful manner. However, it was known that there was a hard knot of dissenters at the heart of England, men who would stop at nothing to bring down the King and his friends and set up Catholic rule again.

Rupert had been drawn in because Lord Henry was one of the investigators and a friend of his family. He had never thought when he left London for Cornwall on a daring adventure that he would find a woman he could admire and value so much.

Damn it! His feelings went much deeper than admiration. At first he had taken his need to touch and kiss her as being merely lust, but then he had begun to realise he wanted more. He was not certain he understood how he felt, because love was something he had never experienced.

At least, this kind of love was new to him—a love that burned deep in his guts and made him aware of pain.

What if Morwenna had gone willingly? She had given herself so sweetly as she lay in his arms the previous night. Surely she would not leave without a word?

No, she had been stolen away and by her own brother. How could Michael do such a thing to her? Where had he taken her and what did he plan?

The thoughts went round and round in Rupert's head as he dressed and shaved, cutting his chin in his haste. He swore as he dabbed at the trickle of blood with linen soaked in cold water.

Where should he look first? Michael might have taken her on board his ship. Would he head for Cornwall or for France?

What would Rupert do in his place? If he suspected that the plot had gone awry, that his friends were being sought, where would he run? Or did he think himself safe? If he were not involved in the actual plot, but had been used to convey the goods…

Hearing pounding at his front door, Rupert ran down the stairs as the maidservant opened it.

'Lord Henry sent me,' the man said. 'You are to come at once, my lord.'

'What is it? I have no time.'

'It is important. Lord Henry insists you are needed, sir.'

Swearing beneath his breath, Rupert grabbed his hat from the stand, then barked an order at his footman, who had returned with his horse.

'I shall return within the hour. I shall need you to take a message so be ready.'

'Yes, my lord.'

Still furious at the delay, but knowing it could hardly matter, because Michael was already too far away to be followed, Rupert left the house with Lord Henry's man. He knew that something important must have happened or he would not have been summoned at this hour. He was on fire to begin his search for Morwenna, but in truth there was little he could do, for nothing would be gained by running around town like a headless chicken.

In his own mind he was certain that Michael had taken Morwenna, which meant she might even now be on her way to Cornwall or perhaps France. Rupert would need to employ agents to help him search for her. Lord Henry might have some idea of where Michael was hiding out. He could gain nothing by refusing to speak to his father's friend and might gain much.

In his first panic he had been ready to ride off in search of her, but now he realised that he needed help. It might take weeks or months to find Morwenna if she had been taken out of London.

His heart felt as if it were in the grip of a strong hand, being squeezed so tight that he could hardly breathe, and his head was pounding. If anything happened to her, he did not think he would forgive himself.

'We discovered Fawkes guarding the gunpowder,' Lord Henry said excitedly as Rupert was shown into his parlour. 'There were six and thirty barrels. Enough to blow the House of Lords to pieces. None would have survived such a blast.'

'Good grief. Are all the plotters taken?'

'No. Most will have fled by now. We know Robert Catesby is one of them: also Thomas Wintour, John Grant, Sir Ambrose Rookwood, Digby, Thomas Percy and others, I dare say. We shall have them soon enough, for Fawkes has been arrested.'

'You say Fawkes was guarding the hoard?'

'Aye. He had ten years' military experience on the Spanish peninsula during the Dutch revolt. We believe he may have been selected to do the wicked deed, though I do not think him the ringleader myself. They will have the other names out of him before many hours have passed.'

'The plotters will flee London as soon as they hear he was discovered.'

'We shall pursue them with all speed and arrest them. It was for this reason I sent for you. I wish you to take a party of men and join those appointed for the pursuit.'

'Forgive me, sir. In this I must disappoint you, for I have other business.'

Lord Henry frowned, clearly annoyed. 'I want you there when the men are taken. There are certain others who may escape because they have friends in high places and I know I may trust you. I would not have the little fish caught while others carry on their misdeeds.'

'Michael Morgan has taken his sister, kidnapped her because of her association with me. I must find her and rescue her before I can do as you ask.'

'This is a matter of the highest importance. What can this woman mean to you?'

'More than my life, sir,' Rupert said grimly. 'You know that I would serve you in this if I could, but I must search for Morwenna.'

'You are but one man. I have agents who may know the whereabouts of this girl. Do as I ask you, Rupert, and I will engage to find the girl. Return to me when the plotters are taken and I shall know where the girl is being held.'

Rupert stared at him, his emotions churning. How could he leave Morwenna to the mercy of her brother? Yet where did he begin to look for her? He had already acknowledged in his own mind that it might take weeks to find her.

His gaze narrowed. 'You give me your word that you will set your agents to finding Morgan? I believe he may have taken her either to Cornwall or perhaps to France.'

'If he knows the plotters are taken, he will try to get to his ship,' Lord Henry said. 'I ask again, what is this girl to you?'

'I intend to wed her as soon as I find her.'

'Then I give you my word to find her, or her brother if she is dead.'

'Dead?' The word was like a knife thrust in his breast. He had suspected Michael meant to trap him, to exact some kind of revenge, but would he kill his own sister? 'He will find no profit in her death. I should pursue him to the ends of the earth and kill him.'

'He was involved in the plot to kill his Majesty and all his lords at the opening of Parliament. Michael Morgan's life is forfeit when we find him.'

'She must be safe first. You give me your word?'

Lord Henry frowned. 'I shall order it so, but when a rat is caught in a trap he may turn on that which is nearest to him.'

'Find him and leave the rest to me. I want your word on it, my lord.'

'My word then, but bring me news of the traitors: who is taken and who lives and is imprisoned.'

Rupert inclined his head. He was on fire with impatience as he left Lord Henry's house. He had given his word to join the hunt for the conspirators and must keep it, but first he would send his messages. Jacques would want to know his sister's fate and he might be able to find his brother if Lord Henry's agents failed.

'You cannot keep me here against my will.' Morwenna glared at her brother across the room. He had brought her to this bedchamber and dumped her on the bed, then locked her in, leaving her for hours without either food or water. 'Do you think to starve me into submission?'

'If I wanted you dead, I would have killed you.' Michael glared at her. 'Had things gone to plan you would be on board my ship and on your way to France by now.'

'No! Take me back to where you found me. I shall not come with you.'

'You will do as I tell you, Sister.'

'You cannot keep me close for ever. I shall run away again as soon as your back is turned.'

Michael swore furiously. 'If your interfering lover had not poked his nose into my business, you would not be here. Someone betrayed us and I think it was he and Jacques, I dare say, for he knew of the gunpowder.'

'Gunpowder?' Morwenna felt sick as she looked at him. 'What have you done, Michael?'

'I have helped certain men obtain the goods they needed and taken certain Jesuits to safety in France, no more. If there were more religious tolerance in this country, I would not have been involved. The King and his ministers have only themselves to blame. Besides, it is over, the plot discovered on the very eve...'

'You were involved in treason?' Morwenna was shocked. She sat on the edge of the bed, feeling faint. 'Michael, how could you? What was meant to happen?'

'A group of Catholic gentlemen plotted to blow up the House of Lords at the State Opening. There would then have been a rising in favour of the Princess Elizabeth, who is a Catholic.'

'She is but a child.' Morwenna felt sick. 'To kill so many and rouse a country to revolt. It's wicked.'

'Catholics have been tortured, burned and ruined. Our own father lost his estate because of iniquitous fines. Why should you care about people you have never met?'

'I would have no one die in such a way.'

'You are too soft-hearted,' her brother growled. He sighed and ran his fingers through his fiery thatch. 'I do not wish to harm you, Morwenna. Give me your word you will not return to him and I will allow you the run of the house. It is not safe to try for the coast yet, because they will be searching for the plotters on all the roads out of London. Far better to lie low until the hubbub dies down a bit.'

'I love Rupert and I should not wish to live without him.'

'Then you force me to keep you a prisoner,' her brother snapped, his temper roused once more. 'In time you will forget him. We shall tell people you are a widow and you may find a husband. I have money in France and it is my intention to settle there. Catholics are not persecuted there, as they are here.'

'You seem to forget that my mother was not a Catholic and Jacques and I do not share your religion or condone your actions,' Morwenna said. 'You think to break my spirit, Michael, but know this—I shall love Rupert to my dying day and nothing you can do will change me.'

'If he comes looking for you, I shall kill him and if you remain stubborn I may do the same with you. I shall not allow you to be that man's mistress again. I wonder that you flaunt your feelings for him. You should be ashamed of what you have done. Have you no shame?'

'I wish that I was his wife,' Morwenna replied with quiet dignity. 'But how can he marry the sister of a traitor? His is a proud family, Michael. They have supported the King of this country for centuries past. How could he desert all that his name stands for to marry a girl like me?' Tears were on her lashes as she faced him proudly. 'I love him and I will bear the shame of being his mistress gladly since I must. I would rather die than marry any other man.'

'Stubborn wench.' Michael glared at her, his temper simmering. 'I'll bring you water and bread, but you'll get nothing more until you come to your senses.'

As he slammed out, leaving her alone, Morwenna sank on the edge of the bed, her tears running freely now, silently down her cheeks.

Surely Rupert would come for her. He would not simply allow her brother to snatch her away from under his nose, would he?

Yet how could he find her? She knew they were in London, in one of the narrow rookery of lanes that made up its dirtiest, darkest slums. Here beggars, thieves and hopeless wretches lived in hovels with rotting walls, windows without shutters or glass and broken roofs. The gutters were choked with the filth that was thrown into them: the contents of chamber pots, decaying fruit discarded by market tranters and other debris. Even the rats lay dead, their swollen bloated corpses stinking of decay. It was a place without hope.

Rupert would never think of looking for her

here. How could her brother have fallen so low as to need to hide in such a place? His anger and disappointment had turned him sour and he had been led into such murky waters that he would never find his way back again. He spoke of a new life in France, but if they were searching for the plotters, how long would it be before he was taken? The thought of the punishment meted out to traitors made her feel faint and she feared for him.

And what would happen to her if he went out and left her here alone, locked into this tiny room without food or water?

For a moment the despair overwhelmed her, but then she brushed a hand across her eyes. She would not give way to despair. Rupert cared for her. He would search for her. He was searching for her even now.

'Taken? Fawkes and others taken?' Michael stared at the man who had carried the dread news. 'They will torture them. No man can stand against such pain as they will inflict. We are all doomed.'

'I am for France this night and you should flee while you can.'

'They will be guarding the roads to the

coast,' Michael said. 'You are a fool if you run now. You should lie low until the heat is over.'

'Please yourself.' His fellow conspirator shrugged. 'I'll take my chances and try for a ship. You have your own ship. You could get us all away to safety.'

'Nay, we should never reach her. If I am known, they will be watching her. I'll stay here and wait until the chase cools. Besides, I still have a score to settle.'

'Well, never say I did not warn you.'

Michael scowled as the man left him. Had he not captured Morwenna he might have run like the others, but he felt secure here and the plotters that ran now were sure to be caught. He would wait and when the opportunity came he would kill the man who had shamed his sister.

Chapter Twelve

〜〜〜〜〜

'Some of them made a stand when we caught up with them at Holbeche House,' Rupert said. He was still covered with the dust of the roads as he stood in Lord Henry's hall. 'Catesby was killed as were one or two others, but most were taken. I think only a few of the minor conspirators may have escaped.'

'They will be tried and punished for their crimes,' Lord Henry said with satisfaction. 'My thanks go to you and the Sheriff of Worcester for a task well done. This will stand as a lesson for others and show what happens to those who plan treason against their rightful King.'

'They deserve their fate,' Rupert said. 'Now, my lord, what news have you for me?'

'Concerning the woman, you mean?' Lord

Henry frowned. 'None that will please you, I fear. My spies followed him into a nest of rogues and gave chase, but he got away. Since then there has been no sign of him.'

Rupert cursed beneath his breath. 'You will give me the direction he was last seen?'

'Yes, of course, though he may have moved on. We have kept a watch on the ports and the roads, but he has not been seen. I think he is lying low, holed up in some dark alley where none dare venture after nightfall.'

Morwenna being kept prisoner for so many days in a place of despair! Rupert's guts turned at the thought, and it was all he could do to stop himself striking the older man. Yet he was to blame—for he should never have allowed himself to be turned from his purpose. His first duty had been to Morwenna and he had let her down. He had only himself to blame, but his thoughts would not allow it to be. He would find her. She must be safe, for if she were not there would be no reason left for living.

'I must leave you, sir. If anything happens to her, I shall blame myself.'

'If she is still alive, he means her no harm. Stay and dine with me, Melford. I would hear more of this business.'

'Forgive me, I cannot.'

Rupert gave him the terse answer, striding from the room without another word. It was what he should have done before. Too much time had passed since Morwenna had been snatched. If she were still alive, she would believe he had deserted her and in a way he had, putting his duty before his personal needs.

'God forgive me,' he muttered as he left and strode through the darkening streets towards the house he'd shared with Morwenna for such a short time.

It was as he approached the door that a shadow lurched out of the gloom and he found himself at the end of a wicked-looking blade. He gave a start, his hand going to his hip, but then, as the moon sailed out from behind a cloud, he recognised his assailant.

'What the hell are you doing?' he demanded. 'I am not your enemy. We need each other to find her.'

'You deserted her,' Jacques accused, but lowered his sword. 'You swore to me that you would protect her, but you allowed her to be snatched and then you went off to apprehend the traitors and left her to her fate.'

'I was promised she would be found,' Rupert muttered and then thrust open the front door of his house. 'Come in. I would not argue with you on the street.'

Inside a lantern was burning, hanging from a hook in the ceiling. His footman and housekeeper hovered. He waved them away with instructions to bring food and wine.

'You should not have left the search for her to others. She was but your mistress, yet you owed her a duty,' Jacques accused. 'If she is dead, I shall take your life if it costs me my own.'

'I'll not prevent you if she is dead. Yet I had little choice,' Rupert said and rounded on him with a frustrated snarl. 'I sent you word. I thought you might know where your brother would take her.'

'They are not in Cornwall and though his ship lies in Greenwich harbour waiting to convey him to France, the crew have received no orders.'

'Where the hell are they?' Rupert burst out as frustration overtook him.

'In London.'

'You've seen them? Is she well—unharmed?'

'I've seen Michael. I know where he is living, but I haven't seen Morwenna. I was afraid to go into the house alone, because if I were killed she would have no help left. I came here to ask for your help and was told you were off after the traitors. Had you not returned I would have tried to rescue her myself this night.'

'My hand was forced. I was promised help in the search. I swear to you that I thought she would be found when I returned, but if you have discovered Michael's hiding place we shall go there now.'

'It may be best to wait until it is dark,' Jacques said. 'From what I saw of Michael he had been drinking more than he was used to. He looked desperate—as if he knew he was being hunted like a rat. I almost felt sorry for him.'

'What are you saying?' Rupert was on fire with impatience.

'If she's still alive he means her no harm. I think he will take her to France with him if he can. Michael would not harm her too much or he would have nowhere to hide. Either you or I would find him and kill him. He knows that and in his heart he loves her, too.'

Rupert nodded, a sense of relief filling his mind. 'I thought something of the kind, but I was not sure whether he was too far gone to care for anyone else.'

'Michael is ruthless. Yet in a way he had always tried to protect his family. He put money by for Morwenna's dower, but she refused to marry the man he suggested.'

'Perhaps she will marry me, though by now she may think I have deserted her. If Michael has been drinking and she is stubborn…'

'Morwenna will never give in whatever he says to her. I have not eaten for hours. We should dine now and then it will be time to discover if my sister is where I believe her to be.'

Morwenna stuffed the last piece of bread into her mouth, chewed slowly, swallowed and then drank two mouthfuls of water. It was poor fare and she was starving, but she refused to give in, because Michael didn't deserve that she should. The food he gave her was less than at the start and sometimes he seemed to forget her for hours. She believed he was drunk most of the time and hardly knew which day it was.

A surge of anger went through her. He had no right to dictate to her, keeping her a prisoner in this wretched place. It was bitterly cold now without a fire and few blankets and she did not like the way he'd let himself go these past few days. She wasn't sure how long she had been here. Just a few days or was it three weeks? At first she'd tried to count the days, but now her mind was hazy and that was because she was feeling so ill. The cold and lack of food was taking its toll on her and she was not sure how much longer she could hold out.

When would Rupert come for her? Had he given up his search or was he finding it hard to discover where her brother had hidden her?

She looked at the window, which was boarded up, the shutters nailed into place and impossible to open. The cracks in the old wood let in a little light and air, but otherwise she had only the candle, the bread and water. Michael had kept to his word and would give her only enough to keep her alive. There was not enough water to spare for washing and her skin crawled because she'd picked up fleas from the bed and they were in her hair and her clothes. She felt dirty and tired and she was getting weaker each day that passed, but still when Michael asked, as he did each time he visited, she refused to give in. She would not go with him to France and she would not marry anyone but Rupert.

Of course Rupert would never marry her. Sometimes her hazy mind thought of the house he'd taken her to on the way to London and she dreamed she was living there with her husband and her children. Such a dream of a happy future that it brought a lump to her throat. Surely Rupert must want this, too? Yet why had he not come for her before this if he loved her as he'd claimed the night she was captured?

'Please come soon,' she whispered. 'Find me, Rupert, I beg you or I may die.'

Hearing a crashing sound below stairs, Morwenna tensed. It sounded as though Michael was drunk again and had knocked something over. He had been drinking more and more these past days and she had begun to fear him. The man who stared at her with wild eyes was no longer her brother, whose rages she had never truly feared, but a stranger who might do anything.

Now she could hear shouting, more crashes as though furniture was overturned in a fight and then a shot. Had someone found Michael? Had they killed him? She heard screaming and then another shot and then she started to scream and bang on her door.

'Help me. Please help me. I am a prisoner.'

There was silence downstairs. Tears ran from her eyes. If they went away and left her, she would die here, for she had not been able to break out no matter how hard she tried to force the window shutters. Her strength was almost gone now and she sank to her knees, her head bowed. Then she heard running steps. Someone was coming up the stairs. Who was it? Would they help her or kill her?

She lifted her head, looked at the man who entered, gave a cry of relief and tried to stand, but found she could not. A moan of despair left her lips as she sprawled on the ground at his feet.

'Is she dead?' Jacques asked, holding his arm, blood running through his fingers. 'Damn him. I hope his soul rots in hell for what he's done to her.'

'I do not doubt that he is already there,' Rupert said grimly. 'I had no choice but to kill him. He would have killed you had his aim not gone astray.'

'He was too drunk to know what he was doing,' Jacques replied. 'We were many and he was but one man. We could have taken him alive.'

'For what purpose? Would you have him hung, drawn and quartered as the rest of the traitors?'

Jacques stared at him, then shook his head.

'I would have seen him on his ship and away to France.'

'Then you are a fool,' Rupert muttered furiously. He had been examining Morwenna for signs of life and sighed with relief as she moaned. 'Thank God we were just in time, but see for yourself what he has done to her. If you would let him live, you are more forgiving than I.'

'I would have thrashed him,' Jacques said, but looked concerned as he saw Morwenna's state when Rupert lifted her. Until that moment he had not realised how weak she was. 'Damn him for what he has done to her. It is as well you killed him. I did not know what she had suffered.'

'She has lost weight and she is ill. I think that devil tried to starve her into submission.'

'His own sister!' Jacques was stunned. 'I thought she had just fainted at the shock of hearing pistols fired. Michael will receive no prayers for his soul from me.'

'We granted him too easy a death,' Rupert said grimly. 'Had I known what he'd done to her, I'd have given him to Lord Henry. He should have experienced some of the suffering he has inflicted on her—damn his soul to hell!'

'If 'tis merely starvation, she will recover. Surely a few days of good food and rest...'

Rupert ignored him as he walked down the stairs carrying his precious burden. Jacques was lucky to be alive—it was his warning that had made him throw himself to one side and thus Michael's ball caught his arm rather than his chest. The pistol had only fired once and then Michael had grabbed for his sword, which lay on the table before him, amongst the dirty dishes and an empty skin of wine.

Rupert could have disarmed him and given him up, but he had killed him, deliberately, intending his death. It was the most merciful end for a traitor and one that his fellow conspirators would have blessed him for. The survivors of the traitors, many of whom had died resisting arrest, would be tried, condemned and hanged, but they would suffer torture first and then be cut down alive to be disembowelled. It was a terrible fate and Rupert had been merciful, but his expression was grim as he left the house accompanied by his men. Jacques clearly blamed him for his brother's death. Despite his anger at the way Morwenna had been treated, he would have given his brother the chance to escape.

Rupert was not that forgiving. Michael

Morgan was a traitor to his King and country, but above all he had treated his sister shamefully, keeping her a prisoner and trying to starve her into submission.

For that he could never be forgiven. Rupert had done what must be done in the most merciful way he could, but would Morwenna understand that he had no choice?

Or would she hate him for killing her brother? It was the chance he'd had to take.

She had been in a fever for some days. The physician had been each day to see her, leaving mixtures for her to swallow when she would, but still there was no change.

Rupert looked down at her as she tossed and turned on the pillows. She was burning up, her skin as hot as fire, yet damp with sweat. Mistress Janet had sponged her with cold water several times, but though it took the heat down it came back again.

'Rupert.' The cry burst from her fevered lips, as it had over and over again as she lay on her sick bed. 'Why does he not come? He does not love me…he does not love me…'

Her cheeks were wet with tears. Rupert bent

over her, stroking back her hair from her damp forehead as he whispered words of comfort.

'I am here now, dearest. Forgive me for not coming sooner. Damn his soul to hell! I hope he burns for what he did to you. Death was not enough.'

Rupert wrung out the cloth in cool water, sponging her face, neck and arms. She was so very ill. If she died, he would not know how to bear it. Her death would lie heavy on his conscience. He had left her to the mercy of that brute while he obeyed his political master. His upbringing had been to serve the Crown and Parliament, but now his spirit revolted against all that he had been taught to respect and honour.

Why should he care what happened to the traitors? Why had he believed Lord Henry when he'd promised to find her? Had it not been for Jacques, she might still be lost to him—she might be dead. Another few days and she would have gone beyond the skill of the physicians. Even now her life hung in the balance and she might still die. She was crying out again, begging him to find her, believing that she meant little to him. His heart turned over with pain and he cursed aloud.

How he had hurt her with his carelessness. He had taken all she gave greedily and without thought for what it meant to her to be his mistress with no hope of more.

Regret swamped him, shaming him.

'I swear I shall make you happy,' he said as he bent over her, touching his lips to her fevered brow. 'Please do not die, my love. Live for me, I beg you.'

'Rupert.' The sobbing cry smote at him like a heavy blade. 'Why does he not come for me? He does not love me…he does not love me…'

He had hurt her so badly by his carelessness. Whatever her brothers, she was a gentle lady and he'd treated her as if she were a whore.

'I swear I shall make reparation,' he said as he sat by her bed and watched her struggle for breath. 'Give me a chance, please let me show you how much I love you.'

Could she forgive him for what he'd done? He had killed her brother and nothing could change that fact, but would she see he'd had no other choice, or would she hate him?

If she could not bear the sight of him, he must make certain she was provided for. Yet how could money pay for what he had taken so carelessly?

* * *

Morwenna cried out as she tossed feverishly on her bed. Her body ached all over and she felt so ill. She was hot and she threw back her covers, but then she was shivering and someone covered her again. She felt cool hands touching her head, stroking her, talking to her in a soft voice she knew, but could not name.

'Mother…' she cried. 'Please help me. I need you. I need you so much…'

'Your mother cannot come,' the voice said. 'I am here, dearest one. You are safe now and I shall care for you. I shall always care for you. I give you my word. You have to get better for my sake, my love.'

'Rupert?' Morwenna struggled through the fog, tears on her cheeks, but she could not see him. 'Rupert, please come for me. I won't let him take me away, but it's so hard. Please come for me.'

'I'm here now, my love. You are safe with me.'

Her eyes opened and she looked up into the man's face. It was Rupert and yet he looked so different…gaunt and haggard, as though he hadn't slept in an age. 'Rupert…you came for me.'

'Of course I did, my love,' he said and stroked her brow with his gentle hands. 'You've been very ill, but the fever has broken. You must eat now. Just a little broth to start and then everything you like. We are going to make you strong and well again, my love.'

'You were so long finding me.' She sighed. 'I thought you would never come.'

'I came as soon as Jacques told me where to find you. It was he that discovered where you were, dearest one.'

'Where is Michael? He was so frightened. We have to help him get away, Rupert. You will help him, won't you?'

'I'll do what I can, but you need to rest now. You shouldn't worry about Michael after what he did to you.'

'Poor Michael. He was so unlucky, he lost everything. He never meant to harm me.'

Her eyes closed and she fell back against the pillows, somewhere between waking and dreaming.

'I told you she wouldn't want him dead,' a voice said, but she didn't know what came next for she was asleep. The fever had broken at last and she slept from exhaustion, peacefully and without dreams.

* * *

'It is not our business what Rupert does, Mama,' May said and looked at her mother anxiously. At times the Dowager Marchioness had a fearful temper and when she felt herself thwarted there was no telling what she might do. 'If this woman means so much to him, he will surely tell us of his plans soon. Besides, Sir Henry had no right to tell you.'

'Sir Henry spoke to me in confidence. She is the sister of a traitor—a man involved in that terrible plot against his Majesty and Parliament. Would you have your brother marry such a woman?'

May's bottom lip trembled, but she faced her mother bravely. 'Rupert's life is his own, Mother. He must be allowed to choose—' She broke off with a cry as her mother slapped her across the face.

'Silence, Daughter. You will show me respect. I knew your brother was ashamed of what he did, otherwise he would have brought her here to us. He has hidden her away and now he speaks of wedding her. I shall not allow him to shame us so. He must give her up or I shall not see him again.'

Holding a hand to her cheek, May was silent. To say the things in her mind would only bring her mother's fury on her once more, but she could not think that Rupert would give up a woman he loved for such a threat. All she could hope was that her brother would not turn his face from her.

'Well, I have done something about it,' the Dowager Marchioness said. 'A marriage has been arranged and Rupert will not dare to go against what I have done or he will never be able to show his face in London again.'

'What have you done, Mother?' May was aghast. 'Rupert will not thank you for interfering in his life.'

'Go to your room and stay there. I will have obedience from my children.'

May turned and ran from the room. Her mother was unkind and she longed to escape her bitter tongue. She had never been the same since her elder son's death. Surely she could not still blame Rupert for what happened to Richard? She must know it was not his fault?

Yet what else could all this be about? Tears were falling as May escaped to her room. If only Rupert would come home and rescue her...

Rupert broke the seal and read though his mother's letter, tossing it aside with a grunt of disgust. She had been busy interfering in his life again, though he had told her to desist. Her letter spoke of her disquiet. She had learned from an unimpeachable source that he was consorting with a woman of undesirable birth and standing and she exhorted him to come home and tell her that it was merely a liaison and that his intentions were not marriage. She was certain that her informant had been mistaken, for she could not believe her son would bring shame on his family name—a name that had gathered lustre down the years.

To quash any rumour of your misalliance I have begun negotiations for you with the Duke of Marley. His daughter Annais is of a proper age for marriage, being just sixteen. She is well favoured and a sweet girl. I am sure that once you see her you will recognise your duty to the family. It is time that you settled down and took a wife. Do not disappoint me, Rupert. Remember your promise.

I remain your loving mother…

Rupert swore, looking up anxiously as Jacques entered the parlour.

'Is she worse? Should I send for the physician?'

'He has just this moment seen her. It is his opinion that she is through the crisis at last. All she needs is good food and nursing and she will be well again.'

'The fever broke once before and then returned. Is he certain now that she is recovering?'

'As certain as he can be. She seems cooler and is sleeping peacefully now.'

'Thank God for it. If she is truly well, I must leave you for a time, Jacques. I have been summoned home by my mother and must attend her. I shall give you my direction and you will send for me at once if Morwenna takes a turn for the worse.'

'Of course.'

'I have your word on it? I would not leave her, but this business will not wait. My mother has begun something that may lead to more trouble. She is foolish and meddlesome, but she does not understand what harm she does.'

'I shall call you if Morwenna needs you, but I hope the worst is over. It should now be a matter of rest, good food and recovery at her own speed.'

'I shall return as soon as I can. Tell her that I would not have left her were it not important.'

'She will understand that you have business, sir. You have hardly moved from her side in days.'

'I would not leave if you were not here, but I know you love her—and there is something important I must attend without delay.'

'You do not need to explain yourself to me.'

'My message is for her. I would not have your sister think I left her without a second thought.'

'Do you wish me to tell her of Michael?'

'If she asks, you must tell her the truth. I pray that she can find it in her heart to forgive me, but there was no choice.'

'You felt you had none, but had I been alone I might have acted otherwise.'

'Had you been alone you would have died. Michael showed you no mercy so why should you mourn his death?'

'Had you a brother you would know how it feels.'

'I had a brother once. He was older and would have inherited the estate, but he died when we were young.' Something flickered in Rupert's eyes. 'Excuse me, I must go before my mother commits me to something I cannot reverse.'

'Go with God. I hope that you return soon. My sister has suffered enough and I would not see her break her heart for you.'

'She shall not do so if I can prevent it. You have my word. It is my intention to change things for the better, but say none of this to her. I would tell her myself.'

Rupert looked down at the face of the woman he loved as she slept. She had been burning up with a fever for days, but now she looked peaceful. Yet even as he bent to kiss her forehead, she threw out an arm and called something.

'Michael,' she sobbed. 'Michael, please do not hurt me. Rupert...'

She was crying in her sleep. He cursed and bent to stroke her head, torn with regret that he must leave her. Despite being through the fever, she was still not well—and he loved her.

It was because he loved her that he must leave her to her brother's care. His mother had begun marriage negotiations that must be stopped before they went too far. He had no intention of wedding the girl his mother had chosen, but he must act quickly for all their sakes or more harm would be done.

'Take care, my love,' he said and kissed her

brow. 'I shall return as soon as I may. Forgive me for hurting you, my dear one. I love you and I shall return soon to claim you.'

He knew that she could not hear him in her sleep and he would not wake her, for she needed her rest. His heart heavy, he took one last regretful look and left her. Surely she would come to no harm in her brother's care and yet he had a feeling of unease as he walked from the room.

Morwenna woke and stretched. After days of being ordered to eat, having her servant wash her and her brother visit her briefly, she was fully awake for the first time since becoming ill. She frowned as she looked at the fire burning brightly in her chamber and felt its welcome warmth. She frowned, trying to recall what had happened just before she was rescued. In her mind she thought she'd heard shouting and a shot—or was there more than one? What had happened when her brother rescued her—and Rupert, had he been there? She was sure he had been here in her room when she first woke from the fever. He'd ordered her to eat something, but since then she hadn't seen him. Perhaps he was too busy to visit her. The thought was painful and she shut it from her mind.

'Morwenna.' Jacques entered the room. She noticed that he was wearing a sling on his left arm. Had he been injured during the fighting? 'So you're awake at last. I was beginning to think you would sleep for ever.'

'What happened to your arm?'

'Michael shot me,' Jacques said. 'Rupert alerted me or I might have died. As it was, I have little more than a flesh wound. The surgeon patched me up and I've almost healed.'

Morwenna nodded. 'I think I remember a shot. Michael wasn't himself, Jacques. He was drinking because he was so frightened. He knew they were searching for him as well as the other plotters. In his fear and his drunken state he may have thought you had come to arrest him like the others.'

'Michael should never have become involved with men like that,' her brother said with a frown. 'If the soldiers had found him, he would have been tried and then his fate doesn't bear thinking of...' He stopped, his eyes flicking away from hers as he considered how to continue.

Morwenna stared at him. 'What is it you're afraid to tell me, Jacques? Did Michael get away? You mustn't be angry with him. He wouldn't harm me intentionally. And please tell me, where is Rupert? Why hasn't he been to see me?'

'He was here all the time until you began to recover. I think he had some family business. I do not know for sure, but his mother may have needed him. A letter came yesterday. He asked me to take care of you and said he would return as soon as he could.'

'What happened to Michael? You didn't answer when I asked if he got away.' She pushed herself up against the pillows. 'I know he treated me harshly, but I wouldn't…' A little cry escaped her. 'Is he dead? There was a second shot. I heard it just before someone came up the stairs and then I don't remember anything else.'

'Michael was killed in the struggle. It was his fault. He was acting wildly—a danger to himself and others.'

'Did you shoot him? Or was it…?' She closed her eyes briefly as the grief swathed through her. 'It was Rupert, of course. He thought Michael a traitor and would have killed him without a second thought. You would have disarmed him if you could.'

'Rupert did what he had to do,' Jacques said harshly. 'Had we taken him alive, he would have been arrested and condemned as a traitor. His fate then would have been terrible. It was a clean death, Morwenna—and he deserved it for what he did to you.'

'Oh, Jacques—are you in trouble, too, because of what Michael did?'

'Rupert has promised to arrange a pardon for me. I knew nothing of the gunpowder treason plot. I could still be charged for smuggling, but thus far they haven't found the caves and unless someone betrays us I doubt they will. Many have tried and failed; it is a secret the Morgans have kept for years.'

'Yes. If Michael had remained a smuggler, he might still live—and he did it for us, Jacques, for his family.'

'He was successful and grew wealthy. I know where his money is hid. I will see you get your share.'

'I do not want his money.' Morwenna frowned. 'What will you do?'

'As soon as you're well I'm going down to the Melford estate on the Marches. Rupert made me his steward there. The old man is ready to retire, though he's staying on for a while until I know what I'm doing.' His eyes dwelled on her thoughtfully. 'Unless you would wish me to take you away somewhere else?'

'Where would we go?' Morwenna smiled oddly. 'I cannot leave Rupert. Even though I know he does not love me as deeply as I love him, I won't leave him. I do not like the thought that he killed Michael, but he had no choice.'

'Rupert cares for you deeply,' Jacques told her. 'He was distraught when we were not sure if you would live. Yet I'm not sure he means to wed you. His family would not be pleased. I heard a whisper that they wish to arrange a great marriage for him, to the daughter of a Duke.'

'Oh.' Morwenna's eyes shut against the tears. She brushed a hand over her eyes and then looked at her brother. 'The day he marries is the day I shall leave him. I could not share him with a wife, Jacques. It would not be fair to any of us.'

'If you leave him, we could go home. The house is ours now.'

'Yes, it is yours by right. If Rupert marries another woman, I shall come back to Cornwall.'

Chapter Thirteen

'I have given my word that the match will go ahead, Rupert. If you break the agreement you will bring dishonour upon us. You promised me that you would marry well, as your brother Richard would have had he lived. He would have known his duty to his family and me.'

Rupert frowned as he faced his mother across the room. She was a proud woman and used to having much of her own way, but in this he was determined to hold firm.

'It was not your decision to make. Your word is not mine, Mother. I am no longer a child.'

'You were to have wed a girl worthy of your name once, but now you would shame your brother's memory and me. You owe it to Richard to marry well.'

'I would have married my betrothed had she not died, Mama,' Rupert said now. 'But I was a boy then and now I am a man. You may not arrange a match for me. I shall not be treated as if I were a child. This time you have gone too far. Marley will understand when I tell him I have a prior commitment and if he does not then he may sue me for breach of promise. I gave no promise and you had no right to do so in my place. I shall be upheld in court and his daughter will be the loser.'

Tears sprang to the Dowager Marchioness's eyes. 'How could you treat me this way, Rupert? How could you shame your family by bringing this whore into our midst?'

'I have no intention of bringing her here,' Rupert said. 'We shall go down to the country and we shall be wed there. Morwenna is not a whore. You wrong her, Mother. She is a lady, though her family fell upon hard times and lost much of their estate. Her mother came from a good family.'

'Her brother is a smuggler and a traitor—and she has lived with you as your mistress. Do you deny that you have lain with her?'

'That is my affair and none of yours,' Rupert replied coldly. 'I have allowed you to have your way in most things because of what happened to Richard. I know that I should not have inherited the estate if he had lived, but he died that day and I survived. I am sorry if you wish it otherwise.'

'Do not be so foolish,' she snapped. 'I would rather have had both my sons survive.'

'So would I, Mama. Believe me, I have regretted what happened that day a thousand times. Richard slipped as we wrestled. It was an accident, no more, and I have let it haunt me long enough. I have not forgot him or my duty to the family, but I shall not marry this child you have found for me. Nor shall I give up the woman I love.'

'Love? What ridiculous notion is this? Have I not told you that romantic love is a mere fancy? I married for duty, as your sister will and as you should. Family and property are what we stand for. It has always been thus.'

'Has it, Mama? I pity you if that is all you see in life. Yet I know that my grandfather was happy in his marriage. Before I met Morwenna I was not so far different in my opinions, I shall admit. I hoped to find affection in my marriage, but I had no great hope of love or happiness. Now the case is altered. Morwenna is far above me. She will bring fresh blood and a healing wind to blow away the hurt of the past. I need her in my life and I shall not give her up.'

'You could keep her as your mistress if you must.'

'She would not stay if I were married. I know her too well. If I so insulted her she would go away, renounce her claims and tell me I must cleave to my wife. No, I shall offer her my name and my wealth—and I pray she will accept me with all my faults. I am hardly good enough for her, but perhaps in time I may earn her love back.'

'You fool!' His mother glared at him. 'If you shame me, I shall not see you or her. We shall be estranged and you will not see your sister.'

'I should regret that,' Rupert told her with a bow of his head. 'If you set your face against me I shall not see you, but my sister is under my guardianship. I shall not deny her, nor shall I force her into a marriage she does not like.'

'If she must choose between us she will choose me, unless she wishes never to see her mother again.'

'Such bitterness does not become you,' Rupert said coldly. 'I must bid you good day, Mother. I shall call on Marley and explain why

I cannot marry his daughter and that you had no authority to begin negotiations on my behalf.'

'Do that and you will be sorry. I shall make you suffer and that whore you would wed. No one in society will receive her by the time I have done.'

'You would be so cruel?' Rupert threw her a look of disgust. 'I shall bid you goodbye, madam. I think we have nothing more to say to one another. You may remain here if you choose, but in the country the dower house is your only home from now on.'

'How dare you deny me my rights?'

'You have none but your dower, madam. I have let you rule my homes, but unless you acknowledge my wife both in private and in public you shall not enter them again.'

Rupert inclined his head, leaving her staring after him in high indignation as he left. It would not suit her pride to be forced to step back for his wife and he was sure it was the reason she had picked an innocent sixteen-year-old, who would be too shy and nervous to argue with her mother-in-law.

Morwenna would not be cowed whatever was said to her. Rupert smiled as he went out to his horse. He would send Morwenna a note explaining that he must be away for a few days, because he could not afford to neglect this affair. The Duke of Marley would be entitled to complain if his daughter thought herself promised to a man she did not know, only to discover that he had wed another. A swift visit to explain before anything was announced would save a deal of embarrassment and pain.

Morwenna was much recovered. By the time he returned she might be ready to leave her bed and then they could begin to make plans for their wedding.

He had done wrong in taking her to his house—his mother was not the only one who would hear of it and think the worst. Indeed, he had intended it as a love nest for them, but the case was altered. Morwenna had been through hell because she'd denied her brother. She deserved marriage and it was the only way he could make recompense for her suffering.

Besides, her illness had taught him something and he knew that he could not live his life without her. He did not wish to.

'Your letter is from Rupert?' Jacques said, looking up from his own. 'He asks that I take you to Melford Towers and promises that he will follow as soon as he can.'

'I do not mind going there,' Morwenna told him. Rupert's letter was puzzling. He spoke warmly of the future, but made no mention of his forthcoming marriage. Surely he did not imagine he could hide it from her? 'I loved that house when we stayed there on our way to London. I shall be happy to see it again—and the people.'

'No, no, it is not to his old house that I am bidden to escort you, Morwenna. That is in the Marches—the castle is not far from Worcester and I believe it to be his principle seat.'

'Why should he ask us to await him there?' Morwenna stared at him in surprise. 'I thought it was his mother's home when she was in the country. He will certainly take his wife there if he is to be married.'

'I know nothing of that,' her brother said and frowned, 'but his instructions are clear. He is delayed by important business and will join us at the castle as soon as he may.'

'I am not sure I wish to go there.' Morwenna shivered. 'His old home is beautiful and I felt comfortable there—but the castle...' She moved away from him to gaze out of the window. 'What can be his purpose?'

A feeling of unease came over her and she was suddenly restless. Despite the bitter cold the sun was shining and she had a sudden desire to make the most of her last day in London.

'Will you take me out, Jacques? I should like to visit Cheapside. I would buy a gift for Mistress Janet and the Footman John—and something for Bess. I could give her nothing when I left and I have some money in my purse—Rupert wanted me to feel independent when I went shopping.'

'Yes, of course, if you wish it.' He smiled at her. 'We shall make a day of it and perhaps visit the theatre this evening.'

'Yes, I would like that of all things. Rupert took me to see one of Master Shakespeare's plays and I did laugh, for it was vastly amusing.'

'Put on your cloak and we shall go out whilst the sun shines.'

'This is most enjoyable,' Jacques said as he picked up another of Morwenna's purchases and prepared to leave the shop just as a woman came bustling through from the back. 'I do not know when I have known more pleasure in a day.'

'Why, bless my soul,' the shopkeeper's wife exclaimed. 'If it is not Mistress Morwenna—and Master Jacques. Have you come to visit me, my dears?'

Morwenna stared at her and then laughed for sheer pleasure. 'Sarah—Mistress Harding. How are you—and your daughter Jane?'

'We are very well thanks to you.' Sarah's face was bathed in smiles. 'You have been buying cloth from us? Had you asked for me I would have given you a better price.'

'We are well satisfied with our purchase of your beautiful materials. I have bought Bess some good wool for a new gown.'

'Then I shall give her some ribbon to dress it,' Sarah said. 'What colour did you choose?'

'The dark blue, but…'

Sarah would not be gainsaid. She insisted on cutting off a length of her best silk ribbon and presenting it as a gift for Bess.

'I owe you so much more and you would never take a penny for yourself, Morwenna. I am glad to see you prosperous and well. Had it not been so, I would have given you a home here—and work if you cared for it. My husband would welcome you to our family. If he were here he would give you half of what he owns, for he knows he would be alone and a widower had you not saved us from the sea.'

'I helped you recover. It was not so very much,' Morwenna protested, her cheeks warm as Sarah told all her customers how brave and generous the Morgans had been to her when she was pulled from the sea half-dead.

After that she insisted on taking them into her back parlour, where they were given mugs of her special spiced ale, cakes and sweetmeats made with minced beef and fruit, piggy pies and a dish of curds with wine.

Most of the day had fled before she could be parted from them, and when her husband came home he insisted on giving Morwenna a length of his finest silk in a beautiful green and some lace to trim it.

Morwenna's protests were ignored and when they were finally allowed to leave, Jacques could hardly manage all the parcels. He hired a sedan chair to carry Morwenna through the streets and another to carry their parcels, walking beside them. Because the light was fading it was as well that he was wearing a small sword, for there were sometimes rogues who would attack the unwary.

'I think we shall not see the first act,' Morwenna said as the chairs deposited them outside her house. 'We must leave our parcels and then hurry to the boats, else we shall miss the farce and 'tis a comedy of errors that I like the most.'

The door was opened before they could knock and John the footman greeted them with a sombre expression and a look in his eyes that seemed to warn of trouble.

'Is something wrong, John?' Morwenna asked, sensing his unease. 'We are late back, for we met friends and stayed to dine with them.'

'There is a visitor in the parlour, mistress. She came three hours ago and will not leave until she has spoken with you.'

'A visitor?' Morwenna felt a sliver of ice slide down her spine. 'I was not expecting anyone.'

''Tis the Dowager Marchioness, mistress.'

'Rupert's mother?' Why was she here? Morwenna threw an agonised look at her brother. 'What can she want?'

'I have no idea. I shall come with you, dear heart. She cannot harm you.'

'No, stay here unless I call for you.'

Morwenna had taken off her cloak. She smoothed the creases from her silk gown, drawing a deep breath as she went through to the large parlour. A woman was sitting by the fire. She seemed intent on its flames and did not turn her head as Morwenna approached.

'You wished to see me, ma'am?'

At that the Dowager Marchioness turned her head. Her eyes were so like Rupert's that Morwenna felt a shock of surprise, but then she saw the sour line of the other woman's mouth and knew the likeness went no further.

As the woman rose slowly to her feet, her manner was haughty in the extreme as she looked Morwenna over, her gaze intent. For a long moment she merely stared and said nothing, then her mouth went hard.

'I see why he is bewitched by you. That hair is enough to rob a man of his wits. You are beautiful and you have the appearance of a lady—but you are a whore. Have you been spending my son's money while out with another lover?'

'I have been shopping with my brother. Rupert gave me money to spend and I did indeed spend some shillings, but I also visited friends.'

'I have no wish to hear your excuses, mistress. A whore is of little importance in the scheme of things here. My son may do as he pleases for he is a man, but I wished to make sure that you understood you can never be more to him than you are now.'

'I beg your pardon. I do not understand you, ma'am.'

'I thought I had made myself clear. You may be Rupert's mistress, but you will never be his wife while I have breath in my body. He has been betrothed to the daughter of a Duke and must marry her or bring shame on his family. Would you have him ruin himself for your sake?'

'Why should he? Forgive me, you speak in riddles. I would bring no shame on Rupert. I think my family hath more cause to quarrel with me over honour than you, my lady.'

'He cannot flaunt a mistress so openly if he is to marry well. He risks his position at court, a good marriage and his honour if he carries on in this fashion. He is betrothed and cannot in honour break his word to the lady. If you cared for him at all, you would stand back and allow him to marry and hold his position in society.'

'If Rupert tells me he wishes to marry another lady, I shall of course stand back. I should not dream of ruining his hopes or hers.'

'Indeed? I had heard that you were to go

down to the castle. You must know that it would be too shocking. If rumours of your liaison reached the King, Rupert would lose any chance of a good position at court.'

'I did not know that he desired one.'

'He was instrumental in bringing a nest of traitors to account. I am told on the best authority that he was due to be honoured with the Order of the Garter and a position close to his Majesty, but if he continues to associate with the sister of known rogues…'

'Forgive me, ma'am. I think I have heard enough,' Morwenna said, lifting her head proudly. 'I should be grateful if you will leave my house.'

'Your house, indeed? You give yourself airs, Mistress Morgan. This house belongs to my son and I have a perfect right to be here. It is you who should leave before he returns.'

'Rupert put this house into my name because he loves me and wished to provide for me should I bear his children.' She saw the look of shock in the Dowager Marchioness's face and smiled. 'I do not know for certain yet, but it may be that I am to have your grandson, ma'am. Would you deny him the right to be his father's heir?

If Rupert wishes to marry me, I shall certainly say yes…'

'You wicked, wicked girl!' The Dowager Marchioness drew herself to her full height. 'I shall not stay here a moment longer to be so insulted. My son may have fallen for your charms, but I can see you for the scheming hussy you are.'

Giving a scream of rage, she rushed at Morwenna, bringing her arm back to strike. The enraged Dowager Marchioness delivered one stinging blow to Morwenna's face before Jacques flung himself at her and dragged her off. She screamed and struggled and it took both Jacques and the servant John to hold her.

'Unhand me, you rogues,' the woman cried. 'How dare you lay hands on me? I shall have you all whipped and thrown into prison, where you will rot until you die.'

'Take yourself off where you belong,' Jacques yelled, beside himself with fury. 'This is my sister's house as she claims and you are not welcome here, madam.'

'Leave her. Make her go away, but do not harm her,' Morwenna said, holding a hand to her cheek. 'Excuse me, I must leave.'

The tears were close as she left the parlour

and ran upstairs to her room. If the Dowager Marchioness spoke the truth, she would not be able to stay with Rupert, even though she loved him and he swore he loved her.

How could he speak of love and then arrange a marriage with the daughter of a duke? Jacques had spoken of the possibility, but she had not believed him.

Could she believe the Dowager Marchioness?

'Morwenna, are you there?' Jacques's knock at the door had her hastily wiping the tears from her cheeks. 'May I come in, please?'

'Yes, of course.'

Morwenna raised her head proudly, preparing to meet her brother's eyes.

Jacques looked at her gravely. 'Are you all right, dearest? She did not harm you?'

'She slapped me, but her words inflicted the greatest harm. She speaks of Rupert's marriage as inevitable, yet surely he would have told me if it were true?'

'She is a wicked woman to attack you as she did.'

'I pushed her too far. She thought Rupert meant to marry me and it drove her wild with hate. Had I told her that he had no such intention...' Morwenna held back a sob. 'I brought it on myself. It was my foolish pride.'

'No, you must not blame yourself,' Jacques said. 'I think her eaten up with some hatred that is older than your relationship with Rupert. She spoke wildly as her footman led her to the sedan chair. He told me she often loses her temper and sometimes throws objects at her servants. I think she is a selfish, bad-tempered woman.'

'She hates me, but I think she hates Rupert, too,' Morwenna said, feeling the tears burning behind her eyes. 'What am I to do, Jacques? I cannot remain his mistress if he truly intends to marry.'

'He took your innocence. He owes you marriage.'

'No, Jacques. He owes me nothing.'

'Morwenna.'

Morwenna closed her eyes. 'Please, I should like to be alone for a while. I must think.'

'You should ignore her spite. We must do as Rupert asked and go to the castle to wait for him.'

'Please, Jacques. Let me rest. I need to think.'

'As you wish, dearest. You know I want only your happiness.'

As the door closed behind him and her maid,

the tears slipped from her eyes. What was she going to do? If she went home to Cornwall, Rupert would follow.

Chapter Fourteen

'I am glad we had this meeting,' the Duke said and offered his hand. 'Your mother was most insistent that we draw up a contract, but I was reluctant to sign until I heard from you. Indeed, I should not have done so. My daughter is precious to me and I would not have her unhappy in her marriage.'

'Your daughter is a lovely girl, sir. Had I no prior attachments, I should have been happy with the match.'

'I thank you for your honesty.' The Duke shook his head. 'Mothers are apt to be too eager at times. You must prevail upon the dear lady to be more cautious, Melford.'

'I shall make certain of it,' Rupert replied. 'I

am glad that we part as friends, sir. I should not like to have offended you in this matter.'

'No offence given. I have suffered from a mother's ambitions in the past. I wish you well and hope to see you and your wife at court.'

'We shall come when we can,' Rupert replied, smiled and took his leave.

He was thoughtful as he left the ancient castle, mounted his horse and rode away with a handful of men at his back. He must ride hard for Melford Towers, for Morwenna would be waiting for him and she might be anxious as to the reason she had been sent there.

It was as he was leaving the Duke's house that a servant came up to him, bowing deeply as he offered a sealed letter. Rupert glanced at the hand and knew it for his sister's. Why should May have written to him here?

Breaking the seal, he scanned the few lines and frowned. His sister begged him to come to her before he left for the castle. It would mean more delay and he was anxious to speak with Morwenna, make certain she understood that he intended to wed her. He ought to have made things plainer in his letter to her, but had wanted to explain his feelings in person—the reason he'd hesitated for so long.

Surely Morwenna would understand when she knew his past?

Jacques had gone to hire a coach and horses for their journey. Morwenna knew she must use this opportunity to escape from him and Rupert. She loved Rupert with all her heart, too much to ruin his chances of preferment at court.

The Dowager Marchioness had told her that she would bring shame on him. If he continued to flaunt her as his mistress he would not be welcomed at court and his friends would turn against him. Besides, he was betrothed to a young woman and he could not in honour break the contract.

Because she loved him Morwenna must walk away from Rupert. She suspected that she might be carrying his child and if Rupert knew she was sure he would not give her up—indeed, he might break his vows to his betrothed and that would ruin him.

The Dowager Marchioness was spiteful, but what she said was true. If Morwenna continued as his mistress, she would ruin him and it would break her heart to know he was wed to another.

Better to run away now than cause more pain for them both. She must hide until Rupert was wed and ceased to look for her.

'Mother did what? How dared she?' Rupert fumed, as May finished speaking. 'She threatened Morwenna and told her I was betrothed when she knew it was a lie?'

'She was so angry because Morwenna defied her,' May said. 'I think she told her that association with her would ruin you and she slapped her, as she slapped me for trying to tell her your marriage was not her business.'

'I am sorry for that,' Rupert said. 'I have allowed her to have charge of her daughter, but you are my sister and you will not have to suffer her unkindness again. I shall send you to Melford Hall and you may reside there until you marry.'

'Mother insisted that I must marry a man of her choosing, but will you let me choose for myself, Rupert?'

'Of course. I shall introduce you to some gentlemen I think may suit you, dearest, but you shall not be forced.'

'Thank you.' May reached up to kiss his cheek. 'You are a good brother and you will be a good husband. I wish you and Morwenna much happiness.'

'Thank you.' He looked into her face. 'I shall tell Mother that you will live under my protection in future. If she wishes to see either of us, she must mend her ways and apologise to my wife—and to you. You will stay here until I can send you to Melford Hall with an escort.'

'Yes, of course.' May shuddered. 'Make it soon, Rupert. She is angry all the time and I do not think I can stay here for much longer.'

'First I must speak with Morwenna. She is brave, but even she must have been in such distress over this.' A bleak look came to his eyes. 'I have not treated her as I ought. I can only hope that she will forgive me—and in time our mother.'

'You allowed her to run away again? And you think she may be with child?' Rupert stared at Jacques in dismay. 'May God forgive me for what I have brought her to. I am to blame for all she has suffered.'

'No, how could you be? It was not your fault that Michael kidnapped her—as for your mother, I do not think she harmed Morwenna physically. Her letter to me said that she did not wish to shame and ruin you. My sister believes you are to marry a Duke's daughter.'

'It was untrue. I shall not marry another. Morwenna is the woman I would have as my wife. I intend to find her and…'

'Supposing she is too proud to wed you now?'

'You know where she is, don't you?' Rupert was suddenly alert. 'Tell me, damn you! I'll beat it out of you if I have to. I must know where she is.'

'I am not certain, but I believe she is with friends who care for her.' Jacques gave him a twisted smile. 'I am not sure that I should tell you.'

'I cannot just allow her to disappear. I love her and want her so much.'

'Then I suppose I must tell you, though she may hate me for it.'

'What will you do now?'

'With your permission I intend to return to your house on the Marches.'

'Then you may escort my sister if you will. May is very distressed and she does not want to live in London—or at the castle. I have told her she might make her home at the Hall until she marries.'

'It will be my pleasure to escort her. I promise to take good care of her.'

'Better care than I took of Morwenna?' Rupert shook his head. 'I am certain of it. May is a timid child. I know that you would not dream of seducing her.'

'You have my word on it.'

'And now you will tell me where I can find Morwenna.'

'I will tell you where I think she may have gone. The rest is up to you.'

'I shall find her if I have to search the country for her.'

'Then you will find her. I wish you luck.'

'And I you.'

On that accord the two men parted.

Morwenna turned as the older woman entered the bedroom just as she was wiping her mouth after being sick for the second time that morning. She raised her head proudly, saying, 'Yes, I am carrying Rupert's child. I shall not deny it.'

'Does he know?' Morwenna shook her head. 'Is that fair to him, my love? Do you not think you should tell him where you are? You are safe with us and we love having you, but your brother and friends may be searching for you.'

'Rupert may be relieved, for he must know our relationship must end if he is to marry. Jacques must have guessed where I meant to come. If he wanted to find me, he would come here. He knows that I need to be alone for a while. When I am ready I shall tell my brother where I am.'

'Well, I shall not push you, my love.' Sarah smiled at her. 'We love having you here and the children are so fond of you.'

'You have all been so kind to me,' Morwenna said. 'I should like to stay with you until my babe is born.'

'I would not dream of letting you go,' Sarah assured her. 'You saved my life and I am honoured that you chose me when you were in such sore distress. You are as a daughter to me and I love you.'

Morwenna nodded, because she knew it was the truth. She picked up her cloak, for it was her intention to walk to the market and buy fruit for the children. Sarah was always busy in the shop and had little time for shopping, so Morwenna made it one of the chores she had undertaken. Sarah's husband would not take a penny for her board so she spent money on the children and thus far she had more than enough for her needs, though one day she would have to find work or draw on the account Rupert had opened for her with his lawyer.

'Sarah, my love.' Tom Harding came along the landing towards them as they left the bed-chamber. 'Will you come down, please? I have received word that a large order for silks and damasks is to come our way quite soon.'

'Why, Husband, you look excited,' Sarah said with a fond smile. 'What has you all of a-twitter?'

'Lord Melford has sent his man of business with an order for silken curtains for the house he has bought for his bride-to-be. I am told that is a fine big house and there will be many yards of silk needed.'

'Lord Melford?' Morwenna asked, feeling a sudden stab to her heart. 'Are you sure that was the name given?'

'Yes, Mistress Morwenna,' the kindly man said, completely unaware that he was delivering a blow to her heart. 'He is a Marquis, you know, and one of the richest men in England. His illustrious family has served the King for many years.'

Morwenna swallowed hard. She would not cry nor would she grieve. It was, after all, what she had hoped for, that Rupert would forget her and marry. Yet it was so soon. No more than two days had passed since she had fled to this house in Cheapside. How quickly he had forgotten his vows of love.

'Is the Marquis below in the shop, sir?' she asked, proud of the fact that her voice did not betray how close she was to weeping.

'Oh, no, he would not come in person,' Master Harding said. 'He has sent his man of business to inspect our wares. His bride loves green and deep rose and I told him we had a new order of just those colours last week. Do you not recall that you chose them for us when the merchant called, Morwenna?'

'Yes, I did. I hope the Marquis buys your silks, sir,' Morwenna said and forced a smile as she looked at Sarah. 'I shall not forget the plums you asked for—and I shall not be more than two hours.'

'It will not take two hours to walk to the market?'

'No. I think I must ask for the rest of my things to be sent on,' Morwenna said. 'It has been in my mind, as you know, and now I should do it.'

'You are going back to his house?'

'Just to fetch a few clothes.' Morwenna blinked hard. 'The house was supposed to be mine, but perhaps he will wish to sell it now he is to marry.'

'To marry?' Sarah stared at her and then at her husband. 'You mean the Marquis…oh, Morwenna, my love. I am so sorry. Tom would not have said had he known.'

'No, please do not apologise. I am glad to know,' Morwenna said. 'I hoped he would marry and forget me. Now I can truly move on and put all the sorrow behind me.'

'Morwenna, are you sure?'

'Do not worry, my dearest friend. Rupert would never hurt me physically. I shall tell Mistress Janet that I will not be returning and bring back anything I truly need. I shall not need my silk gowns now.'

Pulling her hood over her head, she went down the stairs and out of the side entrance into the bitter cold morning. Of course Rupert had no idea that she was staying with Sarah and Tom Harding. He would not have had her learn of his marriage in such a way had he known.

She hoped that he had chosen his bride himself and not let his mother dominate his life.

Blinking back her tears, she passed by the market stalls and then approached a sedan chair waiting for hire. She gave him the address of her house and was taken up by two stout chairmen.

Inside the drawn curtains there was no one to see the silent tears slip down her cheeks. She had held them back in front of her friends, for she knew Tom Harding would feel badly once he realised what he had so gladly revealed.

It had been bound to happen and perhaps it was best that Rupert had decided to move on. Now Morwenna knew what she must do. She would remove her things from the house and ask John the footman to take a letter to Rupert. She needed to know where she could draw a few shillings a month to keep her and the child, for she could not always rely on her good friends. He would not deny her and perhaps now she knew that he was to marry she would be brave enough to face him with the truth—at least she would try once the child was born.

She was feeling unaccountably weary and defeated by the time she reached her destination. Asking the chairmen if they would wait while she collected some of her belongings, she paid the two shillings owed and then went up to the house. She knocked at the door and in a matter of seconds it opened and Mistress Janet stood there.

'Oh, mistress,' the woman cried and a smile broke over her face as she stood back to allow her to enter. 'We've been worried about you. John and me wondered how you were.'

'I've come to fetch some of my things. No one is here, are they?'

'No, mistress. His lordship hasn't been by today. He asked us to send word if you should come and he left some money for you in your room.'

'How kind,' Morwenna said, her throat catching. 'I shall write him a letter and John may deliver it when I've gone, if he will?'

'Of course, mistress. Shall I help with your things?'

'Would it be too much trouble to ask for a hot posset? It is cold out and I need something to warm me. When you come up you can help me, though much of what Lord Melford gave me is no longer suitable.'

'Of course it is no trouble, mistress. I'll bring

you a bite to eat, too. I've been baking the short-bread you like this very morning.'

Morwenna thanked her and went on up the stairs. She felt the welcome of the house sur-round her—it was like returning home and she had not realised how much she missed it.

No, she would not let herself regret anything!

Her bedchamber was exactly as she'd left it. There was a scent of lavender in the air, as if it had been cleaned recently.

Morwenna began to move about the room, opening the chests and taking out the things she would need. Most of the gowns would not fit her in a few months, but the good cloth gowns could either be let out or kept until she had given birth. She would not need the expensive silks and damasks, for she would have no occasion to wear them. They could be sold. She supposed that she might sell them if she wished, for they were hers. She picked up the gown she had been wearing the last time Rupert took her to the the-atre and held it to her face.

Her heart felt as if it would break apart. She had loved him so very much, but he was to marry and she must live her own life.

Morwenna was suddenly very tired. In a few moments she would begin her packing and she must write a letter to Rupert, asking him if he would send the details of the money he would allow her for his child here to the house so that she could easily collect it. She was too tired to think now. A little nap on the bed until Mistress Janet brought up her posset would make her feel much better…

'Is she still here?' Rupert asked as Mistress Janet let him in and put a finger to her lips. 'I was out when John came, but as soon as I returned I rushed straight here.'

'She meant only to stay a short while, but she fell asleep on the bed. When I looked in a moment ago she was still sleeping.'

'Is she ill? Did she look unwell?'

'She looks as always, sir.' Mistress Janet smiled. 'A little tired, perhaps.'

'Thank God,' Rupert said. 'You did just as you ought, Janet—you and John. I cannot thank you enough.'

'Go up now, sir, but let her wake herself.'

'Yes, I shall. I would not startle her for the world.'

Rupert walked slowly up the stairs, his heart pounding. His ruse had worked perfectly. He had resisted the temptation to snatch her from her friends, hoping that news of his new house would bring her here. She had come as he'd hoped and now he had his chance to talk to her and make her understand.

She was still sound asleep as he opened the door and entered her chamber. Lying with her hair spread on the pillows, she looked so beautiful and sensual that his heart caught with need and desire. He loved her so. How could he bear it if he'd lost her?

Rupert knew that in taking her innocence and making her his mistress he had used her shamefully. She had deserved so much more and he was a fool to allow his past to come between them. After what his mother had told her she would believe that he had made her his mistress rather than wedding her because she was not his equal in birth—and because of her brother. Indeed, he had known some reservations regarding her brother, but it was not the reason he'd held back. His reasons went deeper and were more personal, a legacy of the scars he bore because of Richard's death and his mother's bitterness.

All he could do now was to pray that Morwenna would believe him when he told her that he loved her and would be proud to have her as his wife.

* * *

Morwenna yawned, her eyelids flickering. She stretched and then opened her eyes, staring up into the face of the man who sat beside her on the bed.

'No!' she cried. 'Oh, Rupert, no. I thought...'

'You thought I had deserted you,' he said, reaching out to catch her as she would have run from him. Holding her wrist, he bent his head and kissed her lips. 'Did you truly believe that I would marry another when I love you? Surely you know how much you mean to me?'

'Please do not.' Tears started to her eyes. 'Your mother told me it would shame you to wed me. If you renounce your betrothed, you will be ruined.'

'My mother had no right to say such things to you. My sister told me that she attacked you physically?'

'It was nothing.' She hunched her knees up to her chest protectively. 'I made her angry, Rupert, because I said I would not give you up. That I would wed you if you wished...'

'Did you allow her to believe that you might be carrying my child?' Morwenna gave a little cry and turned her face away. 'No, do not hide from me. Were you going to tell me?'

'I would have told you when the babe was born after you were married.'

'Have you so little faith in me?'

Morwenna lifted her head proudly. 'I do not wish to be married out of pity or duty.'

'You insult me, Morwenna. I do not offer you duty but I can hardly blame you for not believing me. I have behaved shamefully. I seduced you, took your innocence and then left you.'

'I gave myself to you willingly, Rupert.' Morwenna's mouth trembled. 'I love you, but I know I am not good enough for you.'

'You are far above me. My mother has much to answer for! Had Jacques not guessed where you were I might have lost you.'

'Your mother's unkindness does not matter,' Morwenna said. 'Nothing would matter if you truly loved me.' Her eyes met his in entreaty. 'You say you love me and yet you made me your mistress and never spoke of marriage. Why? If you do not feel as your mother does, then why did you not wed me when we came to London?'

Rupert hesitated, then frowned. 'Because I was afraid of loving you too much, I suppose. You shake your head, but you do not know my story. My brother died because I pushed him and he fell into the castle moat and later died of a fever. After that my mother hated me, because Richard was her favourite. She made me promise I would marry well, as my brother might have had he lived. I wished to oblige her and was to have married a gentle girl of whom I was very fond, but she too died of a fever. It seems that I lose all those that I love.'

'You are afraid to love?' She stared at him, hardly daring to believe. 'I thought it was because of Michael and his involvement with the plotters and because I am too far beneath you?'

'That is what my mother feels and, I shall admit it, to my shame those things weighed with me for a time. I knew that my mother would never accept you into the family and, at first, I did not understand how much you meant to me. It was not until Michael snatched you and then you almost died...' He stopped, his throat catching with emotion. 'Yes, I know how unworthy that makes me sound, Morwenna. I treated you ill. Why should you love me? I do not deserve you.' He turned his face away. 'If you cannot forgive...'

'Oh, Rupert.' She stared in wonder as she saw tears on his cheeks. 'Do you truly care so much?'

He turned to her, such entreaty in his eyes

that she caught her breath. 'Can you doubt it? I adore you, Morwenna. If you will not have me, there is little left in life for me.'

'Of course I forgive you,' she said and scrambled across the bed towards him on her knees. 'I love you and if we must part it will break my heart.'

Rupert turned and caught her close to his heart, holding her as if he would never let her go. 'You're mine,' he whispered fiercely. 'I want you, love you, need you. You must promise you will never leave me again. Promise me now, Morwenna.'

She gazed into his eyes for a moment in silence, then nodded. 'I promise. I never want to leave you again, but the chairmen wait for me. I should not keep them longer and I must tell Sarah.'

'I paid the chairmen and told them to let your friends know you were safe and would see them tomorrow. I shall take you there and you may introduce me—make me known to your friends. While we are in London we shall also visit your aunt and tell her of our coming marriage.'

'You are quite certain you will not regret making me your wife? If your mother and friends will not know you...' He touched his fingers to her lips to hush her. 'You may lose so much if you wed me, Rupert.'

'If I lose fairweather friends, so be it. I have no desire to spend my life at court, dangling at the King's pleasure for some favour. I want to be with you and our children, Morwenna. We shall find pleasure in the country life, though we may visit London from time to time if it suits us—and my sister will be our constant visitor. If my mother apologises to you, she may visit us now and then. If she chooses to remain a stranger, that is for her to decide. We shall be wed and nothing more matters to me.'

Morwenna looked at him uncertainly.

'But you ordered silks for your new bride.'

'Do you not wish your friends to receive the order for the curtains in our new house?'

'Yes, of course—but how...why...?' She stared up at him. 'The new house is for me—for us?'

'Yes, of course. I hoped it might bring you here, that you would act just as you have out of pride.' He smiled and she glared at him, throwing off his hand. 'Do not be angry. I could hardly drag you from your friend's home.'

'I thought you were to marry the Duke's

daughter…' She choked off and flushed. 'It was not kind of you, Rupert.'

'Would you have seen me had I asked for you at the merchant's shop?'

'No.' Reluctantly, she smiled at him. 'Perhaps I should not, though I was in sore distress…'

'Your pride was nearly our undoing, Morwenna.'

'I suppose Jacques told you where to find me?'

'I threatened all manner of things if he had not.'

'Did you harm him?'

'No. Instead, I asked him to take my sister down to Melford Hall with him. I think they do well enough together.'

'You suggest…' Her eyes widened in surprise.

'Your brother needs a home and she needs a kind husband. May will have more sense than to run away from him, I think.' He ran a finger over her mouth. 'You accuse me of unkindness. Do you know how it hurt me to hear that you had run away from me?'

'Oh, Rupert.' Tears choked her. 'Have I been a fool?'

'Yes, my love, you have but I shall forgive

you. You did not know how much I loved you, for I did not make myself plain. I used you at first and I deserted you after I thought you one of the wreckers. My love and trust grew more slowly than yours, because I had never truly known love. Loving you was a new experience and at first it frightened me.'

'Nothing frightens you,' she challenged.

'The thought of losing you terrifies me. I was afraid of falling in love, and then, when I did, my mother almost destroyed what we had. I do not pity you, Morwenna. I ask you to take pity on me, for if you will not have me I must live alone. I could never risk my heart again. It hurts too much when you are not by.'

'Rupert.' She reached up to touch his face, looking at him in wonder. 'Do you truly love me so much, my darling?'

'With my heart, my soul, my body I thee worship,' he said. 'I would have you to love and to hold all my life long, if you will have me?'

'Oh, yes,' she said and the sob was almost laughter. 'Forgive me for hurting you. I did not think my leaving would trouble you so much.'

'You almost killed me,' he said. 'I thought I might have lost your love and trust.'

'Forgive me,' she said and tangled her fingers

in his hair, bringing his face down to hers. 'Kiss me, Rupert. Love me now and there is nothing in the world that matters outside this room, this bed, except our love.'

Chapter Fifteen

'Are you well, Morwenna?' Jacques asked as he came upon her sitting in the garden at Melford Hall. 'Rupert charged me to take care of you while he was gone. You are very close to your time.'

It was almost the beginning of June and the sun was shining in the sheltered garden. The rain of the previous night had left everything smelling fresh and clean, and the showers had brought on the spring flowers.

'I am quite well for the moment, though my back was aching terribly a short time ago.' She smiled as her brother sat beside her on the wooden bench. 'Where is May?'

'She is talking to the cook, I think. She wanted to make sure they prepared something

light and tasty to please you, Morwenna, because she knows anything rich upsets you at
the moment.'

'She is such a thoughtful girl and so kind to
me,' Morwenna said and reached out to take his
hand. 'I think you like her very well, Jacques.'

'Who would not like May? She is such a
sweet, gentle girl.'

'Not at all like your sister?' Morwenna
laughed as he hesitated, arching one eyebrow.
'I know, I know. My temper hath been pushed
too far of late. I do not know why Rupert puts
up with me.'

'Because he loves you, of course. Good grief,
he has only left you now because there was
an urgent message from the castle saying his
mother was ill and wished to see him before
she died. He was in two minds whether to go,
but felt it his duty to see her if she was truly ill.'

'I know. He is the best husband any woman
could have,' she said and smiled. 'I am foolish
but at times.' She sighed and shook her head.
'It is just my silly fancy. I suppose at such times
women are entitled to be a little apprehensive. If
the child comes too soon and he is not here...'

'Rupert will return as soon as he can,'

Jacques said. 'You are not due for another two weeks—are you?'

'I know. Yet I have been feeling so odd and I keep wishing Rupert was here with me.'

'You have May—and me, dearest.'

'I suppose I am anxious about Rupert. His mother... I am worried, Jacques. Worried that she might do him some harm. He believes she still hates him, because of what happened to his brother.'

'You worry needlessly. Rupert is a strong man, what harm could she do him? Since she asked to see him to beg his pardon and make her peace before she dies it is most unlikely that she wishes him harm. He will be home before the child is born.'

'Yes, I know I am foolish.' Morwenna rose to her feet, took a step forwards and twisted her foot. As she fell, Jacques tried to catch her, but was too late. She caught at him and stead-ied herself, landing on her knees. He knelt by her side, looking down at her anxiously. 'How silly of me...'

'Here, let me help you, dear heart.' Jacques lifted her to her feet and held her as she swayed. 'Have you hurt yourself?'

'My ankle caught. It was just a little tumble.

A shock, no more. I shall be perfectly fine in a few moments.'

'Take my arm. We shall go in together. I will help you to your room. I think perhaps you should rest this afternoon.'

'Yes, I shall.' Morwenna smiled at him. 'Forgive me for worrying you. I know Rupert will be safe enough. It was just a queasy feeling inside—perhaps the berry tart I had earlier.'

'You will feel better soon,' Jacques told her. 'Look, May has come to meet us—perhaps she has some news.'

'A letter has come from Rupert,' May said as she came up to them. 'I think it must be grave news for the courier had ridden hard to bring it. Shall I open it for you, Morwenna?'

'I will open it.' Morwenna took it with shaking fingers. She saw at once that it was not Rupert's writing, but that of his agent. 'He says...' She gave a little cry and clutched at Jacques's arm. 'Rupert is hurt! There was a fire in the castle tower and he tried to save his mother.'

Jacques put his arm about her as she swayed. He took the paper from her nerveless fingers and read the last paragraph aloud.

'The Dowager Marchioness is dead. She had

been ill of a fever and we think she turned dizzy on rising and knocked over a candle, setting fire to the bedding. The alarm was raised and the Marquis tried to save her. He managed to carry her down to the great hall, but she died soon after. My lord received some burns to his hands and asked me to send this letter. You are not to worry and he will be home as soon as he is able to travel.'

'I must go to him,' Morwenna moaned. 'He may be dying. I knew. I knew something bad had happened…' She clutched at her brother. 'I must go to him. You must take me to him at once.'

'Are you sure, Morwenna? You are so close to your time. Rupert would not forgive me if anything should happen to you or the child.'

'If you will not take me, I shall go alone.'

'Morwenna, you can't travel alone,' May protested, horrified. 'If you go we shall go with you, to care for you.'

'Thank you, my dear sister,' Morwenna said and smiled at her. 'Let us go in and pack.' She started towards the stairs and then gave a little scream as the pain ripped through her. 'No… no…not now. It must not happen now.' She looked down at the skirt of her gown and saw the wet stain. 'My waters have broken.'

'That settles it,' Jacques said grimly. 'Up to your chamber. I'll send for the physician and the midwife immediately. You must give birth to your child before you think of travelling to Rupert's side.'

Morwenna gasped and clutched at herself as the pain swept through her. 'I fear you are right, Brother. My child would be born before I could reach him—but you must go. You must go and discover how he is and send word as soon as you can.'

'I cannot leave you at such a time,' Jacques began to protest, but May smiled and placed a hand on his arm.

'You must go, sir. Morwenna has me to care for her and her servants. I swear to you on my life that I will tend her and love her in your place. She will worry—we shall all worry about Rupert until we have more news.'

Jacques inclined his head. 'Very well, I shall do as you ask. Forgive me that I must leave you in such distress.'

Morwenna shook her head, biting her lip as the pain increased. 'Go and bring me news, for I cannot bear that he should be alone.'

'He has servants.' Jacques saw the look in her eyes. 'But he needs a friend at such a time and he will be anxious for news of you. At least I can tell him your child will soon be born.'

Morwenna gasped, but did not reply. May took her arm, urging her up the stairs to her chamber. The pain was terrible, but she would not cry out until her brother was on his way, for if he guessed how she suffered he would not leave her.

They had thought the birth would be soon after her waters broke, but to Morwenna her ordeal seemed to go on and on, as wave after of wave of pain shuddered through her. She could no longer hold her screams and May encouraged her to pull hard on the rope that had been tied to the bedposts.

'You are a good brave lady,' May told her as she bathed her forehead with a cool cloth. 'I wish I had something to give you, but I do not think a tisane would help. Besides, you must not sleep for you need to push when the pain comes.'

'Something is wrong. Why does my baby not come?'

Morwenna arched, tossing on the pillow as

she felt the pain once more. She did not know how much more she could bear and the physician had not yet come to her.

Even as she screamed out again, the door opened and he entered, a small man with a pointed beard, long dark gown and a grave face.

'Your waters broke an hour gone,' he said. 'Yet the child hath not come. I shall examine you, but I think it may be that I must turn the child—or cut you.'

'Help her, sir, for she is in much pain,' May said, hovering anxiously as he approached the bed.

The physician bent over her and lifted her night chemise, his hands gentle and sure as they carried out a brief examination. He shook his head, looking from the young woman in the bed to her companion and the servant hovering near by with pans of hot water and cloths.

'Where is the Marquis? I need to talk with him.'

'My brother is not here. He has had an accident. You may talk to me in his place.'

The physician looked at Morwenna, then led May aside to give her his opinion. 'I shall try to turn the babe, but if it will not come I may have to use forceps—or, as a last resort, cut the

Marchioness. At such times I would normally ask the husband if he wished the child or his wife to be saved.'

'What?' May gave a cry of distress. 'Why must there be a choice? You must save both of them.'

'That may not be possible.'

'Then you must save Morwenna. She is more important than the child. They can have more children…' She saw the doubts in his face and caught back a sob. 'It must be her, for my brother would not forgive you if you let her die.'

'What are you whispering about?' Morwenna said, reared up and looked at them, then put her legs over the side of the bed and stood up, taking a step towards them. 'Save my child, sir. I beg you to save my child at whatever cost.'

'I shall do my best for both of you, madam. Lie down again or you may do yourself damage,' the doctor said and came to the bed as Morwenna fell back against her pillows. 'What I must do now will be painful for you, but it is the best chance for both. If I can turn the babe and then—' He broke off as Morwenna screamed and arched wildly. 'God be praised! 'Tis a miracle. The babe hath turned itself. I can help you now without harm to either.'

Morwenna was grunting as she pushed. Something must have happened when she moved so violently and the babe had turned and now its head was through and then, all in a rush, it came slithering into the world covered in mucus and blood.

'Is the babe healthy?' Morwenna asked weakly as she lay back, her strength gone as the doctor and May worked over her, making her comfortable and tidy. 'Have we a son or a daughter?'

'You have a son,' May said and smiled at her. 'He has all his fingers and toes—and he is perfect. He looks much like you for his hair is reddish brown.'

'Rupert has a son,' Morwenna said and a tear rolled slowly down her cheek. 'Pray God he lives to see him.'

She touched the babe's head tenderly as he was placed in her arms. 'I think we shall call him Edward Rupert Melford. He is beautiful and he has his father's eyes.'

'Yes, he is beautiful,' May said, watching her suckle the babe. 'As beautiful a child as I ever saw—just like his mother.'

Morwenna reached out a hand to her. 'Thank

you, dear heart, for being with me and helping me through the pain.'

'We are sisters and friends,' May said. 'I know that you would do the same for me if I were ever fortunate enough to wed and have a child.'

Morwenna smiled. 'I do not think it needs good fortune, May. Jacques loves you and I think you love him.' She saw the heat in the younger girl's cheeks. 'If he has not spoken, it is because he thinks you are too far above him.'

'How could he be so foolish? He is all I have ever hoped for.' Her blush grew deeper. 'Perhaps I should tell him how I feel.' She bent down to take the babe as Morwenna finished suckling him. 'You should rest now for a while.'

'Yes, I am tired. I believe you should speak to—' Morwenna was startled as she heard the sound of running feet, heavy feet—a man's feet. As the door of her chamber was flung open, her heart was pounding. Was it Jacques? Had he come to tell her bad news?

A man entered and her heart caught. Rupert had clearly ridden hard, for his boots and hose were covered in mud from the roads. She saw that he had a linen bandage across one eye and half his face—and his left hand was also swathed in bandages.

'Morwenna! I met Jacques on the road and he told me you had begun your labour.' His right eye went to the bundle of swaddling in his sister's arms. 'The child is born. We have a child.'

'We have a son, Rupert,' Morwenna said. 'Show him, May. Show Rupert his son.'

Tears caught her throat, because she could see that her beloved husband had been burned in the fire his mother had started. His right cheek was not covered, but there was a red burn mark across his nose and she knew that his injuries must be serious to be bandaged so heavily. Emotion tore at her. He should not have ridden so far and so hard when he was in such pain. He must be in pain, for it could not be otherwise.

'You should not have tried to reach me yet, my love. You are hurt.'

'It is nothing. The physician says the blindness in my left eye is temporary. No real damage has been done; it was just the heat. There may be some scars, but it doesn't signify.'

'No, it doesn't signify,' Morwenna said and a single tear escaped to trickle down her cheek. 'You are alive and here with me. Nothing else matters to me.'

He came to take her hand, sitting on the edge of the bed as his sister and the doctor left the room together. Rupert reached for her hand and held it. His eyes searched her face.

'You are well? I feared for you because the child came early.'

'I am well. I thought they might have to use forceps, but in the end the babe came itself. We have been lucky, Rupert.'

'Very lucky,' he said and bent down to slide his lips over hers. 'I am lucky that my burns were no worse—and that the fall did not break my neck.'

'You pushed yourself hard to come to me.'

'When I learned what my steward had written I knew you would be distraught and so I came at once.'

'Foolish one. Jacques was coming to you because I could not.'

'He told me so, dearest. I could not bear that you should be in pain and I not with you. All is well now. I am here. We have our son and each other—what more could we need?'

'Nothing,' she whispered and reached out to touch his hand. 'You, too, are in pain, my love. I wish I might tend your hurts, but May will do it in my stead until I am well. We have grown fond and she is dear to me.'

'The pain will ease in time.' He smiled and touched her hair, which was still damp with sweat. 'As long as you are well nothing matters to me.'

'Nothing matters but our love and those we love.'

Rupert might bear scars where he had suffered burns to his face and hands, but it did not matter. His scars would not lessen her love for him. If anything, they would increase it, for she felt his suffering as if it were her own and wanted to ease him, to protect and bear his pain for him.

'I love you, my dearest one,' she said. 'I need a little time to recover, but then I would have another child. A daughter next time. I shall call her May after your sister.'

'Jacques has asked my permission to speak to her about marriage. Do you think she will take him?'

'I am certain of it,' Morwenna said. 'We shall be a true family. Rupert…' She hesitated, then, 'I am sorry that your mother died.'

'At least she had made her peace with me. I think she might have learned to know and love

you, dearest, had she lived. I regret her death in
such a manner, but I know she could not have
lived long. We shall mourn her for a time and
then we'll celebrate the wedding of your brother
to my sister.'

'You are happy that they will wed?'

'Of course, dear heart. I am fond of Jacques.
He has worked well here and I am thinking of
giving them the estate as a wedding gift.'

'Oh.' A little frown touched her brow. 'Where
shall we live—not at the castle?'

'The tower has burned down. I have decided
not to replace it—and we shall not live there. I
have already picked a favourable spot elsewhere
on my estate. I shall set architects to work and a
master builder; they will build us a fine manor
house.'

'I think I should like that,' Morwenna said.
'I love this house and something like it would
be a real home for us.'

'The castle was old when my father bought
it. In winter we may be able to see its towers
through the wood that separates it from our new
house, but in summer we shall hardly know it
is there. I intend to strip it of anything of value
and let the walls crumble.'

'In time it will become a mysterious ruin and

tantalise our descendants as they puzzle over the people who once lived there.'

'Yes, I dare say they will wonder why it became a ruin,' Rupert said. 'Now, I should leave you to sleep, my love, for you are tired.'

'And you, too, should rest. Ask the physician to tend your hurts, Rupert. I am sure those burns must pain you.'

'It is a pain I can bear,' he said and leaned forwards to kiss her softly once more. 'But I shall let him ease me if he can.'

Morwenna nodded, snuggling down into her feather mattress. Her eyelids were heavy and she could feel herself drifting away.

Epilogue

'So, what do you think of your new home, my love?'

They had stopped the travelling coach beyond the entrance to the park and walked over the rise together to see the house from a vantage point. It was high summer and more than three years since the building was begun. Until this moment they had lived in their fine house in London, visiting Jacques and May at Melford Hall for several weeks in summer and at Christmas. They had also spent some time travelling in France and Italy. Now at last their house was ready for them.

'Oh, Rupert.' Morwenna caught her breath. The stones of mellow Cotswold stone were golden in the sunlight, the long windows reflecting the light in tiny leaded panes. The house was larger than Melford Hall, but not huge and rambling, of modern design in the shape of an E with a main building and three wings built around courtyards. 'It is beautiful. I can hardly believe we are to live in such a lovely house.'

'I should not dream of giving my wife anything less. It is a fitting place to bring up our sons do you not think so, my love?'

'Yes, Rupert, I do,' she breathed, her lovely face alight with happiness. 'And, if I have my wish this time, our daughter.'

She placed her hands against her slightly rounded stomach. This would be their third child and the last birth had been much easier than the first, perhaps because Rupert had been with her all the time.

Rupert laughed, reached out and pulled her closer.

'If we have another son we can always try again,' he said and gave her a wicked look. 'I never tire of trying, dear heart.'

'No.' Morwenna laughed, feeling the warmth of the sun on her head as they linked hands and walked down the slope towards their home. 'Nor I, Rupert. Nor I.'

* * * * *

A sneaky peek at next month...

HISTORICAL

IGNITE YOUR IMAGINATION, STEP INTO THE PAST...

My wish list for next month's titles...

In stores from 4th January 2013:

❑ Some Like to Shock – Carole Mortimer

❑ Forbidden Jewel of India – Louise Allen

❑ The Caged Countess – Joanna Fulford

❑ Captive of the Border Lord – Blythe Gifford

❑ Behind the Rake's Wicked Wager – Sarah Mallory

❑ Rebel with a Cause – Carol Arens

Available at WHSmith, Tesco, Asda, Eason, Amazon and Apple

Just can't wait?

Visit us Online

You can buy our books online a month before they hit the shops! **www.millsandboon.co.uk**

1212/04

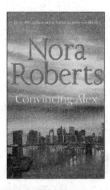
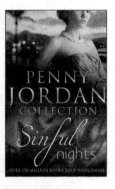